Finley Acker

Pen sketches

Streets of Cairo, Sphinx and Pyramids, Bedouin Wedding Festival....

Finley Acker

Pen sketches
Streets of Cairo, Sphinx and Pyramids, Bedouin Wedding Festival....

ISBN/EAN: 9783337096236

Printed in Europe, USA, Canada, Australia, Japan

Cover: Foto ©Andreas Hilbeck / pixelio.de

More available books at **www.hansebooks.com**

ABORIGINAL WEDDING AT FERNANDO PO.

TEN YEARS' WANDERINGS

AMONG THE ETHIOPIANS;

WITH SKETCHES OF THE MANNERS AND CUSTOMS OF THE CIVILIZED
AND UNCIVILIZED TRIBES, FROM SENEGAL TO GABOON.

WATERFALL AT BATANGA.

BY THOMAS J. HUTCHINSON, F.R.G.S.;

FELLOW OF THE ROYAL SOCIETY OF LITERATURE; FELLOW OF THE ETHNOLOGICAL SOCIETY; H.B.M.'S
CONSUL FOR THE BIGHT OF BIAFRA AND THE ISLAND OF FERNANDO PO; MEMBRE TITULAIRE DE
L'INSTITUT D'AFRIQUE; CORRESPONDING MEMBER OF THE LIVERPOOL LITERARY AND
PHILOSOPHICAL SOCIETY; AUTHOR OF "NIGER, TSHADDA, BINUE EXPLORATION,"
"IMPRESSIONS OF WESTERN AFRICA," &c.

LONDON:
HURST AND BLACKETT, PUBLISHERS,
SUCCESSORS TO HENRY COLBURN,
13, GREAT MARLBOROUGH STREET.
1861.

The right of Translation is reserved.

LONDON:
PRINTED BY R. BORN, GLOUCESTER STREET,
REGENT'S PARK.

TO

WILLIAM BINGHAM BARING,

LORD ASHBURTON, F.R.S.,

PRESIDENT OF THE ROYAL GEOGRAPHICAL SOCIETY,

THIS VOLUME IS,

WITH HIS LORDSHIP'S GRACIOUS PERMISSION,

RESPECTFULLY DEDICATED,

BY

THE AUTHOR.

PREFACE.

WITHOUT any fear or trembling, I come before the public with my third contribution to literature on the subject of Africa.

If I be accused of sketching in this volume a less favourable portraiture of the African character than I have done in either of my former works, I shall only advance the plea of never having set forth anything in my description of these people but the naked and unadorned truth as it stood before me.

That I have met native Africans conscious of their own inferiority, and anxious for knowledge to develop the industrial riches of their country, I have already confessed,—that "the slave population is destined to be the future working power in drawing forth Africa's resources for their own and their country's good," I still hold as an abiding faith—that I have witnessed a cannibalistic sacrifice during the past year in one of the most important commercial ports of the Bight of Biafra, these pages will attest to the reader.

More than three hundred years have passed since Shakspeare made the Prince of Morocco thus address Portia, the rich heiress in the play of the "Merchant of Venice":—

> "Mislike me not for my complexion,
> The shadowed livery of the burnished sun,
> To whom I am a neighbour, and nigh bred.
> Bring me the fairest creature northward born,
> Where Phœbus' fires scarce thaw the icicles,
> And let us make incision for your love,
> To prove whose blood is reddest—his or mine."

Despite of the opinion recently given in a work by Dr. Bucknill, "On the Medical Knowledge of Shakspeare," that the bard, who "wrote not for an age, but for all time," had sound views in physiology and pathology, the foregoing extract from his writings leads me to doubt it, even after making a broad allowance for poetic license. In our days more is required to enable us to judge of the attributes of humanity than the colour of a man's blood; and although any negro between Cape Bojador and the Cape of Good Hope may possess as healthy life fluid as the most vigorous member of the Caucasian tribe, it gives me pain to feel obliged to record facts that prove the Ethiopian is not exactly a "man and brother" in that sense of perfect equality which the mistaken enthusiasts who advocate the claims of his race represent him to be.

Yet, amid such anomalies as I feel it my duty to describe here, it is my impression that the little which is known of the vast continent of Africa—even with the labours of Livingstone, Barth, Burton, and Speke—may be considered but as a drop in the great ocean of discovery lying hid, and some day to be brought to light. When such an occurrence as the butchery at Bonny comes to our knowledge, only in the present year, who would presume to define the limits of the strange things yet to be revealed?

Not I, at all events. For every day of my ten years' connexion with Africa brought to light some feature of the country, or of the people, whereof I had previously been ignorant. Indeed, so sombre is the cloud of mystery enveloping all things in that land of heathen darkness, that it was only within the last eighteen months I became cognizant of the facts connected with the horrible system of anthropophagy prevailing there.

If I am asked to suggest a remedy for the barbarity of the people amongst whom this custom exists, I freely confess I have none to offer.

For I pin my faith to an axiom laid down by one of the critics [*The Spectator*, March 20th, 1858] of my "Impressions of Western Africa"— that "neither slave-dealing nor marsh-malaria causes human sacrifices or gross superstitions, accompanied by grosser crimes"—leaving the reader to deduce his own inferences from my "Ten Years' Wanderings."

THE ROSERY, BROADWAY, WEXFORD.

CONTENTS.

CHAPTER I.

CHAPTER II.

CHAPTER III.

CHAPTER IV.

CHAPTER V.

CHAPTER VI.

CHAPTER VII.

CHAPTER XIII.

CHAPTER XIV.

CHAPTER XV.

CHAPTER XVI.

CHAPTER XVII.

CHAPTER XVIII.

TEN YEARS' WANDERINGS

AMONG THE

ETHIOPIANS.

CHAPTER I.

Domestic **Slavery** of Western Africa—Difference between this **and** the Foreign Export of Slaves—Its **Varied Phases**—Women—**Palm-Oil Trading** Cockswains—Pull-a-boys—Emancipated **Servants—Blood-men—Egbo-bos**—Mangangas—Dikuku—Mikuka—Bangolo—Of Domestic **Slavery at Lagos—At Cape** Coast, and **in the** Yoruba Country—Of the Pawning System in these Places—Domestic Slavery regarded as a Natural Institution by Rev. **Mr.** Wilson—Social Phase in Bonny—Importance of considering **seriously** the Pawning **System as** an Incipient of Civilization.

CONNECTED with **Western** Africa, there seems to me no subject on which the general public has received information so minute and so extensive as on that of the slave traffic.

It may be needless to explain that there is a vast difference between the exportation of slaves,

B

which constitutes the slave trade, and the domestic social slavery which exists as indigenous to the whole continent.

The former part of this subject I leave to the blue-books and the African squadron, for both of which it is still quite sufficient. On the latter there is much more to be spoken and written than I possess ability or have had opportunity for doing.

We find many classes of social slaves in Western Africa—first amongst which are the women. In all African states they are the work-day labourers—in many they constitute the artists— and in whatever position they may be, whether wives of kings or of serfs, they are handed over to the successors of their lords and masters, who have liberty to kill, sell, or dispose of them in any other fashion. There are the slaves who have the cockswainships of palm-oil trading canoes, and who consider themselves an aristocracy above the mere commonalty of the pull-a-boys, whose work is to tug night and day by paddling canoes. To these may be added an indiscriminate class, who are to be found at different places inhabited by Europeans along the coast, nominally in the character of servants, but who have been bought as human cattle.

Some of these **last** named **have** undergone the mockery of being emancipated. Yet I have no hesitation in saying—because I know it—that **the** social treatment of these poor creatures has **been,** and still is, as bad and as brutal as **it is** possible for *soi-disant* civilization to inflict.

It **is** a melancholy anomaly to be obliged to confess that the black man has no **master** so cruel **as** the civilized negro. Sierra Leone, the **Gold** Coast, and Mrs. Stowe's model republic **of** Liberia can show numerons instances **of this.** I **do not** make such a statement without having had ocular, and still possessing written, evidence **of** the fact before me.

In many of the palm-oil trading rivers slavery is purely mythical—except in reference to **the** preposterous superstitions on which the authority of the governing powers is upheld. In Bonny, the men who rule the roast in political **debate, as** well as on **the palm-oil** 'change, are **of the** slave class; and the same **condition of** affairs, only perhaps in **a** lesser degree, exists in Old Kalabar. The bloodmen of this latter place, as well as the Egbo-bos of Brass, rank in a very trifling **degree** inferior to the freemen.

A very apt illustration **of the** influence which

the domestic slaves possess, and sometimes demonstrate, is apparent from what we find in Kameroons. Here, as in Kalabar, there is an Egboship amongst the freemen. There are also two orders of Egbo, entitled "Mikuka" and "Bangolo," to which freemen and slave boys are alike admitted; not, however, to the enjoyment of equal privileges; for the masters or freemen are the governing heads, and oblige the serf party to be satisfied with what they can get. The slaves have also orders of their own, to which the titles "Mbwe," "Kosso," and "Kella Remba," are given. Of the minutiæ of these nothing is known, more than of their Egbos elsewhere, for they are all kept as secret as freemasonry is with its professors. That they are invariably used as engines of oppression, is patent by every deed of their regulations. On the death of a late chief, his son energetically carried out a despotic principle in the "Mikuka" order, rendering it incumbent on candidates who were going through the routine of initiation into the body, that other people's yards and houses should be plundered of any goats or fowls to be found. The slaves, being the least protected class, were chiefly the parties on whom these forays were made, particularly that portion of them getting into comfortable position from their palm-oil trading. The freebooterism was carried on in the night, as the neophytes, during their period of probation, are kept locked up all day, in order to maintain a fable of their invisibility. So the slaves were driven to a reprisal, and established a new order, entitled "Manganga," whose doctrines they brought with them from the interior country of Abo. One of the chief provisions of this was to be opposed to the kings and chiefs in everything—acknowledge no allegiance to them, and use every exertion tending to the subjugation of royalty.

Another of its codes gave power to a slave buying oil at an interior market for his master to demand one "big ting" (a form of apocryphal currency, representing from fifteen shillings to a pound in value) for his commission, no matter how trifling the amount of oil purchased. If it were not paid, the slave belonging to the "Manganga" order had the power of placing a supposed witchcraft stick, called "dikubu," outside the freeman's door; and from that moment the fate of the latter was doomed. The presence of the dikubu before his house sentenced him to drink sangaree (or test-poison) water.

No one was allowed to communicate with him, and on the first time of leaving his home (if he escaped the sangaree) his dwelling was burnt or razed to the ground.

With the notable exceptions of Dahomey and Ashanti, the domestic slavery of Western Africa is, in fact, little more than a *nominis umbra*, as regards the difference in position between the children and slaves of a chief. Such horrors of daily life as those described by Mrs. Stowe as existing in the United States, and those recorded as taking place on board slavers in the middle passage, are not known in Africa. Neither the ordainers of, nor the victims to, superstitious sacrifices, look upon this institution as a cruelty. It sometimes, and not unfrequently, happens that a slave is more wealthy and more powerful than his master or owner. In such a case it is where the terrible Egbo law of Old Kalabar acts with so much despotic power.*

Domestic slavery differs from the feudalism and vassalage of English history, chiefly in reference to the brutalities and superstitions by which it is upheld.

A very good definition of this domestic sla-

---

* Vide "Impressions of Western Africa," chap. x. Longman, Brown, and Co., 1858.

very is thus **given by Mr.** John Chillingworth, of Lagos, **in** a shrewd letter to the *Cotton Supply Reporter*, dated October 10th, 1859 :—
"It is argued in favour of the slave trade, that slavery is indigenous to Africa, and that the Africans but change a black master for a white. But the domestic slavery of Africa is altogether different; the slave, or rather vassal, is on a par with his master physically and morally. There **is no strong** line of demarcation. It is difficult, **indeed, to say** which is master and which is **man.** Frequently the master gives his daughte. as a wife to his 'boy,' as he calls him, and when the master dies without a direct heir, his boy becomes possessed of his property. This sort **of** 'boy'-hood comprises all the domestic slavery, provided cupidity is not excited, **and evil** passion aroused by the European slave-dealer. Nearly everyone you meet is a boy, **who** has in turn a boy, and that boy has another boy."

This system is explained more fully in a communication I have had on the subject from Mr. Bannerman,* of Cape Coast. On the Gold Coast he **says**:—" Everywhere **domestic** slavery

* This gentleman **has established a new** paper, the *West African Herald*, at Cape Coast, whose contents are invariably characterised by **a spirit** of manly independence.

prevails. It is not easy to convey to the mind of a stranger precise notions of this institution as it exists amongst us, nor to give clear ideas of the nature of the tie existing between master and slave. Here there exist hundreds of families in which it is quite impossible for even the members to discriminate who amongst them are slaves, and who free. Thirty and forty years communion from intermarriages obliterate the distinction. A man may be a slave to his own son. For example, I buy a slave and marry him to my niece. (Here the line of succession is usually, but not invariably, from uncle to nephew or niece). If they have a son, the child, on my death, becomes possessed of my property, and his own father is one of his slaves. But 'slave' is not the proper term for this class of persons; for in very truth they are in general nothing less than members of the family, who have become part of it by purchase instead of by birth. About forty or fifty years ago, when the Ashantee invasion had upset the whole country, thousands of families were broken up, and people were sold right and left around the Gold Coast. Now natives of the coast are not accustomed to be sold. The slaves are brought down from the far interior. They are of all ages. Purchasers prefer buying them at the ages of between ten and twenty, for then they can be trained up. The old fellows are usually very lazy and obstinate (having been probably sold on that account). If brought down to the seaside, these slaves fetch from thirty to forty dollars a-piece. They are all marked in a peculiar manner on the face."

I need not, I trust, explain that this statement is meant to describe the sale of servants to residents of a British colony, whose social ordinances must need thus chime in with the social arrangements of the country in which it is situated.

The domestic slave on the eastern coast of Africa does not seem to be the same marketable article that he is on the west coast. Dr. Livingstone writes:—"These various chiefs, though nearly independent of each other, are by no means independent of their people. Suppose a man is dissatisfied with one chief, he can easily transfer himself to another; and as a chief's importance increases with the number of his followers, fugitives are always received with open arms."

The fugitives cannot so easily transfer themselves on the west coast, and, indeed, desertion of this kind, when it does occur, 'is frequently the primary cause of civil war.

Superstitions, in their various forms, constitute the chains which bind the slaves to obedience, and these are justified as necessary to be upheld by some magical influence amongst a people, two-thirds of whom are born and live in slavery, subject to the governing authority of the remaining one-third.

Serfdom of this kind cannot be said to originate in the strong oppressing the weak, or in the majority overpowering the minority, and therefore the justification may be admitted.

The system of pawning, as it exists in the countries interior to Lagos and the Gold Coast, may be described as one of the most despotic features of domestic slavery.

The Rev. Mr. Mann, Church Missionary at Ijaye, in the Yoruba country, writes to me :— "The home slave was as the child in the house; no contempt was cast upon him. Bad treatment was prevented by taking the slave away. Now every one treates his slave as they like. Three days they work for the master, and one for themselves. A child of a freeman with a female slave was not a slave; also children of slaves belonged to the family of the master.

" The **system of** pawning the body is largely prevailing, **to the** disadvantage of **morals,** industry, and the peace of families. **It enables** the head of a family to put his relatives, whose **natural** watchman he is, into the hands of **strangers.**

" **He cares** then very little for the pawned relative (who is little better than a slave), **and squanders the levied** money in idleness."

The **Rev. Mr.** Mann further explains **that the money thus** raised by pawning **is spent in** buying "additional wives," and in expensive funeral orgies.

At Cape Coast, according to Mr. C. Bannerman, "the system **of** pawning is infinitely more complicated than that of domestic slavery. **If** a person be pawned to another, an amount **of fifty per** cent. interest must be paid before **he can** be redeemed. Children born whilst the mother is in pawn need to be redeemed at four and **a half** dollars each. If a pawn die, his or **her** relatives cannot take the dead body for the purpose **of** burial till they have paid redemption money. **To** this a compromise is sometimes made by allowing whoever buries the body to be security for **the debt.**"

The following very curious **fact** is recorded

by the principal judicial functionary of the Gold Coast settlement,* regarding " domestic slaves, who are commonly looked upon and considered members of the family, more particularly in the rural or bush districts—working side by side with their masters—eating from the same dish, and constantly addressing each other by the titles of father and son. The master usually provides a wife or husband for his slave; frequently, if it be a female, taking her to wife for himself, or giving her to his son. Indeed, the relations of master and slave are here so much on the same patriarchal footing that we read of in the Old Testament, as, in concurrence with many other facts, to convince me that the systems are derived from a common origin; and I have more than once availed myself of the provisions of the Mosaic code in deciding between master and slave, quoting my authority, with a short account of its origin. These decisions, as far as I could judge, have been all the more respectfully and cheerfully obeyed from being found to be based on ancient authority, and a code of laws with which many of their own are identical."

The opinion of this gentleman upon the

* Vide *West African Herald*, July 27th, 1860.

pawning system is directly opposed to that of the Rev. A. Mann, already recorded, as well as to the provisions of the Supplementary Slave Trade Suppression Act,* which places pawns on the same footing as slaves, so far as British subjects are concerned. His opinion on this matter is well deserving of serious consideration, inasmuch as the first grand obstacle standing in the way of African civilization is the relative position and mutual dependence of master and slave.

With reference to the act of parliament just mentioned, he observes : — "This enactment, although doubtless well intended, I consider to be a mistake, much to be regretted, for it destroyed, as it seems to me, a most powerful means of the gradual abolition of slavery in these countries, and of introducing in its stead a system of contracts for labour. For *in principle,* pawning, when voluntary, as it is commonly, is nothing more. If, therefore, instead of being put on the footing of slavery, and so made unlawful for British subjects to deal with, it had been regulated so as to render the terms of the contract equitable, it might have been the means, I think, of *gradually superseding sla-*

* 6 and 7 Victoria, cap. 98.

very altogether, as the regular enforcement of such contracts would render pawns more valuable than absolute slaves to persons living under British rule, which, while on the one hand it checks and restrains the master, can on the other hand enforce obedience by the slaves."

An opinion which my humble judgment presumes to endorse as worthy the attention of our government.

The Rev. Mr. Wilson* looks upon domestic slavery in southern Guinea as "a natural institution, growing out of the wants and circumstances of society, but in this case greatly promoted and strengthened by foreign traffic." It appears to me extremely probable that the change for the worse recognized by the Rev. Mr. Mann, in the Yoruba country, as existing in the social usages of the inhabitants now-a-days, may be traced to what they have learned of the degradation of the foreign slave trade. I allude more especially to the custom of a chief putting his own relatives in pawn.

It may be recorded here, as a peculiar phase of the social system in Bonny, that when a man

* "Western Africa, its History, Condition, and Prospects; by Rev. J. Leighton Wilson, sixteen years a missionary in Western Africa." Harper Brothers, New York.

is being conveyed into that place for the purpose of being butchered, **the fact of his finding anything eatable—even a grain of corn—in the canoe, is** sufficient to ensure **his** liberation.

CHAPTER II.

BELIEVING as I do in a doctrine of Archbishop Whately, that "no savage tribe has ever yet been known to have generated *per se* the faculty of working out its own civilization," and without going into a description, which would be too lengthened, of the benefits derived by the native Africans from the missionary stations along the coast—the various British colonies of Gambia, Sierra Leone, the Gold Coast—the intercourse of supercargoes at places where trade is established, I come at once to consider how far, from the facts before me, the intelligence of the negro race, as it exists in the present day on the western coast of Africa, appears to be developed, or gives us hopeful signs of its growing progress in that regard.

One of the most remarkable peculiarities of the native Africans, as I have stated elsewhere, is their faculty of imitation. The words "saby" and "palaver" are derived from the French and Spanish. These two expressions are used by all the negro tribes who can mutter some words, however few they may be, of other language than their own, and comprise all that has been engrafted into their mongrel dialects from these languages. The latter word is frequently used with English descriptive epithets. For example, the term "sweet mouf (for mouth) palaver," means what is understood in Ireland by "blarney," in cockneydom by "soft sawder." "Fool palaver" expresses what we would entitle nonsense; "sarce (for saucy) palaver," means abusive language; and the term "god-man palaver," is applied to missionary teaching.

A few specimens of the peculiar idiomatic forms, which owe their origin entirely to derivation from the English tongue, will show at once the pathway in which their chief imitative faculty is tending.

The word "lib" with some, and "live" with others, is used to express the presence of inanimate as well as animate things. "Your hat no lib dere, sir," or, "Your tick no lib dat place you put 'im," are pieces of information frequently given by a negro Mercury if sent in quest of either of these articles, when one is about to proceed out of doors. "My mudder done lib for devil-ly," is an expression in which a Bonny man once conveyed to me the information of his mother's death.

The customs-duty paid to kings or chiefs for the privilege of trading within their districts is expressed by the word "comey," as the nearest approach which their philologists can make to custom.

A present which it is considered essential to give to every African potentate, and which is indeed expected in all cases of conference with them, is expressed by the term "dash"—a very free and easy style of nomenclature—in its origin no doubt intended to signify that the gift should be (literally) dashed at the recipient without any stinginess. There is no harshness about this word, like that of the Turkish "backsheesh," although possessing the same meaning.

"Changey for changey" is a very musical way of describing one thing changed for another, and refers to loves and hates, as well as to palm-oil and British goods.

The phrase, "We go for jam-head," does not mean that skulls are to be jammed one against another, as goats or rams do in combat or playfulness; but that the thinking powers of the brain shall be exercised by two or more persons in mutual cogitation and decision.

Whenever an African talks of his having an enmity against any one, he describes it by confessing that "some bad ting lib for him tummac for dat man;" thus constituting the stomach the organ in which the agency of spite and malice is engendered and nurtured.

"One day no be all day," is a very significant way of expressing the hope of a better day.

The term "bob" has a meaning in some degree resembling that signified by palaver, and seems to me an abbreviation of the slang word "bobbery." There is a trade "bob" and a war "bob," as well as a hate "bob" and a respec' "bob."

At first acquaintance with the native Africans the errors which they commit in sexual nomenclature seem very absurd. A man talks of his daughter as being "his son," of "bullocks' milk," and of a "cock-jackass." A woman up the Niger was introduced as being, in the absence of her brother, "the biggest man for town." To shew the estimation in which the soft sex are held, the brigantine, "George," was fired at by some of the Aboh country people, when dropping down the Nun from the confluence of the Kwarra and Tshadda, because it was inferred the vessel was a "woman ship," therefore helpless, inasmuch as she was unprovided with engines or machinery, and consequently considered incapable if she got into a difficulty.

But these blunders soon lose their novelty by daily repetition in conversation; and there is not much chance of their being assimilated to the high style of those inoculated with the *cacoethes scribendi*. Whether it be to individuals in a private or official character, such communications as the following are frequent amongst the scribbling class. I extract it from the *New Era*, a paper published a few years ago at Sierra Leone :—

" To Daddy Nah Tampin Office.

" HA, DADDY !—Do, yah, nah beg you, tell dem people for me, make dem Sally-own pussin know.—Do yah. Berrah well.

" Ah lib nah Pademba Road—one bwoy lib dah oberside, lakah dem two docta lib overside you Tampin-office. Berrah well. Dah bwoy head big too much—he say nah Militie Ban— he got one long long ting, so-so brass, someting lib da dah go flip flap, dem call am key. Berrah well. Had! dah bwoy kin blow !—she-ah !—na marnin, oh !—nah sun time, oh !—nah evenin, oh !—nah middle-night, oh !—all same—no make pussin sleep. Not ebry bit dat—more lib da ! One Boney bwoy lib oberside ; nah he like blow bugle. When dem two woh-woh bwoy blow dem ting, de nize too much too much.

" When white man blow dat ting, and pussin sleep, he kin tap wah make dem bwoy carn do so? Dem bwoy kin blow ebry day—eben Sunday dem kin blow. Wen ah yerry dem blow Sunday, ah wish dah bugle kin go down na dem troat, or dem kin blow them head-bone inside. Do, nah beg you, yah tell all dem people 'bout dah ting wah dem two bwoy dah blow. Tell am Amtrang Boboh hab febah bad. Tell am Titty carn sleep nah night. Dah nize go kill me two pickin, oh!

"Plabba done.—Good by daddy.

"CRASHEY JANE."

For the information of those not accustomed to the Anglo - African style of writing or speaking, I deem a commentary necessary, in order to make this epistle intelligible.

The whole gist of Crashey Jane's complaint is against two black boys, who are torturing her morning, noon, and night—Sunday as well as every day in the week—by blowing into some long, long brass ting, as well as a bugle. Though there might appear, to some unbelievers, a doubt as to the possibility of the boys furnishing wind for such a lengthened performance, still the complaint is not more extravagant than those made by many scribbling grievance - mongers amongst ourselves about the organ nuisance.

The appellative "Daddy" is used by the Africans as expressive of their respect as well as confidence. "To Daddy, in the stamping (*alias* printing) office," which is the literal rendering of the foregoing address, contains a much more respectful appeal than "to the Editor" would convey; and the words "Berrah well" at the end of the first sentence are ludicrously expressive of the writer's having opened the subject of complaint to her own satisfaction, and of being prepared to go on with what follows without any dread of failure.

The epithet "woh-woh" applied to the censured boys means to entitle them very bad; and I understand this term, which is general over the coast, is derived from a belief that those persons to whom it is applied have a capacity to bring double woe on all who have dealings with them.

"Amtrang Boboh," who has fever bad, is Robert Armstrong, the stipendiary magistrate of Sierra Leone, and the inversion of his name in this manner is as expressive of negro classicality as was the title of Jupiter Tonans to the dwellers on Mount Olympus.

One of the most remarkable features of Anglo-Africanism is what may be entitled the mendicant. From the highest king to the lowest slave begging seems to be indigenous—indeed, with the former class much more than with the latter. For those possess a certain degree of *mauvaise honte*, arising from the dread of remorseless refusal to their caste—the only idea that keeps them from its indulgence.

All the "sweet mouf palaver," all the "daddyism" that can be advanced, is used to effect the success of these appeals, whether oral or written. In the rainy season especially the trading supercargoes in the rivers frequently receive letters narrating the writers' promised *intention* of bringing down ivory, palm-oil, or other produce, and begging in conclusion for a dash of rum, for which a jar is generally sent. In the following specimen, addressed to a " dear brother," there is a beautiful style of fraternal affection shewn by the alternative offered—if he to whom it is addressed does not undertake a voyage of about two thousand miles to see the writer's children, that he will send the few things enumerated therein, which are to " make him satisfy."

The request for " coral and silver rings," and the " pair of ladies' shoes for the wife," seem to be rather *mal-à-propos* for the mother of children in a state of nakedness. It is redolent, too, of the aristocracy of mendicancy amongst a people who, as soon as they are able to read or write, cease to be negroes, and become developed into " coloured ladies and gentlemen."

" F. Po., 2nd September, 1855.

" DEAR BROTHER,—This is to inform you that

my childrens, Name of them **John, Emily,** and **William, sent there** best compliments to you; I am glad to see your Evan this moment **come to me,** because I have sent **you** this **four letters, and no answer from you.** Aidoouka and Abbian come and your grandfather Name is Aisain In-tear; dear brother, **as you don't wish to** come here as I wish you to come to see my children, my wife, and myself, because **I** hope and trust that all of them to see you with **love, joy,** and gladness. Also all our country people give there best compliment to you, **and your wife and** children, and if you can't able to come, sent me something to make me satisfy. Give my best love to **all the Callenban (Kalabar?)** people who join your company; I am quiet **well. Also my** wife beg you for Close, and her children, for they are Naked sent shawl Hondkercif for **me** **and the** one to tie head, also sent me a large coat. Also sent me some corrill and silver Ring and the childrens want shoes two blue caps for John and William a very nice on and my wife sent **to beg** you for one pair of ladies shoes and I want a blue cap or a nice hat. Mouguan jour-ton Nhan Obeng Anook" (this must be a private phrase in some African tongue—perhaps a sort of masonic appeal or hint) " give their best love to you.   Even I myself and children.   I remain your truly brother in love.

"T—— B——."

The passion which rules

> "The court, the camp, the grove,
> And men below, and gods above,"

is very limited in its poetical existence.   It in fact seems to be crawling into life only in one or two places where our language is the established standard one.   In the majority of African kingdoms the gentle god is unknown, and I believe the vile system of polygamy very much tends to keep him so, as well as the fact that woman in all these places is a slave.

In the colony of Liberia, which has been established by the American Colonization Society, and is now a free republic, the civilization of love seems to have taken root, as may be judged from the poetry, speeches, and a considerable amount of amatory Anglo-Africanism which may have been observed in the *Liberia Herald*, a newspaper published at Monrovia, the capital.

I give here an original effusion of a native of that place—not, however, taken from the newspaper—addressed to a " coloured lady," with whose charms, it appears, he was smitten.   Delicacy, of course, obliges me not to reveal the names :—

"January 23rd, 1852.

"To P. R.

"My Dear Miss,—I tak my pen in hand to Embrac you of my health, I was very sick this morning but know I am better but I hope it may find you in a state of Enjoying good health and so is your Relation. Oh my dear Miss what would I give if I could see thy lovely Face this precious minnit O miss you had promis me to tell me something, and I like you to let me know I am very anxious to know what it is give my Respect to the young mens But to the young ladys especially O I am long to see you O miss if I don't see you shortly surely I must die I shut my mouth to hold my breath Miss don't you cry O my little pretty turtle dove I wont you to write to me, shall I go Bound or shall I go free or shall I love a pretty girl a she don't love me give my Respect all enquiring Friend Truly Your respectfully,

"J—— H——.

"Nothing more to say O Miss."

I believe that amongst the gentlemen of this republic more specimens can be adduced of varieties of literature than on any other part of the coast. Before me is a copy of a letter, bearing no date, which was sent from shore to the commander of a man-of-war steamer that had just dropped anchor in the roadstead of Monrovia. It runs thus, and the writer held the position of a colonel in the Liberian militia :—

"GENTLEMEN OF THE MAN-OF-WAR,—I shall be rejoiced to see you on shore. Mrs. H—— sends her love, and will be happy to wash your clothes. I have the honour to be, gentlemen, yours affectionately,

"J—— H——, COLONEL."

Here is a specimen of pathetic sublimity of appeal, from two chiefs who were rescued from slaughter up one of the palm-oil trading rivers, and who, in consequence of not being able to return to their native district, owing to family feuds still existing there, addressed this letter to the British supercargoes :—

"July 15th, 1856.

"GENTLEMEN,—Though several months have now elasped [*sic* in orig.] since we were driven away from B——, we trust that our remembrance may not be obliterated from your memory. We are the same your former friends who now addresses you, but oh, how changed from that persons whom you then knew. Where is now our former flow of spirits, and our prosperity?—they were all fled, all fled, and their places usurped by melancholy, poverty, and the sneers and contempt of an unfeeling world. This to a person of your sensibility must be as painful to read as it is for us to write. It is not our object to practice on your feelings by artful languages. But our distresses have increased to that degree, that speak they will in some guise, and we urged on them, we have stifled our repugnance of disclosing them to you. Without further circumlocution, let us tell you then at once that our state is that of the bitterest poverty, in fact, of destitution, and we make our appeal to your kindly feelings in the name of that friendship which once existed between us. We have said enough. We need add no more.

"We subscribe ourselves to be your most unfortunate friends,

"F—— P——.

"G—— H—— P——."

The conclusion, "We have said enough. We need add no more," may have appeared to the composer as emphatic as the end of Sheridan's great speech on the Warren Hastings case seemed to the servant of the former; for, as Moore tells us, he admired the expression with which was delivered the finale, " My Lords, I have done," much more than he did any other part of that famous three days' oration.

In Fernando Po, where the majority of the inhabitants in its capital have been liberated from slave-ships by British men-of-war, there appeared stuck on a garden paling, one fine morning during my residence there, a notice, of which the following is an exact copy :—

"Notice is hereby given, that person or persons whom will attend in company of play, and dance at the residence of W—— L——'s house, Esquire, (B——t House) I beg respectfully that whom attend in decent and manners, in the presence of the Co., and may require glass of wine and spirits, will attend with sixpence real in the Co., put in subscription of for the company on the 9th instant, in the evening, at 5 o'clock precisely, the undermentioned signatures are the holders of the Co. affixed :—

                  T. E. W—s.   Wm. D—o.

" Bandmasters   Bn. K—y.   Jn. F. M—e.

                  Jo. B—t.

" Clarence, Jan. 5th, 1858."

The band whereof the above signatures purported to represent the masters, comprised only the five musicians, so that each was a *soi-disant* bandmaster. The instruments consisted of two asthmatic flutes, and three noise-making, though far from melody-generating, drums.

I shall not weary my readers by giving more than another example of literary composition. It is a compact history of an old palaver, which I requested a Kalabar man to put on paper for me. Although the main points are here briefly laid down in less than twenty lines, a detail of them occupied the narrator for nearly two hours, when he came to see me on board H. M. S. S. V——.

"In King Archibodg's time Henshaw Duke's family, that time all chop 'be very dear, send seven big canoes full of yams and konkeys to sell at Ikpa market. Then one of King Eyos people come and steal some of Abara Ikang's coppers, then bob come up and fight, then King Eyo's people tief everything that live in the seven canoes. Then when Henshaw Duke's people come home, Duketown gentlemen want to make palaver. Then King Eyo send down and say he will to pay for all de coppers his people tief. Then Henshaw Duke's people say they no want nothing for Eshian Eyo, King Eyo's head man at Ikpa, had beg pardon of

Abara Ikang, and make sorry, and so palaver set one time."

No less remarkable, as a specimen of brevity, was a proclamation once issued by the bellman at Fernando Po, according to the governor's instructions. It was intended to tell the owners of all pigs, without rings in their noses, that these animals were destined to be shot if found abroad. The bell, of course, being tolled as he walked along, he thus spoke to the crowd gathered at each corner:—

"I say—I say—I say—I say—suppose a pig walk—iron no live for him nose!—gun shoot!—kill 'im one time! Hear ee, hear ee."

Not the most accomplished lexicographer, from Johnson's time to ours, could have proclaimed the governor's ukase so happily, because so intelligibly, to those for whom it was intended.

When we come to consider that some of these productions are emanations from grown-up men, who have received an education in missionary schools, it may be wondered at that so little continuity of ideas or coherence of composition is observable in them.

The present development of the mental powers of the native African is one upon which a variety of opinions exist.   On this subject there appears to me a sound philosophy in the following observations, written by my friend, Captain Sir Henry Vere Huntley, of which he has given me liberty to make use. Few men have had more opportunities for acquiring experience in Western Africa than Sir Henry, in his connexion with the Naval as well as with the Civil service of Her Majesty's Government :—

"I fear the intellect of the Tropical African is not of that order which some few who have, and a vast number who have not, visited Africa proclaim it to be. Had it been so, the chiefs long ago would have seen the ruinous consequences of slave-dealing with foreigners, and of slavery at home ; or otherwise the Tropical African himself would have broken from his bondage, and asserted his liberty, as every intellectual race, sooner or later, has done.

" In the origin, no nation had more favourable opportunity than others of emerging from barbarism, unless it is admitted that some were gifted with a higher standard of mental capacity than others, which enabled them to rise to the heights of civilization and sound religion. But such an admission crushes the claim of Tropical Africa to any even moderate scale of intellect.

D

With some nations, of the higher order, superstition fell before religion sooner than in others, and primitive ingenuity was earlier developed into skilful mechanism; whilst Tropical Africa remains unchanged. Even nations which have completely succumbed for a time, have, when events threw open their gates and ports, shown themselves to have been long in possession of highly civilized practices and feelings, as well as much advanced in arts and sciences, in spite of their self-imposed isolation. Extraordinary powers of perception and adaptation have distinguished these nations on coming into contact with others. With Tropical Africa there is no trace of such indigenous, or, as some wildly believe, suppressed mental powers.

"I am aware that there are persons who strangely argue, that whoever thinks the Tropical African less intellectual by nature than the inhabitants of other countries, must of necessity be an advocate for the slave-trade, and for all manner of unmitigated oppression in Africa. We reply that there is nothing inconsistent, but the reverse, in those who see deformities, defects, and even vices in the African character, maintaining towards them at the same time the Christian attributes of commiseration and mercy ; and that there is little charity in that mind which can argue that the perception of a low intellect in the negro must necessarily lead to the treatment of him with injustice, cruelty, and oppression."

Probably we shall be able to judge whether this reasoning be correct or otherwise, if tested by an illustration from our own time, when we come to examine the intellectual features which are in existence, according to their own showing, amongst the citizens of the republic of Liberia.

CHAPTER III.

IT may be asserted by the over-captious that I ought to search for and adduce illustrations for this chapter amongst the Africans, who are component parts of the population of British Colonies, and who may, therefore, be expected to give evidence of a more highly developed intelligence under the fostering care of a Government establishment. But I deem it an act of justice to the black men, who claim an equality with whites, rather to show of what stuff they are made, according to their own advocates ; and to point out how erroneously writers of their own class describe them before the world as possessing qualities of which they have as yet shown no palpable evidence.

The republic of Liberia has been pictured by Mrs. Beecher Stowe as the Eden into which one of the characters in " Uncle Tom's Cabin " retires to spend the evening of his days. It has been acknowledged as a free and independent republic by the majority of European governments, and it is frequently pointed out to us as evidence of what the native African can do in establishing his independence.

Frederika Bremer, in all her beautiful works, never arrived at a conclusion more true than the following* :—" To imagine that the emancipated slaves of America could, beyond the sea, in Liberia in Africa, establish a community according to

* " Homes of the New World, Impressions of America." By Frederika Bremer. Translated by Mary Howitt.

the American republic, is, I believe, a grand mistake." No greater mistake has ever been made by the friends of the African. In the organization of this republic, there was deficient —or rather discarded—what Miss Bremer writes of as " that great influence which a man of the white race, by his natural intellectual superiority and systematic turn of mind, will always have over the black." I do not go so far as to say the white *will always* have superiority over the blacks ; but I hold that, in the present state of their relative development, such a condition of supe- riority does exist. I maintain this more strongly, for the purpose of showing how the Rev. E. Blyden—literary champion of that republic— damages his own position as an advocate of progress, by assuming a condition of perfection which we know does not exist amongst his re- publican brethren. Moreover, he flings down the gauntlet of defiance at the whites, without whom neither he nor his compatriots would be free this day in the republic of Liberia.

Let me not be misunderstood. I have perused sentiments from the pen of this gentleman which oblige me to respect him. I have seen his ad- vocacy of the spirit of self-reliance, as spoken to the people of Monrovia, set forth in language worthy of the illustrious Ellery Channing. For these reasons I regret to read thus from Mr. Blyden's pamphlet, entitled a "Vindication of the African race" :—

" Cases are not wanting of coloured persons fleeing from American bondage to Liberia, who, meeting a few difficulties, and unused to the task of self-reliance, wish to return and live their former life of ease and freedom from care. Some do return, and bear back evil reports of this good land. These cases are painful; but they are not surprising: they are illustrations of the invariable effects of slavery. Nor is it to be wondered at that even in Liberia, an African Government, free, sovereign, and independent, there should be, as Bishop Scott alleges, 'a degree of deference shown to white men that is not shown to coloured.' This will be the case in every African community for a long time; even after the entire abolition of slavery in the Western world. This reverence of the oppressed for the oppressor, as we have just seen in the case of the Israelites, is not easily shaken off. Such is the influence of the latter upon the former, that their voice, on any question, has the effect to hush into the profoundest silence the least murmur of dissent on the part of the former.

"It is, however, incumbent upon the intelligent among the African race to discountenance, as much as possible, this servile feeling, and to use every means to crush it wherever it appears; for its influence on the mind and morals, and general progress of the race, is fearfully injurious."

There is a querulousness of petty vanity in this which almost forbids us to hope for good from such a source. In a republic where no white man is allowed to have a voting or executive influence in government, "a degree of deference to white men" is complained of. We cannot wonder at this, indeed, when we remember that a few pages previously we read :—

"Let the candid among the enemies of our race take, as far as they know, all the cases of Africans who have enjoyed any opportunities of intellectual development and improvement, and see if the majority have not profitably availed themselves of those opportunities: or take an African of ordinary mind, and a Caucasian of like capacity; place them both under the same instructions, with equal privileges, and we hazard nothing by saying that the Caucasian will not excel the African, if, indeed, he keep pace with him. This has been tested, and the result has turned out in favour of the African. If, then, under given circumstances, the Caucasian will arrive at a certain point of intellectual improvement, and under the same circumstances—as the facts of a fair induction show—the African will attain to the same point, where is the absolute superiority of the Caucasian? Where is the peculiar mental obtuseness of the African? Where?"

I take it upon myself to answer the latter question—that we have, in the very query itself, a most palpable proof of "mental obtuseness," following up, as it does, the writer's classification of all white men as the "oppressors" of the African race.

Throughout the whole of Mr. Blyden's pamphlet he follows the very style of reasoning which he himself condemns in others. "It cannot be truly affirmed," he says, "that inferences proceeding on such assumptions wait for refutation; but those who avail themselves of them follow *prejudice* more than *judgment*. And so strongly does their prejudice against the African bias their minds, that we often find even the profoundest of them indulging in such one-sided argument."

And yet because John C. Calhoun, of South

Carolina, employed " bold and unblushing sophistry with reference to the African race," and because Mr. Blyden was refused admittance to a literary institution in the United States, on the ground that the faculty had failed to realize their expectations in one or two coloured persons whom they had educated, the white people all over the world are enemies of his race, and their oppressors.

Mr. Blyden's objection to "isolated cases the most unfavourable being taken as fair specimens of the character of the whole race," might seem to be very fair, if he would allow this sentence to be applied to the few cases he adduces to prove the non-existence of intellectual obtuseness, and would permit the single change of *un*favourable to favourable.

What hopes there may be from Liberia can be gathered from his concluding sentiments, which contain much that is good, and beautiful, and true, with a considerable amount of what cannot be defined as anything more elevated than vapid rhodomontade :—

" The position of the people of Liberia invests them with peculiar ability for doing good in behalf of the downtrodden race to which they belong. If they properly use that ability, they

may exert no inconsiderable influence in bringing about the universal disenthralment and
elevation of Africans.   They should not, in
order to benefit their enslaved brethren, 'render
evil for evil' to their oppressors.   Such a course
is productive of no good; it is a plan of proce-
dure that finds no sympathy in these enlightened
days—it is a progeny of the dark ages.   These
are times when, by argumentation and demonstration, the moral sensibilities of men must be
appealed to.   Physical inconveniences, employed
for the purpose of correcting moral evils, have
no true reformatory effect.   Men must be led—
not driven.   No desirable effect can be produced
by reiterating doleful complaints and harsh vitu-
perations against men on account of their prejudices.   But a great deal is accomplished by
furnishing practical demonstrations that such
prejudices are destitute of foundation.   And
this is the work of the people of Liberia in
particular and of coloured men in general.   We
must prove to our oppressors that we are men,
possessed of like susceptibilities with themselves,
by seeking after those attributes which give
dignity to a State; by cultivating those virtues
which shed lustre upon individuals and communities; by pursuing whatever is magnificent

in enterprise, whatever is lovely and of good report in civilization, whatever is exalted in morals, and whatever is exemplary in piety. Then shall we prove that we do possess 'rights which white people are bound to respect;' the decision of an enlightened Chief Justice to the contrary notwithstanding. But so long as we contentedly remain at the foot of the ladder at whose top *our oppressors* stand, it is unreasonable, it is absurd, to call upon them to recognise us as equals in every respect; and it is worse than absurdity to abuse and vilify them for their opinions and prejudices with respect to us. We must make our way to the position which they occupy. And having overstepped the interval which has so long separated us from them, and standing with them on the same summit, we shall be welcomed as equals. Then will Shem, Ham, and Japheth dwell together as brethren, in 'liberty, equality, and fraternity.' There will be no more slavery; for Canaan, the 'servant of servants,' has been exterminated."

"We must make our way to the position which they, our oppressors, occupy," is language which, in fact, involves a true principle; but Mr. Blyden ought to see the inconsistency of boasting of what the Liberians can do for the downtrodden

race to which they belong, till *they* get to the top
of that ladder "where their oppressors stand,"
and at whose foot they acknowledge themselves
as still remaining. Before they attain that position, too, the boast of intellectual and mental
equality is a piece of flagrant bombast, and
nothing more.

With the instances advanced of the Anglo-
African tendency, opposed although they be to
what I cannot avoid designating as erroneous
reasonings from the Liberian republic, the
question may be asked—Are there no other obstacles than these latter standing in the way of
African civilization, and opposing the development of that country's inexhaustible riches?

Civil wars all along the Gold Coast do not
indicate anything like a condition of happiness
or prosperity; and as we approach the neighbourhood of the palm oil rivers, there rises up
before us a panorama such as I believe no other
part of the world can show.

The sacrifice of twin children, as well as of those
who cut their upper teeth first, is carried on at New
Kalabar as in Aboh and Old Kalabar. Even as
late as 1856 an Albino child was sacrificed at
the bar of the first-named river to the shark,
who was, up to a late period, the ju-ju of this

country. Some of the natives up the creeks having been devoured by these carnivorous fish, the family of the shark species got into disfavour, and now goats and fowls are their favourite sacrificial offerings.

At the mouth of Brass river, when an Albino girl is sacrificed, the officiator at this ceremony is an old man named Onteroo. He has an enormous tuberosity on the back of his head; but whether his divinity is believed to exist in this or not, my informant cannot say. Several canoes accompany him and the victim, who, it seems, is quite satisfied with her fate, as she is indoctrinated with the idea that her future destiny is to be married to a white man. As soon as they reach the bar, the canoes are all turned with their heads homewards; the word is given, and the girl is thrown into the water, with a weight round her neck to prevent her floating, thus obviating the possibility of an escape.

The Brass people have likewise an interior (to their country) territory, entitled the god country, to which they resort for oracular purposes. Keya, the King of the Obullum Abry side of Brass river, was known to have recently paid a visit there to ascertain whether he or a powerful chief, named Amanga, was to be the head man.

On his return, a number of the " god country" people came with him, and lived at his place, on the fat of the land, whilst they were deliberating. Amanga, of course, was now and then present at the festivals; but one morning he became very sick, and was dead in a few hours afterwards.

In parts of Benin it is the custom to sacrifice two men at the appearance of a new moon.

The Rev. Mr. Crowther's journal of his last ascent of the Niger records :—" After the inspection of the lands at Idda, as we were returning to the ship, Kasumo, the Arabic interpreter, who had fallen in with a brother Mallam here, and also with a Yoruba slave, was privately informed that, about three months ago, an Albino slave boy, whom we saw here in 1854, about nine years of age, was offered in sacrifice as a peace-offering in the settlement of their political disputes; that the hands and feet of the poor boy were dislocated, after which he was put alive into a pit prepared for him, over which a large pot was placed; so the poor creature had to linger the remaining days of his miserable existence in torture and agony. He was there three or four days before he expired, when the pit was covered up."

Something similar to this brutality, but of a more aggravated nature, is the mode in which punishment for murder is inflicted by the aborigines of Fernando Po. When the murderer is discovered, his crime is proved before a meeting of the magnates of his district—not with any form of trial by jury, or of test by ordeal, but simply by the deposition of evidence, be it confirmatory or circumstantial. The body of his victim is then carried to some distance in the bush, and he is tied to it by withes plucked from trees. He is left in that horrid position, without a bit to eat or a drop to drink, until death puts an end to his sufferings. The prolongation of a man's life under such circumstances, bound night and day to a dead body advancing to putridity, is a fate that one shudders to think of.

Yet perhaps we should not regard this with equal horror, did we reflect that in our own Christian country of England, and about A.D. 1190 — in the glorious old times of the Crusaders —the first " articles of war " issued by

Richard Cœur de Lion, for the government of the Navy, contained a primitive code, which punished the murderer by lashing him to his victim's body and throwing him into the sea.

It may be considered a strange coincidence that amongst the tribes of the interior, who can have no communication with those on the coast, similar brutalities are in existence, as if such things were racy of the African soil. Dr. Livingstone records* that "in several tribes a child which is said to 'tlola' (transgress) is put to death. 'Tlola,' or transgression, is ascribed to several curious causes. A child who cuts the upper front teeth before the under, is always put to death among the Bakaa, and, I believe, also among the Bakwains. [A practice similar to this exists at Aboh, New and Old Kalabar.] In some tribes, when twins are born, one of them is put to death. [A modification of the Old Kalabar custom of burying twins alive.] And an ox which, while lying in the pen, beats the ground with its tail, is treated in the same way. It is thought to be calling death to visit the tribe."

On the occasion of a civil war at Bonny this year (1859), the following incident occurred:—

* " Missionary Travels and Researches in South Africa," p. 577. Murray, London. 1858.

A canoe, paddled by four young boys, the eldest not more than seven years of age, and steered with a paddle by a man in the stern, was observed crossing the river amongst the shipping. It was pursued by another canoe, in which were eight men propelling, and a man standing up in its fore part with a rifle in his hand. As soon as the latter had reached to within fifteen or twenty yards of the former, the armed man fired at and killed one of the boys. He coolly reloaded his rifle and shot the other three boys in succession. The murderer's canoe having soon arrived at that which had now but one occupant, he (the last-named) jumped into the water, out of which he was soon dragged by his pursuers, to be stabbed to death in their canoe with knives.

The idea that men who had committed a murder " should be condemned to the same fate they had bestowed upon another," is practically carried out in the very mode in which the butchery had been consummated—as thus recorded to me, by Mr. Oates, of its occurrence at New Kalabar :—

" On the 4th January, 1859, as Dr. Saunders and I were leaving the beach, a great commotion was raised through the town, in consequence of the ju-ju king having been attacked and severely wounded in the ju-ju house. We returned, and on going up to the place, found it full of natives. On a table in the centre was stretched the unfortunate ju-ju potentate, suffering from a severe stab in the abdomen and a fearful gash in the wrist. With such appliances as the natives could furnish, Dr. Saunders stitched and dressed the wounds. It was then related to us that a head man of the ju-ju king's establishment had been mad for a few days; that while he was making ju-ju, with many of the people attending at the ceremonial, the lunatic had rushed into the temple and inflicted the wounds on him; and that, before the madman could be seized, he had rushed away again, supposed to have gone into the bush (as the thick wood around is termed).

" Dr. Saunders wished the king's bed to be made up in the ju-ju house, that the wounds might not be disturbed; but all those around objected, giving as a reason their dread of the assassin coming back and doing something worse. Preparations being then made to take him on a door to his dwelling-house, we proceeded to accompany the bearers, when, on going outside, we saw no less than three hundred men armed with guns, daggers, spears, and knives. Such is the respect shown to white men, that over a hundred of these armed people formed a body-guard around us to conduct us in safety to the beach, where our boats were, as it was then getting dark, and the madman might be roaming about; for in his flight he had stabbed two women, though not mortally wounded them. Some of this escort carried torches, and the flashing light in darkness revealing the blades of weapons, with the moving ebony of their nearly naked bodies, and the glistening savagery of their eyes, was a picture not often seen, even in Africa.

"*January* 5.—The ju-ju king died this morning. After the ceremonies of his funeral were over, he was buried in his own temple, a number of armed men afterwards going in pursuit of the murderer. They found him in a tree and shot him. Athough he fell down dead, they inflicted upon him like wounds to those he had given to the king—namely, a stab in the belly and a gash across the wrist. His body was then cut in two and thrown into the river for shark food.

" In a very few days afterwards upwards of fifty persons belonging to the murderer's family were put to death in a similar manner—by wounds in the belly and across the wrist. Indeed, there was not a single one of his kith or kin left in the town that was not sacrificed in exactly the same manner as he had butchered the king."

Although the natives of New Kalabar had great faith in this ju-ju king—ranking him on all state occasions before king Amakree—they hold in veneration a superior spirit, believed to exist in a country some three months' travel from New Kalabar, and in a direction tending towards Aboh, up the river Niger. I believe it to be in some part of Oru ; and it is entitled by them, when they speak of it in English, the " Long ju-ju country." Parties are sent there to undergo an ordeal for serious crimes. It is believed that the ju-ju at that place, who is supposed to be a woman, knows everything—the names of all the ships trading in the river, of the merchants to whom they belong, and of the supercargoes. The country in which this Delphic oracle resides is described as a species of amphitheatre, surrounded by hills. As soon as the accused arrives near a certain bush—only one person being allowed to approach at a time—his accuser makes the charge against him in a loud voice. He is then called on to say if he be guilty or not guilty. Of course the charge is invariably denied. Upon this he is told to return. The simple people of New Kalabar, who never have been there, believe that if the accused be innocent he can go back; but that if he be really guilty, his feet become fastened to the ground; that water springs up, which rises, rises, rises gradually, till it mounts over his head, when he is drowned; and that, as soon as the water subsides after his death, the victim is found fastened in the earth, with nothing of his body visible except his head.

Mr. Oates informed me that, on one occasion, a hundred men were sent away by the authorities, being accused of some witchcraft, the particulars of which he was ignorant of. Of these thirty-nine returned, bringing with them an accusation against twenty other persons, who had not previously been suspected, and who thus, by the revelation of the long ju-ju, were declared guilty. These were executed, having been first made drunk—a privilege which is likewise granted to all condemned to die by Egbo authority in Old Kalabar. The mode of execution at New Kalabar is hacking the convicted with swords, knives, and cutlasses, till death puts an end to his sufferings.

CHAPTER IV.

Wilhelm Humboldt's idea of the human family being one fraternity.—Baron Von Humboldt's concurrence in these opinions.—Adherence of native Africans to gri-gris, ju-jus, and fetishes.—Cannibalism.—Probability of languages assimilating their nature to these practices.—Of the sale of human flesh at Sierra Leone.—Mr. Caulker's explanation of reasons for burning or burying alive the Negroes.—Cannibalism at Omun, amongst the Boola tribe and the Ejoemen.—Sale of Negro flesh at Old Kalabar.—Cannibalism at Brass.—Reasons given for eating the slaughtered bodies of their enemies.—Of the Pangwes taking carcasses out of the ground to eat them.—Reprisal cannibalism at New Kalabar.

In the first volume of Baron Von Humboldt's "Cosmos," * an extract is given from a work of his brother Wilhelm, in which the following passage occurs :—

" If we would indicate an idea, which throughout the whole course of history has ever more and more widely extended its empire, or which

* Page 368.

more than any other testifies to the much con-
tested, and still more decidedly misunderstood,
perfectibility of the whole human race, it is that
of establishing our common humanity; of striv-
ing to remove the barriers which prejudice and
limited views of every kind have erected amongst
men, and to treat all mankind, without reference
to religion, nation, or *colour*, as one fraternity,
one great community, fitted for the attainment
of one object—the unrestrained development of
the psychical powers."

Bearing upon these observations, the Baron
likewise remarks* :—"The principle of individual and political freedom is implanted in the
ineradicable conviction of the equal rights of one
sole human race."

This philosophy puzzles one who contemplates
such scenes as I have recorded, and am about to
go on with. There may be allowed a palliation
for the deeds of the American Indians in scalp-
ing those who fall into their hands by the for-
tunes of war, or the chances of raid and foray.
A plea may, perhaps, be advanced for the
atrocities committed by Sepoys in the recent
Indian rebellion, urged on as they were by the
despotic creed of Islamism. But the thirst for

* Humboldt's "Cosmos," vol. ii., p. 568.

blood which marks the lives of many of the Negro races, seems to me very incompatible with the foregoing, as well as with another idea of Humboldt's * :—

"Whilst we maintain the unity of the human species, we at the same time repel the depressing assumption of superior and inferior races of men. There are nations more susceptible of cultivation, more highly civilized, more ennobled by mental cultivation, than others ; but none in themselves nobler than others."

I fear that "mental cultivation" can have little effect on individuals who cannot be classed as humanized. Although not denying that a few, very few—the *rari nantes in gurgite vasto*—have manifested an intellectual capacity equal to that of white men ; still, even those who for scores of years have been intermixing with European traders, mostly Englishmen, cling to their gri-gris, ju-jus, fetishes, and cannibalism, with as much pertinacity as they did a hundred years ago.

It might be assumed that their languages, assi-milating the practices of their daily lives to natural organization, may have something to do with this adherence to old practices. No doubt arguments can be advanced to prove that

* "Cosmos," vol. i., p. 368.

they, with all their thirst for their fellow-crea-
tures' blood, are entirely innocent and unconscious of many abominable crimes, which are of
daily occurrence amongst civilised communities
of Europe. Caligulas and Neros may be said
to exist amongst these tribes; although they
have not yet arrived at that stage of civilization which produces a Robson or a Redpath.

People in England, who imagine Africa to be
a land of palms and gold, of elephants and lions
—even those less poetic and more commercial
folk who look to the growing development of
that country's resources in the increasing production of palm oil and ivory—would scarcely
believe that in these days—whilst I write—cannibalism is almost as rampant on the west coast
of Africa as it has ever been.

Let us turn backwards a few hundred miles
from Liberia to the British colony of Sierra
Leone, where we can read the following paragraph in the "African" newspaper of April 5th
last. It is contained in a report of the sixty-
eighth (!) anniversary of the Countess of Hun-
tingdon's connexion in that colony :—

"Mr. Samuel Priddy, who is employed by
the Society, and has been labouring as a native
missionary at Bompeh in the Sherbro country,

supported the same (*i.e.* a resolution). He stated that the cruel and barbarous practices of cannibalism were indulged in during the late war, and that he saw hampers of dried human flesh carried on the backs of men, upon which they intended to feast. He called for help, and hoped that such pecuniary means would be provided as would prove sufficient to send him back to the sphere of his former labours."

The editor, in a foot-note, says he would like to see the statement confirmed, as if a doubt could be thrown on the spoken words of a respectable and truth-telling missionary, who recorded only what *he saw!*

In a subsequent number of the same paper, we observe a Mr. Caulker denying that cannibalism exists in the Bompeh part of the Sherbro country, and asserting that the Boorhdy country must be the one meant by Mr. Priddy; thereby acknowledging that cannibalism *does* exist in his neighbourhood. With what a graphic coolness is the following palliation given in his defence of the Bompeh people against the charge of being man-eaters :—

" Only when one is sick, they would request the sick party to confess all that he or she had done in order to live; and if the sick party acknowledges to have entered into a leopard or an alligator, to eat any one that may have been killed by such animals, or to have sucked the blood of a deceased person while living, then the parents of such deceased person (if the deceased party was a chief or some high one) will flog such person to death, or burn, or bury such person alive."

This is quite enough of the peculiarities of the "white man's grave" for the present, so we pass Monrovia again and speed down the coast.

Cannibalism exists in the Omun country, up the Cross river; and I am informed that the Boola tribe, who reside far interior to Corisco bay, come down the Mooney river to get some of the sea-shore dwelling people to make "chop" of them, because they are reputed to have a salt-ish, therefore a relishable flavour. This may be defined to be the epicurism of man-eating.

My late colleague at Lagos (B. Campbell, Esq.), giving me some information about the Ejoemen or Jomen—a tribe spread over the countries adjacent to many creeks in the Delta of the Niger—observes, "When I wrote to you about the Ejoemen I forgot to tell you that they are generally considered to be cannibals. Some Krooboys, who had been badly treated on board a Liverpool ship, a few years since, took one of the boats and went off. Hunger and thirst compelled them to enter one of the rivers between Benin and the Nun. The Ejoemen fell in with them, and after a desperate struggle captured the Kroomen, first killing two of their number. The survivors of the Krooboys were eventually sold at Warree town, and redeemed by Mr. Henry. They declared to Mr. Henry that the Ejoemen had eaten those boys who were killed.

"When Captain Denham was surveying this part of the coast, he sent up one of the rivers a boat, in which were two young officers. They were attacked by the Ejoemen, overpowered and killed, and if the surviving Kroomen's story be true, were no doubt eaten also.

"Mr. Carr, of the model farm (second Niger Expedition), was most probably killed by these people, or by King Boy, who was an Ejoeman."

During the year 1859 human flesh was exposed for sale, as butcher's meat, in the market at Duketown, Old Kalabar.

In Brass (or the Nimbe country), cannibalism often occurs. Even within the last year a chief of that district, named Imamy, killed two of the Acreeka people before mentioned, who were sacrificed to the manes of his father, and eaten.   In Brass, as in Bonny, they eat all enemies taken in war; and they put forth, as a justification for this, that devouring the flesh of their enemies makes them braver.

Captain Townsend, who is very familiar with the internal economy of all the negro tribes, has related to me the following illustration.

The Pangwes, who reside up the river Gaboon, exhume, for the purpose of eating them, the dead bodies of their friends, when they have been from six to eight days in the ground. A Gaboon black trader, in the employment of a white supercargo, died suddenly. His family thinking that the death had resulted from witchcraft, two of his sisters were authorised to go to his grave and bring his head away, in order that they might test the fact. This testing is effected in the following manner: An iron pot with fresh water is placed on the floor; at one side of it is the head of the dead man; at the other side is seated a fetish doctor. The latter functionary then puts in his mouth a piece of herb, supposed to impart divining powers, chews it, and forms a magic circle by spitting round the pot, the head, and himself. The face of the murderer, after a few incantations, is supposed to be reflected on the water contained

in the pot. The fetish man then states he sees
the murderer, and orders the head to be again
put back to its proper grave, some days being then
given to him for deliberation. In the meantime,
he may fix on a man who is rich enough to pay
him a sufficient bribe to be excused of the charge;
and if so, he confesses that the fetish has
failed.

In the case just mentioned, when they returned
with the head, the body left behind was nowhere
to be found, and on making inquiries into the
facts connected with its disappearance, it was ascertained, beyond doubt, that some Pangwes, who
had been present at the disinterment for the purpose of decapitation, had returned to the grave,
taken the body therefrom, and eaten it.

Mr. Oates, who was trading for Captain Straw,
supercargo to Messrs. Horsfall and Sons, of Liverpool, has drawn out for me a picture of his experience in New Kalabar:—

"It seems that some few weeks previous to this
occurrence (27th August, 1858), two natives of
New Kalabar were on their way to the Aboh
palm oil market, when they were caught by the
natives of a district called Acreeka, killed, and
eaten. On hearing of this, the New Kalabarese
determined on reprisal. Accordingly, a palaver

was held, and a message sent demanding that the murderers should be given up, at the same time intimating that if this request were not granted, a war with no mercy to young or old would be commenced forthwith. The men, four in number, were delivered over, along with a boy, who turned king's evidence, in the hope of not being included in the punishment. They were tried before the ju-ju King, as well as the chiefs in the ju-ju house, and condemned to the same fate as they had inflicted on the others. They were then brought into the market place, which is hard by a sheet of water opposite King Arnakree's residence,* and the boy informer was compelled to perform the most disgusting mutilations on his unfortunate countrymen whilst they stood in the water. Worse than tiger-like, the spectators drank the water, in which was mingled the blood of the victims. The latter were then dragged out, hacked and cut limb from limb by the Kalabarese executioners, whilst pieces of their flesh were distributed amongst the natives of the town, some of whom roasted, some boiled, and others made soup, rendered pungent, no doubt, by palm oil and red peppers."

* Vide "Impressions of Western Africa," p. 101. Longman, Brown, & Co., 1858.

CHAPTER V.

Author's doubts of foregoing **brutalities**, removed only by what he saw carried out—Reprisal Execution at Bonny preparatory to a Cannibalistic Feast—Private Arrangements to obtain a View of the Scene of Execution—Sensations on seeing the Ju-ju house at early dawn—No Similarity between it and Newgate—The Executioner and the Victim—Appalling Nature of the Silence prevailing at the Butchery—Manner in which the Execution was carried out—Decapitation—Boys **and** Girls Carrying Bits of the Carcasses away with them—Two Women Squabbling for a Morsel of Negro Flesh—Inutility of Moral Force Preaching to prevent such Scenes—The Ju-ju Executioner's Reason for not Eating his Brother Negro's Head—Accounts of Similar Butchery and Cannibalism at Dahomey—Heroes Wearing Necklaces of Human Teeth.

I must confess that the stories which I had only recently heard of cannibalism did startle me—as I believe they will many of the public, to whom they are new, with reference to this part of the world.

The incidents recorded by Mr. Oates set me seriously to think. I was already aware of the door-

pillars, as well as the inside flooring, of the Bonny
ju-ju house being ornamented with negroes' skulls.
I had seen within this heathen temple arm and leg
bones of human bodies arranged on its high altar.
These were the mortal remains of their enemies
in the Andoney country, whom they did not
deny that their forefathers had devoured. But
I entertained not the slightest suspicion that any
leaven of the old anthropophagy existed in the
present time, till I had ocular proof of its appalling atrocities.

On the occasion of an official visit to Bonny,
in the early part of last year, I was privately informed that a reprisal execution, prefatory to the
eating of a body, was to take place on the following morning, opposite the ju-ju house. It
was in return for a similar murder of one
of the better class of slaves, who had been a
palm-oil trader—and who was reported to have
been killed, as well as eaten, the week before, in
one of the creeks leading up to the Humballah
country. The poor fellow captured, and now
doomed to death, was to be eaten too. No white
man in the river was expected to know anything
about it. Indeed, if a white man were seen near
the place of execution when the victim was about
to suffer, his presence would have either caused

an adjournment to another time and place, or have been the subject of a "big palaver," involving the payment of a considerable fine.

Communicating my intentions to nobody, I landed, on the evening of our arrival, at the sandy beach close by the river's side, and opposite to where the trading ships are anchored, instead of going the usual way round by the creek into town. I sauntered in the direction of the ju-ju house, seemingly with no purpose, and a few minutes' survey shewed me a small house, with a loop-hole in it, commanding a view of the temple's front—nothing intervening between it and the creek but a heap of garbage. The door was within a few yards of the creek, which runs at a right angle with the main bed of the river. It was empty and unoccupied, and had probably been used as a store in past times by some trader, who had now grown rich enough to buy or build a larger magazine elsewhere.

Making a detour by another route, I returned to H. M. S. S. S.——; and the commander, entering into my wishes, gave orders to have a boat ready at any time on the following morning when I desired it. I suggested the small dingy, with four Krooboys using paddles.

Starting from the vessel at half-past four o'clock

in the morning, after taking my shower-bath, cup of coffee, and glass of Quinine wine, the Krooboys paddled noiselessly along. The man-of-war steamer being anchored a considerable distance down the river, we turned into the creek, as a faint greyness, indicative of coming day, appeared in the eastern sky. "Softly, softly," the Krooboys sculling, we approach the nearest landing-place, between which and the river's corner arises a dense mangrove bush, ten or twelve feet high above the water's surface. I am removed from the boat to shore on the shoulders of a Krooman. Then, telling the men to go back to the ship for their breakfast, and to return to the front beach for me in two hours, I slipped into the small house, and closed the door.

I know not of what kind are the sensations felt by those around Newgate, waiting for an execution in the very heart of London's great city; but I know that on the banks of an African river, in the grey dawn of morning—where the stillness was of that oppressive nature which is calculated to produce the most gloomy impressions, with dense vapours and foul smells arising from decomposing mangrove, and other causes of malaria, floating about, with a heaviness of atmosphere that depressed the spirits, amidst a community of cannibals, I *do* know that, although under the protection of a man-of-war, I felt on this occasion a combined sensation of suspense, anxiety, horror, and indefinable dread of I cannot tell what, that I pray God it may never be my fate to endure again.

Day broke, and, nearly simultaneous with its breaking, the sun shone out. As I looked through the slit in the wall on the space between my place of concealment and the ju-ju house, I observed no change from its appearance the evening before. No gibbet, nor axe, nor gallows, nor rope—no kind of preparation, nothing significant of death, save the skulls in the pillars of the ju-ju house, that seemed leering at me with an expression at once strange and vacant. It would have been a relief in the awful stillness of the place to have heard something of what I had read of the preparations for an execution in Liverpool or London—of the hammering suggestive of driving nails into scaffold, drop, or coffin—of a crowd gathering round the place before early dawn—and of the solemn tolling of the bell that chimed another soul into eternity. Everything seemed as if nothing beyond the routine of daily life were to take place.

Could it be that I had been misinformed—that

the ceremony was adjourned to another time, or was to be carried out elsewhere?

No. A distant murmur of gabbling voices was heard approaching nearer and nearer, till, passing the corner house on my left, I saw a group of negroes. An indiscriminate crowd of all ages and both sexes, so huddled together that no person whom I could particularly distinguish as either an executioner or culprit was visible amongst them. But above their clattering talk came the sound of a clanking chain that made me shudder.

They stopped in the middle of the square opposite the ju-ju house, and ceased talking.

One commanding voice uttered a single word, and down they sat upon the grass, forming a circle round two figures, standing upright in the centre—the executioner and the man about to be killed. The former was remarkable only by the black skull-cap which he had on him, and by a common cutlass which he held in his hand. The latter had chains round his neck, his wrists, and his ankles. There was no sign of fear or cowardice about *him*—no seeming consciousness of the dreadful fate before him—no evidence even upon his face of that dogged stubbornness which is said to be exhibited by some persons about to undergo an ignominious death.

Save that he stood upright one would scarcely have known that he was alive. Amongst the spectators, too, there was a silent impassiveness which was appalling. Not a word, nor gesture, nor glance of sympathy, that could make me believe I looked at beings who had a vestige of humanity amongst them.

As the ju-ju butcher stepped back and measured his distance to make an effectual swoop at his victim's neck the man moved not a muscle, but stood as if he were unconscious—till——.

Chop! the first blow felled him to the ground. The noise of a chopper falling on meat is familiar to most people. No other sound was here—none from the man, not a whisper nor a murmur from those who were seated about! I was nearly crying out in mental agony, and the sound of that first stroke will haunt my ears to my dying day. How I wished some one to talk or scream, to destroy the impression of that fearful hough, and the still more awful silence that followed it. Again the weapon was raised to continue the decapitation—another blow as the man lay prostrate, and then a sound broke the silence! But, oh, Father of Mercy! of what a kind was that noise—a gurgle and gasp accompanying the dying spasm of the struck-down man.   Once more the weapon was lifted—I saw the blood flow in gory horror down the blade to the butcher's hand, and there it was visible in God's bright sunshine to the whole host of heaven.   Not a word had yet been uttered by the crowd.   More chopping and cleaving, and the' head, severed from the body, was put, by the ju-ju executioner, into a calabash, which was carried off by one of his women to be cooked.   He then repeated another cabalistic word, or perhaps the same as at first, and directly all who were seated rose up, whilst he walked away.   A yell, such as reminded me of a company of tigers, arose from the multitude—cutlasses were flourished as they crowded round the body of the dead man— sounds of cutting and chopping rose amidst the clamour of the voices, and I began to question myself whether if I were on the other side of the river Styx, I should see what I was looking at here through the little slit in the wall of my hiding-place?—A crowd of human vultures gloating over the headless corse of a murdered brother negro —boys and girls walking away from the crowd, holding pieces of bleeding flesh in their hands, while the dripping life fluid marked their road as they went along ; and one woman snapping from the hands of another—both of them raising their voices in clamour—a part of the body of that poor man, in whom the breath of life was vigorous not a quarter of an hour ago !

The whole of the body was at last divided, and nothing left behind but the blood. The intestines were taken away to be given to an iguana—the Bonnyman's tutelary guardian. But the blood was still there, in glistening pools, though no more notice was taken of it by the gradually dispersing crowd, than if it were a thing as common in that town as Heaven's bright dew is elsewhere. A few dogs were on the spot, who devoured the fragments. Two men arrived to spread sand over the place, and there was no interruption to the familiar sound of coopers' hammering, just beginning in the cask houses, or to the daily work of hoisting palm-oil puncheons on board the ships.

Before quitting the house, which I managed to do at a moment when all around was clear, I asked myself, is this the eighteen hundred and fifty-ninth year of the Christian era?—are these the people amongst whom British commerce has been exercising its civilizing influence for more than half a century?—two questions which it is melancholy and saddening to feel obliged to answer by a simple affirmative.

Two days after, on passing the ju-ju house, I saw a small scaffold made of twigs, erected at the distance of a few yards from the front of the house, on the top of which were deposited leg, thigh, arm and rib bones, which had all the appearance of having been grilled first, and well picked afterwards.

These executions, and the subsequent harpyism, are generally confined to families or houses, and therefore cause little or no excitement on the part of the general population not directly interested. Hence the small number of people present at this affair in a town whose population amounts to nearly eight thousand. Such scenes may now be considered of more frequent occurrence than formerly, as the Bonny people have sworn an oath (or, as they call it, taken ju-ju) to exterminate the Obetta tribe, who occupy an interior district, and their *modus operandi* of effecting this resolution is by waiting for them in ambush, and then capturing, killing, and eating them.

It may be asked, is there no moral or social law amongst these people to prevent such occurrences? My answer is simply, that moral and social obligations are things of which they are as ignorant and unconscious as of the language of Kamschatka, or of the condition of affairs in the moon. Many persons might suppose that the "moral force" presence of a man-of-war in the river ought to have acted as a prohibition to this butchery. No doubt it would, had the steamer been anchored nearer to the town, or had it been suspected that a knowledge of the event had arrived on board.

But all the men-of-war in the British Navy could have had no power to prevent the execution being consummated elsewhere, away in some private creek, or swamp, or bush. And if stopped for the time being, it would have been carried out *sub umbrâ* as sure as the day dawns and the night darkens over Bonny country.

Lecture these people on the sin and shame of such things, and judge by what I am about to record of the effect which such remonstrance is likely to have.

Six or eight months subsequent to my having witnessed the foregoing slaughter, Mrs. Hutchinson accompanied me to Bonny in a man-of-war steamer, as she had had fever, and required change of air. Whilst we were there staying with Mr. Straw, supercargo of the hulk "Ambrosine," belonging to Messrs.

Charles Horsfall & Sons of Liverpool, there came on board one morning the very same ju-ju executioner that I had seen at his bloody work during my former visit. Rumours had been afloat that another affair, like the previous one, had come off a few days before. Indeed, so much of certainty was attached to these rumours, that Mr. Straw asked the ju-ju man, in the presence of myself and my wife, how he could have so little shame as to stand unabashed before a white lady, who had heard of his having eaten the head of a brother black man? With the most imperturbable *sang-froid* he replied, that he had not eaten it, " as his cook had spoiled it, by not putting enough of pepper upon it ! "

That a cruel and barbarous practice analagous to this has existed from time immemorial in other parts of Africa is evident from what is recorded by travellers to Dahomey in the year 1727.* On their being conducted to the king, Guaja Trudo, at that time the fourth monarch of this kingdom, they passed by two heaps of human heads piled on two large stages. These, they were told, were the heads of four

* Vide *West African Herald*, July 27th and August 13th, 1860, in which is a very interesting paper "On the Origin and History of Dahomey."

thousand of the Whydahs, who had been sacrificed to celebrate a late victory, which was the finishing stroke of King Trudo's invasion, and consequent subjugation of the Whydah territory, a few months previous to the travellers' visit.

At the ceremonial of reception on this occasion were present the king's body-guard, amounting to forty, who were armed with muskets and swords, and ornamented with strings of human teeth round their necks, hanging down to the waist before and behind. These were the teeth of enemies slain in battle, which the king's worthies or heroes were allowed to wear as trophies of their valour. It was death for one of these heroes to presume to wear a tooth whose owner he could not prove he had killed with his own hand.

Very similar to the sacrifice described in this chapter was the following one recorded as having been celebrated on the latter occasion—more especially so far as regards the practice of giving the head to the king, the blood to the fetish, and the body to the common people to be eaten :—" After they had dined on some ham and porter, which they brought with them from Whydah, the travellers repaired to the place where the prisoners were

to be sacrificed. Four small stages were erected,
at about five feet from the ground, by the side
of one of which the English captain took his
station. The first victim was a comely old
man, between fifty and sixty years of age, with
a firm countenance and undaunted bearing. He
was brought to the side of the stage with his
hands tied behind him; and as he stood erect
the fetishman, or ju-ju priest, laid his hand upon
his head and made a speech, which lasted
about two minutes. This ended, he made a sign
to the executioner, who was standing behind the
prisoner (?), and who immediately severed the
head from his body with one stroke of a broad
sword. The multitude gave a great shout. The
head was thrown upon the stage, and the body,
having lain a short time that the blood might
drain from it, was carried away by slaves, and
thrown on a spot near the camp. The like scene
was doubtless exhibiting on the three other
stages at the same time. The Englishman was
informed that the blood belonged to the fetish,
the head to the king, and the body to the
common people, by which last he understood
that it was given to them to be eaten. The
king, it was said, intended to build a monu-
ment of his victory with these and other skulls."

CHAPTER VI.

Appalling consideration suggested by the foregoing Inhumanities—
Difficulty of devising Remedial Measures for them—Paucity
of British as well as Missionary Stations amongst the Native
Africans—Questions regarding Great Britain's duty in aiding
African civilization—No faith in the obligation of a National
Compensation—From Serious and Sanguinary to Recreative and
Refreshing—Sydney Smith's appreciation of Tropical Delecta-
bilities—The village of Twa and its Attractions—Passage up the
Creek from Brass Harbour to Twa—Architecture in the Village
—Our trip to Brass town, the capital of Nimbe country—
Richard Lander's description of it thirty years ago—Our night
at the King's Country Palace—Variety of Serenading and other
Attractions—The King's Fisherwomen—Ebony mermaids—
Sensations on parting company.

THE most appalling consideration arising from our
knowledge of incidents like those recorded in the
preceding chapter seems to me that we cannot consider them to be isolated, if for no other reasons,
from the fact of their being for the most part consummated in the sight of our fellow-countrymen.
It pains me very much to have it in my power to

add, that savageries more inhuman than any I have recorded here, truculent and indecent enough to create a shudder in the nerves of the most de= praved, are of frequent occurrence amongst the tribes within my jurisdiction. To attempt civi- lizing such a race before they are humanized, would appear to me beginning at the wrong end. I have passed many a serious hour in cogitating and trying to suggest to myself some sort of education to root out this fell spirit, but I fear that ages must pass by before any system, even of the simplest form, can produce impressions of ame- lioration on temperaments such as they possess. The few British stations on the coast, and the pau- city of missionaries amongst the immense popula- tion (two hundred and fifty millions) of the African continent, although producing beneficial results within their limited spheres, are but as drops in the ocean of Ethiopian barbarism and darkness.

The question of duty in aiding the civilization of Western Africa, is simply one of rendering com- pensation for the many miseries our legitimi- zation of the slave-trade has caused to these people. The spirit of Christian love alone can enable us to discharge our duty in this respect to that race in the oppression and degradation of which we have borne so large a share. The world's past history affords very few instances of

such a palpable penitence as this would imply;
for if we look to the records of the desolating
wars that have overwhelmed dynasties all over
the habitable globe during the last twelve centuries, succeeding to none of them can we find the
proposal of a " national compensation."

Does our nation constitute itself a public
schoolmaster for the untutored African? I ask
not the reasons for doing so, if so it be. But, for
the sake of our common humanity, let it assume
this office in a manner different from that which
obtains at the present time.

Before leading my readers into anything
further connected with the socialities of African
life, I shall ask them to accompany me into some
of the scenes which are to be enjoyed here, and
leave them to relish these as a whet to their philanthropy; for a little recreation is needed
after what we have just gone through.

Many—indeed I consider myself safe in writing—the majority of my friends at home, have
little idea of the delectabilities incidental to a
residence within the Tropics. Sidney Smith has
described, with his usual graphic power, the
pleasure of finding centipedes crawling over one's
bed, and of seeing flies drowning in a milk jug,
or ants dancing quadrilles over the bread and

butter. Of all places in the world—between the Tropics of Cancer and Capricorn—I believe Western Africa to possess a variety of features amongst which even a philosopher of Mark Tapley's school could "feel credit in being jolly."

I am on board a man-of-war, in the harbour interior to the mouth of Brass* river, and it is the middle of the rainy season. A creek, about a quarter of a mile in length, and from six to eight yards wide, leads down to the village where the native pilots reside. This village is called Twa; and though the course of the water may be defined as like what the "Irish Sportheen" designated a "turpentine* sthramelet," it certainly would require a more intensely poetic imagination than I possess to discover in it any resemblance to the stream of Bendemeer, with its "bower of roses," where "the nightingales sing all the day long."

As the boat goes ahead, the giant stems of the mangrove trees seem like vegetable monsters, grasping handfuls of earth; lizards and amphibious mud-fish, with occasionally a small waterfowl of the crocodile species, are observed; a grey king-fisher flits past me here and there; an odd canoe, fastened to a mangrove branch, is

* No doubt a poetical expression for "serpentine."

passed as we move along; and in this craft I see a few lazy negroes stretched on their backs, enjoying the *dolce far niente* to an intensity impossible to be realized by a European.

The village of Twa contains about a hundred huts, in the very best of which no one with a spark of feeling in him would compel a pig to reside. The fish of the stream and the cocoa-nuts of the trees are the only sources of subsistence for the inhabitants; as against the cultivation of yams their ju-ju (which in this case may be interpreted to be their laziness) places an interdict. The ground-floors of their houses—and these are all constructed like Donnybrook tents, having no "upstairs" in them—are very little higher than the water of the adjacent creek. In the passages between the dwellings, stagnant pools of muddy slough are everywhere collected; and when I saw the soft sex splashing and puddling through these, it struck me as very fortunate for every *paterfamilias* in Twa that long-tailed crinolines, or even the bloomer costume, with patent leathers, have not yet become the mode in this part of the world. If you go into a house, you would do well to inquire into the possibility of getting out again, as the greater number are so low in the roofs that people can talk at each other from opposite sides by looking over the roof-ridge. Should you require a seat, there is a log of mangrove wood for you; and, in case you are thirsty, you must not be particular about the style of earthenware that is presented in order to quaff some cocoa-nut milk or palm wine thereout.

This, however, is but a petty village; and it is not fair to judge of the manners or morals of a people by the character and customs of those dwelling on their borders. Let us proceed to Brass Town, the capital of the Nimbe country.

So we are off next morning in a boat, not much cheered by perusing the following description of it, written nearly thirty years ago: —" Of all the wretched, filthy, and contemptible places in this world of ours," observed Richard Lander,* " none can present to the eye of a stranger so miserable an appearance, or can offer such disgusting and loathsome sights as this abominable Brass Town. Dogs, goats, and other animals, were running about the dirty streets, half-starved, whose hungry looks could only be exceeded by the famishing appearance of the men, women, and children, which bespoke the penury and wretchedness to which they were reduced; whilst the skins of many were

* " Travels into the Interior of Africa."

covered with odious boils, and their huts were falling to the ground from neglect and decay."

But who knows whether civilization, progressing in the usual *festina lente* style characteristic of everything in this country, may not have changed the picture by this time? I am not much cheered into this belief by my voyage; for I find that the passage, as it has been described to me by the supercargoes, is a wearisome continuation of creeky water for upwards of thirty miles —one of the most remarkable illustrations of sinuosity in the delta of the Niger; not a square inch of *terra firma* along the whole route—only mud, mangrove, sky, and water; no beds of primroses, buttercups, or daffy-down-dillies; no hotel or place of rest on the way—not even a "Mangrove Arms." Of water there is a superabundance around, as well as above and beneath us; for as our boat is rowed along, the rain comes down in drops as large as gooseberries — as tropical rain always does — and though the atmosphere is murky, very much resembling a London November fog, our pilot knows every corner and turning as well as if it were bright sunshine. No sign of life is observed the whole journey up, save occasionally a solitary female paddling a canoe loaded to the water's edge with firewood—thus clearly proving that the social condition described by Dr. Livingstone as existing in Eastern Africa, by which "a newly-married man is bound over for life to carry home firewood for his mother-in-law," has not yet reached the Brass country.

But here we are at the capital, and find it, like many important cities at home, divided into two segments by water running between. One side is Obullumabry, of which Keya is the head magnate; the other is Bassambry, over which Orishima "rules the roast." Either side might be taken as an example confirmatory of Lander's portrait. The debris of a small periwinkle-looking shell, styled in the native language "semèè," seems to constitute the earth upon which the residences are constructed. The only thing varying the monotony of the hundreds of similar habitations, is the ruin of an old slave barracoon, fabricated of tin plates, which is now falling into decay. A visit to the ju-ju house, that Delphic oracle to which the high-priest would like, no doubt, to see us coming with "a dash," is not to be accomplished without an elephant or a canoe to carry us across the intervening pools; and as neither happens to be come-at-able, we wander about in the dirty passages, seeing nothing but masses of mud, diversified by quantities of shells of the mangrove oysters and of the aforesaid semèè periwinkle tenements; heaps of firewood; odd puncheons for holding palm oil; snarling, long-tailed, long-eared curs; naked boys and girls; and a sloughy gutter everywhere. King Keya meets us in the street, and offers an invitation to his country house to spend the night there, as evening is approaching, and our Krooboys are not made of iron to pull back the thirty miles. So, having had *satis superque* of African scenery for one day, we accept his hospitality, and forthwith proceed to the royal suburban residence.

If I were not alive now, and conscious of writing this in the cabin of H. M. S. V. ——, I could not believe that I ever should have been fortunate enough to enjoy such an uninterrupted continuation of delights as those experienced during that night's stay in the royal abode at Brass.

My bedroom was about twelve feet by four, with holes in the bamboo roof—about eight feet high—that let the rain and rats come in, and holes in the floor, probably to allow both to make their exit. There was neither stool, chair, nor table, nor any article of furniture except the bed. This was made of two empty gun-chests, covered with a native country mat, and having no pillow save a log of wood. The creek by which we voyaged up was within five yards of the door, and when the tide was low bull-frogs, crocodiles, and mud-fish could gambol about in their native parterre, in the remorseless swamp of which a human being trying to walk would certainly be swallowed up. The odour from this place at the time of our visit was indescribable, and the sensation that it brought to my olfactory nerves was far from being like that of the south wind " breathing o'er a bed of violets—stealing and giving odour."

As soon as I had seated myself on the bed (?), with a cigar in my mouth—for to sleep with all those accessories would have been a vain attempt —and had blown out my palm-oil lamp, down came the musquitoes in showers—followed by some rats which descended after them without waiting for an invitation. A few of the latter fell near to where I was sitting, and I made a furious tilt at them with a stick I had placed near me. This of course alarmed them, and made them beat a retreat for some time. But as if in mockery of my chivalry within doors, outside the bull-frogs commenced croaking in dozens, communicating as agreeable a sensation by their music as the rasping of a file over a rusty saw.

I lay down and tried to sleep, but it was no use. In a few moments the rats were again gambolling on the roof. A slight shuffling movement which I heard on the floor made me fearful that at any minute I might be rendered conscious of something slimy in contact with my hand or face, probably a mud-fish (or jump-fish, as it is called by Kroomen), a kind of amphibious reptile, that appears like a cross-breed between a conger-eel and a chameleon. How stupid I was to have blown out my light!

What noise is that? Female voices outside! Who in the name of goodness are they?—passing and repassing by the king's harem — ever gabbling, gabbling, gabbling. This amusement going on during the whole livelong night, with the companionship of the rats, musquitoes, and bull-frogs, put a thousand strange notions into my head. Can they be going to the creek-side to sacrifice—perhaps infants? Are they on their way to undergo the process of laving in that sweet stream? If the former be their purpose, they must be out-Heroding Herod—if the latter, a Turkish bath, with shampooing of currycomb, would seem very appropriate for the majority of the ladies whom I saw to-day in the streets (!), and whose bodies were daubed over with a greasy cosmetic of red (styled in the Nimbe language "Umbia"), which gives the anointed the semblance of a highly-tinged Red Indian. But down they go and back they come—never tiring—never relenting—never shewing compassion, till morning dawned, when I opened the door cautiously and looked out!

Some were standing in the mud—others were lifting fish and nets out of canoes! They were the king's fisherwomen. Following their professional pursuits during the night, they had kept me in this condition of restless curiosity! Talk of Billingsgate, indeed! I looked at them, and there they were—wet, muddy, and slimy, like so many ebony mermaids—but still prattling and talking, their tongues clattering as if these organs were so many untireable steam-engines.

There was no use in giving them a "bit of my mind," for I did not understand a word of their language, and they did not comprehend mine. It may be useless to record that I did not go down on my knees in the mud to pray for them. I was unheroic enough to imagine that a wiser thing than that—as far as my own comfort was concerned — would be to quit the Nimbe country as soon as I could. So my boys having got into the boat, I gave his sable majesty a more fervent than friendly shake of the hand— and turned my back on his territory, with feelings in which I cannot say there were any sentiments of regret

CHAPTER VII.

Three glorious nights of jollity between Bimbia and Kameroons—
Reflections on land about Sea-sickness—Preparing our Bivouac
—A Game of Nine-pins with Cocoa nuts—My first Night's Comfort—Conjecture as to the possibility of M. Soyer's making a
Palatable Dish from Leeches and Ship's Biscuit—Attractions in
the Wrecked Ship—Pleasure of a Night passed on Board—Mingled attractions of Rats and Leeches—Thudding of Waves against
the Ship—Of a Thirty-mile Walk along an African Beach, subsequent Sleep, and refreshing Dreams—Sensations of Waking in a
Boat half-full of Water—At sea once more—Dread of becoming
a second edition of the Ancient Mariner—Safe at last.

ONCE again in a man-of-war steamer, and away
to a wreck on the shore between Bimbia and
Kameroons. Anchor being dropped outside
Bimbia harbour, I start from the steamer, accompanied by three boats, two officers, a number
of the crew, and several Kroomen. A pull to
the scene of disaster was about twelve or fourteen miles from the place where we had left our
man-of-war. The vessel to which we were pro-

ceeding was stranded in the midst of the breakers, close by the beach; and as it was the time of spring-tides, with a very high wind blowing, it was deemed advisable by the officer in charge to let the boat's anchor drop when about a quarter of a mile seaward of the wreck, in order to wait till what he styled a "half gale," then sniffling about, should take a notion of subsiding. I entertained a "mental reservation" about the "half gale," yet did not express it; but it was something to the effect of declining acquaintance with a whole one, if those seas and that wind were to be designated only as "a half."

The swell of waves was so enormous near the wreck, and the rollers made such a "line of beauty" (as a mad poet would call it) in their curl, that our pilot, the aforesaid officer, expressed his dread of the boats being swamped if we attempted to land.

"Cease, rude Boreas, blustering"—I had not time to finish the line before a peculiar kind of drowsiness came creeping over me; after that a sensation as if the boat were playing leap-frog with the waves—then nausea of the stomach— after this the awkward prostration, insensibility, and apathy of that ridiculous malady called sea-sickness. I felt conscious of being alive, and of people talking together in the boat, but no more. I fancy, if you have ever been sea-sick, you will agree with me, that the most horrible aggravation to one's sufferings in that state is that of being conscious of persons talking around you, who are not sick at all—who express their sympathy in voices as grating as a saw-mill, and who, you cannot help thinking, have as much sensibility or sense of human-kindness in them as so many Egyptian mummies. There is no use in my attempting to describe what I felt during a time that seemed four weeks to me, but which was recorded by my fellow-passengers as being only three or four hours. If but little pity is felt for the actual sufferings of those prostrated by the *mal de mer*, how can we expect to excite the sympathy of others by any mere description, however elaborate, of them?

I found myself on the beach, as damp as a shark or a salmon in its native element, at about five o'clock in the evening, having had sufficient salt spray over me in getting ashore to rouse me from my dulness and apathy. I was too happy to stand up and walk, so I sat down on the edge of one of the boats, that had been hauled up on the beach, and commenced to think.

"To think"—of what Byron meant when he wrote of "loving the ocean, and his joy of youthful sports upon its breast to be"—and of Haynes Bailey's rhodomontade about the " blue, the fresh, the ever, ever free"—feeling at the same time a malignant desire to see both of these poets, in company with the sea-god Neptune, riding on the billows before me "sated on a low-backed car," and in a condition something approaching to that under which I laboured a few hours gone by. The recollection now flashed on my mind, perhaps it was as a punishment for this demoniacal spirit, that although our three boats were hauled up high and dry upon the beach, the getting them launched again through such a surf as that which raged there was a perfect impossibility. Therefore wreck or man-of-war was equally unapproachable; we had only one meal's provision with us, save a bag of bread for the sailors; we were all conscious of being endowed with stomachs—we had not a change of clothes—there was no hope of a bed save in the boats, or in the thicket of tall Guinea grass around, where the company of snakes, centipedes, musquitoes, land crabs, with other horrid reptiles, was not likely to be of the most attractive kind.

As night approached, our bivouac was prepared by the sailors and Kroomen rigging the sails upon the oars, so as to form a covering over the after-parts of the boats. This being accomplished, the tars, true to the lightheartedness of British sailors all over the world, commenced playing at nine-pins with a quantity of cocoa-nuts that were strewed over the beach. A fire was kindled, and I stowed myself away in the stern of my own boat; but to sleep, with hundreds of musquitoes serenading around, delighted, no doubt, at having the opportunity of exercising their skill in phlebotomy on my face, was a thing that Morpheus would not sanction. The operations of these blood-suckers were diversified during the night with showers of rain, which only drove them in greater numbers beneath the awning.

Morning dawned, and shewed us the breakers raging more angrily; while the wind was likewise blowing with greater fury. One of my Kroomen advanced at my call, and, shaking his head ominously, mumbled, " Wathery be sarcy (saucy) too much, for any dem boat to lib (live) in dat say."

Breakfast was soon got over, as it consisted only of ship's biscuit and water from a leech-pool hard by, materials that even M. Soyer's artistic skill, with his most piquant condiments, could scarcely transform into a savoury dish.

When the tide reached its lowest ebb, we advanced in a body to the wreck up to our middles in the water, for the ship was so near the beach that we could talk to those on board. The gangway ladder had been taken from the ship's side, and suspended from the bow, so we clambered up and ejected some native as well as British pirates who were in the vessel.

Taking possession of the derelict, and making arrangements for setting about saving the cargo, occupied so much time, that when I looked over the ship the tide had reached in so far, I saw it was impossible to regain the shore, so I turned into the cabin.

Here there was a desolation out of my power to describe. All the meat, wine, and brandy had been abstracted by the natives, and the cabin had been dismantled of its furniture— tables, chairs, and lockers. There was plenty of biscuit on board, but no water ; and the latter was only attainable when the efflux of the tide would permit a Krooman to go on shore to fetch it. However, here we were for the night, as returning, even if we could, to the boats would seem to be an " out-of-the-frying-pan-into-the-fire" sort of change.

From the moment I came on board until I left, next day, there was a continuous thundering against the ship's stern, caused by the waves rising and breaking with a furious thud, as if of a battering-ram, shaking every plank and nail, and making every mother's son of us within the sphere of these planks and nails to quiver in sympathy.

A Krooboy was sent ashore for some water, which he brought back in a calabash-bottle, ingeniously tied on the top of his head, and we had a cup of tea, with bread, before retiring to rest.

To rest, indeed! The only places on which we could lie down were either wet sails or hard boards. The rats, driven from their abiding places below, after the ship's bottom had been stove in, were running "for safety and for succour" about the cabin deck. Now and then a volume of spray dashed over the sky-light, the " biggest half" of it coming down in showers on us in the cabins without compunction. The waves beat furiously against the sides of the ship; while the abominable odour of the bilge water, united with that of the palm oil which escaped from the casks, was indescribable.

There was no use in calling the steward, as he had nothing at command to comfort us. Some water might be left in that calabash, which would serve as a refreshing drink, but there might also be some leeches in it; and was there not the possibility of one of those blood-augers getting into a man's stomach, and giving him the sensation of a gimlet going through the diaphragm? Oh! faugh! is morning never to come?

It did come, but with it no signs of improvement from yesterday. Goodness gracious! when is this wind to subside?—when are the waves to become quiescent?—and, if the "half gale" continues, how long can the ship endure this billowy battering? I must do something to get out of this; for two days and two nights of such knocking about are quite enough for one fit of recreation. If the wreck should break up!

But that thought is too horrible to dwell upon. "Here, steward, place a Krooboy to report to me when the tide is out sufficiently to let me try and scramble ashore; get me some tea, with a little bread, and I shall be off."

"Off! where to?" you may ask. Clambering down the ladder, I reached the shore on the shoulders of my Kroomen; took off my boots and stockings, tucked up my trousers, told two of the boys to accompany me, bringing with them a Union Jack, some biscuit in a bag, and water in a bottle—taking care to include no leeches in the latter.

Away we trudged for a walk of sixteen miles along the strand, nearly as far towards Bimbia as the western outlet of Mordecai Creek, in order to try a chance of signalling to H. M. S. V——, a request to send us some means of delivery. I knew that her place of anchor was about eight miles from the nearest point of land at which we could arrive; but if the sky, at the time we reached that place, happened to be clear, some of her look-outs might observe our flag. When we arrived at the end of our journey, we could barely distinguish the outline of a steamer; and the wind was blowing, the surf beating, and the rain falling, just as vigorously here as in the place which we had left. With these was that haziness of atmosphere which is the invariable accompaniment of such weather in Western Africa; and I could not give myself credit for possessing the "animagosity" of a human donkey, when half an hour's flag-waving proved to me that all my signalling was vain, and that my only alternative was either to toddle back the sixteen miles, or to try to roost for the night in one of the adjacent palm trees.

You may guess, **if you** can, with what an amiable temper I turned to retrace my footsteps. There was no virtue in carrying out this resolution; for an old proverb says, "There is no virtue in necessity." The prospect of my night's lodging was not very inviting. Nevertheless, I tried to persuade myself that the exercise would do me good, as walking only made me feel as if I were becoming more vigorous. I was even beginning to sing, when I was startled by the appearance of the dead bodies of two black men on **the** beach, whom neither I nor my Krooboys had recognised on our way up. This may be explained by the fact that on our first journey we had walked through **the surf, as** the tide was just beginning to come in, while on the return we **were** obliged to keep close to the bush, as it was nearly up to high water. The bodies were those of **two** poor fellows who had been drowned by the upsetting, on the day before, of a canoe that was sent to our assistance by King William of Bimbia.

Thirty miles walk, even along a smooth sand, forms no bad anodyne for a sound sleep. Having despatched a messenger to the wreck for some tea, I partook of a basin of it with bread ; and as it was near dark when I arrived at my hotel, I huddled myself up in the boat's stern—first causing a fire to be lighted at each side, in order to keep off the musquitoes. I was soon asleep. Some time in the middle of the night I got into a conglomeration of horrible dreams. I fancied that the wreck was in Lagos harbour—that the pounding water was gradually breaking it asunder—and that the prospect of a speedy separation of its component parts was very much enlivened by the sight of a few hundred sharks swimming about, with jaws open for their prey, and eyes gloating in anticipation over their promised feast.* I thought that the grand smash came at last, and that I was in the water swimming for my life, when—

Suddenly I awoke, and found myself, though not in the society of sharks, floating in a pool that had collected at the end of my boat—her bow was a little raised—the result of a fall of rain that had continued perhaps for hours, with *no outlet*. It had *an inlet* sufficiently spacious, for the whole of the boat was uncovered save the part wherein I was sleeping.

Here was a pickle, to be sure! The acmé of my three glorious nights' pleasures and comforts.

* Any one who has been at Lagos must know that numbers of sharks may be seen, many with their back fins out of the water, prowling about every ship.

Pitch-dark; the fires of course extinguished by the rain, which was still falling. No change of clothes; and therefore, of course, no refuge from this condition of wretchedness. The sparkle of a light in the Krooboys' hut, however, caught my eye; and I was out of the boat in a twinkling—indeed, I believe that I shivered and shook myself out of it, called up a few of the boys to make the fire larger, took off my clothes, rolled myself in a boat's awning, and waited till my garments were dry. No quinine wine to be had—no tea nor coffee till morning dawned, and the stranded ship was approachable; biscuit and leech-pool water were the only things at hand — or leech-pool water and biscuit, by way of variety.

Flesh and blood could stand this no longer; so, as daylight glimmered, I asked one of my Krooboys to go out and look at the sea. His reply, " Wathery sarcy still all same " almost tempted me to knock him down. Another Krooboy, whom I soon became weak enough to respect, gave it as his opinion that the " wind no be so throng," and that he thought " the sarcy wather go down when tide done for go out next time."

His prediction was verified. The large cutter belonging to the man-of-war was launched first, and got away with safety, having one of the

officers on board. My gig was shoved off soon
after, and as soon as we had got outside the
breakers, and I found myself once more safe
afloat, I began concocting what kind of certifi-
cate I should give to my weather-wise Krooman,
to obtain for him meteorological promotion, perhaps at Greenwich Observatory. Being rowed
in a boat for several hours at sea—seeing the
cutter with sails set going ahead of me as fast as
the Flying Dutchman—and a state of mind and
body such as any man would be in after four
days and three nights of such rustication as I had
endured—are not at all predisposing to placidity of
temper. The cutter had been out of sight for a
few hours; no steamer was yet visible, and we had
nothing to steer by but land-marks. These, too,
were often obscured by heavy showers, which
made the sky thick and gloomy. But we were
getting along even against a strong current, and
I was congratulating myself on soon having a
refreshing bath, with a comfortable change of
clothes, on board the man-of-war, when—oh !
horror of horrors !—the sky clearing up disclosed
the steamer about ten miles off—anchor up—
steam up—and her paddle-wheels propelling her
in quite a different direction from that in which
I was advancing.

Nevertheless, I did not faint, and having a dread of becoming a second edition of the Ancient Mariner, I at once roused my energies. For I knew that the steamer was not going away, leaving me behind, but that the commander had determined to come nearer to the wreck for future operations, as I had suggested through the officer when leaving that morning, and was now making a round through the proper channel. To accomplish this purpose he was obliged to bring the steamer by a detour out of the shallow water in which my boat could float.

So up with my flagstaff and flag at the stern ! Putting the helm hard a starboard, we turned out to sea, and I urged my Krooboys to pull cheerily, although they had been tugging at the oars for five hours already.

Another half-hour's pull—the steamer is coming towards us—the look out espies my flag —the engines are stopped, and—here I am !

CHAPTER VIII.

CHIEFLY illustrative of the colony of Sierra Leone is the peculiarly interesting fact, that the mere mention of its name is regarded as suggestive of malignant disease and death.

Our purpose is to view it in its three most important phases—namely, the commercial, the social, and the sanatory points of view.

The history of the world in past ages does not exhibit such evidences of pure and high-minded philanthropy as have been manifested for many years by our Government and the benevolent people of Great Britain towards the natives of Africa. Conspicuous among these has been the enormous outlay of millions of money for the suppression of the slave-trade, with the ulterior view of civilizing the Ethiopian race.

To express my belief that philanthropy is an exotic not suited to the climate of Africa, nor calculated to produce all the effects anticipated on its people, is in no way intended as a disparaging reflection on the philanthropic exertions of my countrymen. But it is saddening to feel a conviction, as I do from the multitude of sombre facts before me, that these efforts bear little better fruit than did the wheat in the parable, which is recorded to have fallen amongst briars and thorns.

From M'Culloch's Commercial Dictionary, I learn that the first importation of settlers to this colony took place in the year 1792, when about twelve hundred free negroes, who had joined the Royal Standard in the American war, were obliged to take refuge in Nova Scotia, and were thence transferred, from motives of humanity, to

Africa. From that time to the present Sierra Leone has cost our Government nearly ten millions of money in civil government expenses—in naval expenses—in cash laid out on captured slaves—and in salaries to the executive officers of the Mixed Commission Court. The value of its exports was—

In 1850 . . . . . £123,150
1856 153,347
1858 225,349

The largest amount being, to use the words of Mr. Jameson, in his pamphlet on the Niger Trade, "not more than the value of produce annually passing through the hands of any second or third-rate commercial house engaged in trade with India, China, or America."

By the table of its commerce during 1858, which is appended, and which I have obtained at the Colonial Office, it will appear that our exports to that part of the world very much exceed the financial worth of our returns from its produce.

In the adjoining settlement of Gambia a like condition of affairs may be observed; and it is a fact that the French derive from both colonies a much more considerable amount of exports—chiefly of ground nuts—than we do.

SIERRA LEONE, 1858.

COUNTRIES.	IMPORTS.	EXPORTS.
United Kingdom—		
Great Britain . . .	£108,007 8 7	£86,532 5 6
British Colonies—		
Bathurst, Gambia .	720 10 7	3,204 18 11
Foreign Countries—		
France	1,456 6 1	25,271 16 11
Madeira.	11 13 10	.. ..
Teneriffe	87 5 6	.. ..
Goree	3,460 4 11	34,795 10 11
Leeward Coast . .	1,178 5 9	28,531 16 7
America	18,563 11 2	47,013 0 6
	£133,485 6 5	225,349 9 4

GAMBIA, 1859.

COUNTRIES.	IMPORTS.	EXPORTS.
United Kingdom—		
Great Britain . . .	£33,603 2 7	£19,984 15 0
British Colonies—		
Sierra Leone . . .	5,829 7 6	1,077 6 0
British West Indies .	456 1 8	470 0 0
British North America	.. ..	210 0 0
Foreign Countries—		
France	8,398 7 1	52,366 6 3
Canary Islands . .	277 3 0	.. ..
Cape Verd Islands .	222 14 0	739 3 0
Goree and Senegal .	5,023 8 5	2,167 6 0
Leeward Coast . .	7,717 10 9	7,421 1 10
Windward Coast. .	119 14 0	154 5 0
Foreign West Indies	100 0 0	.. ..
United States . . .	14,402 2 1	25,774 9 6
	£76,149 11 1	110.364 12 7

It appears that in this year there is an increase of £1,082 6s. 8d. in the revenue collected, as duty on wine and spirits, above that of 1858.

This is accounted for by bonds given in 1858 falling due in 1859. There is a decrease of duties on the imports of Foreign and British vessels, to the aggregate amount of £938 16*s*. 7*d*.; and the Colonial Secretary attributes this in a great measure to the failure of the ground nut crop, the staple article of trade, which therefore required a lesser quantity of goods for its purchase.

According to Martin's work on the British Colonies, the population of Sierra Leone in 1836 was—

	Males.	Females.
Whites . . .	83	22
Coloured People	19,895	15,678

Total, 19,978 .. 15,690—Gross Total, 35,668.

And by a return which I procured at the Colonial Office, I find the total population in 1858—

	Males.	Females.
Whites . . .	82	25
Coloured People	19,660	18,551

Total, 19,742 .. 18,576—Gross Total, 38,318.

I do not put forward any arguments against our colonial possessions in Africa on the ground refuted by Mr. M. Forster of the City Chambers, London, as stated in Montgomery Martin's work on the British Colonies—namely, in reference to the attempt said to be often made to depreciate the commercial importance of our settlements on the west coast of Africa, compared with the cost of maintaining them. It may be that the cost of maintaining these settlements—including the presentation of 29,709*l.* 10*s.* for the service of the colony of Sierra Leone in 1859—is as extravagant as some assert it to be. If so, I can only mourn over money so spent, and to so little practical use, to our commerce, or our philanthropy.

Leaving the commercial part of the subject aside, we turn to the educational, and find, according to last year's report sent to the Colonial Office, that in the Jourabah grammar-school, of which the Rev. E. Jones is president, there are nine young men who are being trained for schoolmasters; and in the grammar-school which is subsidiary to this there are ninety-four pupils. These are to be prepared for the Jourabah school, where they are educated for commercial and other pursuits. The subsidiary school has been principally supported by the Church Missionary Society, but most of the pupils pay for their education. The Jourabah Institution is wholly supported by the Church Missionary Society. There is, moreover, a female school, having forty scholars,

supported partly by the Church Missionary Society, and partly by the friends of the pupils.

There are nearly twenty Dissenting chapels in
the colony, in most of which an educational
course is carried on.

In no part of the colony can be discovered
native enterprise, self-respect, self-reliance, or,
amongst its African population, any of the qualities that tend to make a community comfortable
or happy, or to elevate it in the scale of human
civilization. "Dignity balls" and "Goombee"
dances are favourite amusements of the natives
—both being recreations of the grossest immo-
rality.

Bearing on the subject referred to in the first
paragraph of this chapter, it may be unnecessary
for me to remind English readers of the dreadful
mortality that took place in this colony during
the year before last—1859. Of its morbific characteristics few men have had more extensive
opportunities for acquiring experience than Dr.
Clarke, who read a paper entitled "Short Notes
on the prevailing Diseases in the Colony of Sierra
Leone," before the Statistical Section of the British Association at Glasgow, in 1855, which was
published in the Journal of the Statistical Society
of London, in March of the following year.

Although the author has kindly given me permission to make what use I desire of it, I do not consider its tabular records of sufficient importance for the general reader.

They are pre-eminently so for the scientific inquirer, and may be found in the Journal before mentioned.

Some of Mr. Clarke's observations on Sierra Leone are worthy of consideration, as well from the fact of his being an observing man, as from his having lived for eighteen years in that colony :—

" Although Sierra Leone can no longer be justly called 'the white man's grave,' it must not be supposed that the climate has in any degree changed. That the mortality has diminished is unquestionable, but for this several causes may be assigned. The style and comfort of the houses occupied by Europeans are improved, they dress in a manner better suited to the vicissitudes of the climate, a greater degree of temperance prevails, and the general use of quinine has considerably shortened and reduced the amount of illness and mortality."

To these causes of an improved sanitary condition ought to be added the drainage of the town—a very important matter in all African

cities, and whose adoption has led to highly beneficial results at Bathurst.

There is no doubt of the following being an
established fact :—

" It is a fact worthy of note, that the European, after his constitution has become assimilated thoroughly to the climate, is better
able to resist the climatic influences than
persons of mixed colour. The latter class (in
the colonial service at least) are, as a body, more
frequently on the sick list than their European
colleagues."

The *soi-disant* humanitarians, who advocate the
continuance of the slave-system, because it takes
the serf-class of negroes away from their country
for their own personal amelioration, would do
well to read and ponder over the following appalling picture :—

"At the period I took charge of the Kissy
hospitals (1837), the slave-trade was in active
operation, and consequently great numbers of
liberated Africans were constantly received into
hospital. It was a most distressing sight to witness the arrival of these poor creatures; and it
is necessary to make a few preliminary remarks,
in order clearly to understand the difficulties
with which the medical officers had to contend.

The appearance of **the slaves** when landed from the condemned ship was most striking. In some the expression of the countenance indicated sufferings, moral and physical, of the most profound and agonising nature. Others gazed vacantly around in the most utter helplessness. Occasionally among the newly-arrived groups all sense of suffering was merged in melancholic or raving madness. The wizened, shrunk, and skinny features were lighted up by the hollow feverish eye; the belly was, as it were, tacked to the back; whilst the hip-bones protruded, and, in some cases, had become the seat of foul sloughing ulcers; the hand and skinny fingers seemed much elongated by the great and neglected growth of the nails, and they were so deplorably emaciated, that the skin appeared tensely stretched over, and tied down to the skeleton; the legs refused to perform their functions, and the poor creatures reeled and tottered about from sheer debility; their squalor and extreme wretchedness were heightened, in many cases, by the party-coloured evacuations with which their bodies were besmeared. They rushed towards the water provided for their use, fighting with each other to drink and drink again, as if their thirst was unquenchable. They would devour their food, quarrelling with each other for the possession of a bone or fragment of meat, and what was left they would carefully put away in little bags suspended from their necks, to be eaten at leisure."

What a subject for a painter! No doubt the prototype of this sketch could be found in many "middle passages," of which the horrors are only known to Him who knows all things.

Mr. Clarke's observations on fevers and native diseases are very useful, but I must leave them with the statistics. Here follows a synopsis of the present state of medical science amongst the Africans:—

"The liberated Africans, and indeed all classes of the coloured inhabitants of Sierra Leone, put great confidence in country remedies, and, in too many instances, recourse is had to European methods of treatment only after they have tried all the native remedies with which they are acquainted. At the same time, it must be admitted that the more intelligent among them eagerly seek the advice and assistance of the European surgeon, whenever an opportunity is afforded them of doing so. The class of persons in West Africa styled "country doctors," impose upon the credulity and superstitious fears of their fellow-countrymen by means of fetishes and amulets, or gri-gris. They likewise prepare a quantity of crude decoctions, powders, &c., from the roots, leaves, and bark of trees, and from plants culled from the jungles; but their knowledge of the medicinal properties of these is of the rudest and most imperfect nature. Moreover, as the plants are gathered without reference to the season of the year, and to other important conditions, they are uncertain in their action, and often dangerous in their operation. These barbarous remedies are, besides, administered in such large doses, without any consideration as to the age, sex, or strength of the patient, that in this way alone many lives are yearly sacrificed. It will be acknowledged by persons at all conversant with the African character, that this system of jugglery and quackery exerts the most injurious influence in retarding the progress of civilization among the negroes."

His observations on the Hygiene of life in Africa are very sound:—

"It may not be irrelevant to add a few remarks on what appear to me to be the best means of preserving health on the west coast of Africa. In the foremost rank should be placed temperate and regular habits. The moderate use of wine, far from being injurious, is necessary to counter-act the depressing and debilitating influences of the climate. It is a matter of the greatest importance to protect the skin from chills, and this is best done by wearing under-clothing of flannel, or, what is better, a mixture of cotton and wool. Out of doors the head should be well protected from the sun by a thick hat of light fabric; and to all who value their health, it is essential to use an umbrella during the heat of the day. If a person is overheated, and suffers from profuse perspiration, he should at once change the whole of his clothing, and not simply take off coat or jacket, and then sit down to cool himself in a current of air. The *siestas* so much recommended are very good, but they certainly cannot be indulged in by the mass of Europeans resident in tropical countries; and it is undoubtedly true that on the west coast of Africa, as elsewhere, mental and bodily activity contributes largely to good health. It is hardly necessary to recommend retiring early to bed, say nine or ten o'clock, and rising early, say six o'clock, when a cup of coffee or tea should be taken, followed by a cold or tepid bath, the cold bath to be carefully avoided when persons are suffering from hepatic or splenic enlargement.

"The bedroom should be the largest and best ventilated room in all the **house, and** should be provided with a fireplace, **so** that in the rainy season it may be kept dry and wholesome. Piazza bedrooms should be avoided.

" With **regard to** food, it should **be of the sim**plest and most nourishing kind, with a moderate use of fruit, avoiding pastry.

"By duly observing these precautions the Englishman may live almost as safely at Sierra Leone as in his own country; and he will not find, as too many have done, through their own recklessness, that the magnificent scenery which greeted his eyes as he approached the African coast, was but a deceitful screen to conceal the horrors of the charnel-house. The climate has been made the scape-goat of a thousand sins, and those who live most in opposition to its dictates have been the readiest to blame it for their sufferings. If nature wears a perpetual smile in this quarter of the world, **it is** to those only **who** listen to her teachings. To them no sackcloth **and** ashes lie hid beneath her flowery robe; and to them Sierra Leone will no longer appear an object of terror, **as the** 'White Man's Grave.'"

I think it well to insert the following remarks **on** Lunacy, as it appeared amongst the black colonists, not only because they illustrate a novel feature in the character of the negro, but because they demonstrate the improved care that is now taken by the colonial authorities at Sierra Leone to separate and classify the patients :—

"The lunatics seldom lived long, being frequently cut off by dysentery or dropsy, or becoming epileptic or paralytic—complications almost hopeless. The majority, if they did not soon recover, died within two or three years of their admission to the asylum. A few survived for many years, and, in one rare instance, recovery took place after the lapse of twelve years. The larger proportion of the patients treated were males. The disease manifested all its varied forms. Some gesticulated and danced about the yard, uttering the foulest abuse. Religion was the unceasing theme on which others expatiated for hours together, occasionally arrogating to themselves the attributes of our Saviour. These delusions in some instances might be traced to the effect produced on weak minds by the exciting and barbarous exhibitions so often witnessed in their numerous conventicles of 'finding the Lord,' 'finding peace,' &c. The love of finery was shown by several of both sexes who picked up rags, which they fastened to their persons—

or feathers, &c., which they stuck in their hair, or passed through holes in the *alæ nasi* and cartilage of the nose. The raving madman, the melancholic, the imbecile suffering from dementia, the idiot, the religious, the suicidal, the epileptic, were, until 1858, enclosed together, without distinction, in the most miserable cells, where no separation could be effected. On the transfer of the colonial hospital from Kissy to Freetown, in 1858 (a most desirable and much needed change), the lunatics were removed to that building, which, although in many important points ill adapted for the purpose, is, nevertheless, a very great improvement on former asylums."

In the tables one case of hydrophobia is marked down. Mr. Clarke, however, records it as his opinion, concurrent with that of Staff-Surgeon Fergusson and Colonial-Surgeon Aitken, that that disease never occurs in the colony—and therefore doubts the correctness of the record.

CHAPTER IX.

The Gold Coast—Brutalities of the King in Ashantee half a century ago—Sacrifices after his Mother's death—Bloodshed after
his own—The present King of Dahomey and his sanguinary
intentions—Report of Cruikshank's mission to Dahomey, in
1848—Festal Recreations, in the shape of Human Sacrifices, at
Ashantee—Men butchered to do honour to the Portuguese
slave-dealer, De Souza—A like ceremony in compliment to the
Dutch general, Verbeer—The Dahomean King's arguments in
favour of the Slave-trade—The French nation in its early connexion with Africa, especially with the Gold Coast—Their repudiation of the Portuguese claims to primary geographical discovery in this part of the world—Beginning of British legitimate
commerce with Western Africa—First opening of palm-oil trade
—Number of forts on the Gold Coast—Immense wealth of its
interior districts—Its Missionary establishments—Its Colonial
Commerce for 1858.

ON no part of Western Africa have there been
such scenes of turbulence and bloodshed, chiefly
connected with human sacrifices, as still continue to be enacted in the interior countries
contiguous to the Gold Coast.

In the year 1808 (more than half a century

ago), the King of Ashantee sent an army of fifteen thousand men against the Fantees, on the Gold Coast, who laid waste a large extent of country in the neighbourhood of Anamaboe.

At that time our fort at the last-named place was occupied, and even the small number of soldiers which it contained successfully repulsed the army of barbarians, and prevented them from doing any further harm with their savage implements of warfare.

After ravaging the intermediate kingdoms of Akim and Dinkera, in the year 1816, this monarch is reported to have sacrificed three thousand human victims on the grave of his mother. At his own death, some months subsequently, slaves were sacrificed at the rate of two hundred every week for three months—thus making five thousand six hundred victims to the horrible Juggernaut of African superstition.

Knowing as I do the hereditary tenacity with which barbarous customs are transmitted from generation to generation by those of negro blood, it was with no surprise, though with a feeling of horror, that I read, in the *West African Herald* of July last, the following paragraph:—

"DAHOMEY.—His majesty Badahung, king of Dahomey, is about to make the 'grand custom' in honour of the late king Gezo. Determined to surpass all former monarchs in the magnitude of the ceremonies to be performed on this occasion, Badahung has made the most extensive preparations for the celebration of the 'grand custom.' A great pit has been dug, which is to contain human blood enough to float a canoe. Two thousand persons will be sacrificed on this occasion. The expedition to Abeokouta is postponed, but the king has sent his army to make some excursions at the expense of some weaker tribes, and has succeeded in capturing many unfortunate creatures. The young people among these prisoners will be sold into slavery, and the old persons will be killed at the 'grand custom.'"

Doubts as to the correctness of the foregoing announcement are completely set aside by the receipt of a letter, dated Cape Coast Castle, September 16th, which says:—"The atrocities at Dahomey have far exceeded the report of which you are aware. Thousands have been sacrificed. Latterly came a steamer on that coast, and shipped off fifteen hundred slaves. A man-of-war being on the spot, saw the vessel, but suspected nothing of her design. We hear that English people, and other Europeans, have been imprisoned there— most probably from refusing to witness the human sacrifices, or to take part in the rites of diabolical superstition."

By this it will be seen that the only rivalry ever known to exist between those Arcadian neighbours, the potentates of Dahomey and Ashantee, still flourishes with all its pristine vigour.

The report of Mr. Cruikshank's mission to the present King of Dahomey's father, at his capital of Abomey, in the year 1848, showed that the exertions of that gentleman, sent out, according to report, by Her Majesty's Government, pursuant to a motion made in the House of Commons by Lord Fermoy, to endeavour to stop such deeds of bloodshed, had resulted in utter failure. When Gezo, the present king's father, could not be reasoned into a sense of the moral obligation of abandoning the slave-trade, it would seem a hopeless task to endeavour to convert the son from a practice that he had seen carried on in the earliest days of his childhood, and in his growth to manhood.

On the occasion of funerals—and even of festal recreations—thousands of human beings are annually sacrificed in the capital, Abomey. When De Souza, the notorious Portuguese slave-dealer at Whidah, who is also the King of Dahomey's viceroy in that district, visited his Majesty a great number of slaves were sacrificed to do him honour. The same practice was carried out at Comassie, the capital of Ashantee, when the Dutch general, Verbeer, arrived there on a call of courtesy to the king. These two events, which took place within the last twenty years, were nearly contemporaneous in their occurrence.

Surrounded by barbaric splendour, and having early imbibed the thirst for glory as a conqueror, although it was only over brother barbarians, the late King Gezo advanced to Mr. Cruikshank such arguments to prove the inexpediency of his giving up the slave-trade, as were the natural reasonings of a man in his position. They are thus laid down in Mr. Cruikshank's own report :—

"His chiefs had had long and serious consultations with him upon the subject; and they had come to the conclusion that his government could not be carried on without it. The state which he maintained was great; his army was expensive; the ceremonies and customs to be observed annually, which had been handed down to him from his forefathers, entailed upon him a vast outlay of money. These could not be abolished. The form of his government could not be suddenly changed, without causing such a revolution as would deprive him of his throne, and precipitate his kingdom into a state of anarchy. He was very desirous to acquire the friendship of England. He loved and respected the English character, and nothing afforded him such high satisfaction as to see an Englishman in his country, and to do him honour. He himself and his army were ready at all times to fight the Queen's enemies, and to do anything the English Government might ask of him, but to give up the slave-trade. No other trade was known to his people. Palm oil, it was true, was now engaging the attention of some of them; but it was a slow method of making money, and brought only a very small amount of duties into his coffers. The planting of coffee and cotton had been suggested to him; but this was slower still. The trees had to grow, and he himself would probably be in his grave before he could reap any benefit from them. And what to do in the meantime? Who would pay his troops, or buy arms and clothing for them? Who would give him supplies of cowries, of rum, of powder, and of cloth, to perform his annual customs? He held his power by an observance of the time-honoured customs of his forefathers; and he would forfeit it, and entail upon himself a life full of shame, and a death full of misery, if he neglected them. It was the slave-trade that made him terrible to his enemies, and loved, honoured, and respected by his people.   How could he give it up?   It had been the ruling principle of action with himself and his subjects from their earliest childhood.   Their thoughts, their habits, their discipline, their mode of life, had been formed with reference to this all-engrossing occupation; even the very songs with which the mother stilled her crying infant told of triumph over foes reduced to slavery.   Could he, by signing this treaty, change the sentiments of a whole people? It could not be.   A long series of years was necessary to bring about such a change. He himself and his people must be made to feel the superior advantages of another traffic in an increase of riches, and of the necessaries and luxuries of life, before they could be weaned from this trade.   The expenses of the English Government are great; would it suddenly give up the principal source of its revenue without some equivalent provision for defraying its expenses? He could not believe so.   No more would he reduce himself to beggary.   The sum offered him would not pay his expenses for a week; and even if the English Government were willing to give him an annual sum equivalent to his present revenue, he would still have some difficulty in employing the energies of his people in a new direction. Under such circumstances, however, he would consider himself bound to use every exertion to meet the wishes of the English Government."

A curious domestic superstition is thus recorded as existing on the gold coast. It is a custom with the natives of position and wealth to purchase a young slave of their own sex, or sometimes to select one from amongst some of the young slaves previously in the house, and to bestow on him, or her, the title of " Crabbah," or " Ocrah"—the meaning of which is, that the slave thus entitled is in future to be looked on as the soul or spirit of the master or mistress.

These favoured persons wear a chain of gold, or white beads, around the neck, to which is attached a large medallion of gold to denote their rank.

They are treated with great indulgence so long as they behave well.

In Ashantee the favourite Ocrahs of the great men are slaughtered on the death of their masters, it being considered necessary that they should accompany them to the next world. A similar wholesale slaughter of slaves, with a like purpose, is carried out on the death of any big man at Old Kalabar.

Meditating on the early connexion of European nations with Western Africa, we find, in a work entitled "Mémoire sur le Commerce Maritime de Rouen, par Ernest de Freville," that the French claim the honour of a first visit to this part of the world. So early as November, 1364, the merchants of Dieppe sent out two vessels, of one hundred tons each, which arrived at a little river near the mouth of the Sestos, on the Kroo Coast.

Their trade at this place, although its nature and extent are not described, was, no doubt, profitable; for, in September the following year, the Rouen merchants joined with those of Dieppe, and sent out four vessels. One of these passed the Ivory Coast, and voyaged on to the Gold Coast.

Twenty years' commercial connexion between Rouen, Dieppe, and the Gold Coast, inspired the merchants to send out artisans and materials to construct the fort of Elmina, the building of which was finished in 1386.

The civil wars in France having damaged their commercial connexion with all parts of the world, the trade between Rouen and the Gold Coast was necessarily affected; and, according to the French author from whom we derive our information, the Portuguese did not commence their reputed discovery of, and communication with, places on the west coast of Africa till more than a hundred years after.

It was in 1472 that the Portuguese arrived at Prince's Island—in 1484 at the Congo—1486 at Benin—and twelve years afterwards they doubled the Cape of Good Hope.

British legitimate commerce in Africa did not commence till 1553, when two ships left Plymouth and visited Sestos, Elmina, and Benin. Their touching at these places and no others seems to me very strong circumstantial evidence that the French account, previously quoted, is correct. The cargo with which they returned was gold and pepper—the latter was brought from Benin, whence, in the year 1590, was obtained the first cargo of palm-oil, an article of commerce which has since been so largely exported from Africa. The seventeenth century was the great time of African companies—palm oil and slaves being then the two main products. Slave-trading reached its climax in 1771, when one hundred and ninety-two slave-ships left England for Africa.

One particular characteristic of the Gold

Coast is the number of forts that are erected along its seabord. These were no doubt intended by the early European discoverers of that coast as fortresses, to prevent strangers encroaching upon a land at that time supposed to be a veritable Eldorado.

The chief fortress, and the capital of the Government, was Cape Coast; inland from which (Mr. Bannerman writes to me)—" The Wassaws are in possession of a splendid mining country, but they will make no use whatever of the wealth which Providence has placed within their reach. Under the surface of the soil here there lies an almost fabulous amount of wealth. Akim, Ashantee, Gaman, Wassaw—all these countries may be described as one vast mine of gold."

In Gaman, a kingdom tributary to Ashantee, there are mines so prolific that the gold can be procured within six feet of the surface of the soil; the king will not allow them to be worked, reserving them for his fetish.

Apollonia Fort is now dismantled and abandoned, although formerly an extensive trade in gold was carried on there. From a Government report, published in the year 1841, we learn that the king of the country in which Apollonia

Fort is situated was the terror of all the neighbouring districts, on account of the frequency of his human sacrifices.

The forts of Succondee, Commenda, Coromanty, and Tantumquerry, are all now in ruins, presenting an appearance of the utmost desolation. The forts that are occupied are Cape Coast, Accra, Christianburg, and Dixcove, by the English; Elmina and Creve Cœur by the Dutch. Neither French, Portuguese, nor Spaniards have at present any possessions in this part of Africa.

On the Gold Coast there is a territory extending from Cape Apollonia to the fort of Quittah, a few miles eastward of Cape St. Paul's, and inland to the frontier of the powerful kingdom of Ashantee. This territory comprises many distinct tribes, all of whom acknowledge some kind of allegiance either to England or Holland. The Dutch have authority over several towns on the seaside, but almost the whole of the interior is subject more or less to British influence.

As it is my desire to lay before my readers as complete a description as I can give of the social peculiarities of the native African, I copy here a curious sketch, which I know to be correct, from the *West African Herald* of May 31st, 1860 :—

"A few weeks ago an old man died in Ajumor-coong in the interior, leaving to his family over three thousand ounces of gold, three hundred slaves, and much land. The old fellow when alive dwelt in a most wretched hut, and the only piece of furniture he possessed was a mat. The deceased miser's name was Ocrah Taweah. Now, this man was a fair type of a large class of natives in this part of Africa, who are to be found chiefly in those districts of the protected territory that are situated at some distance from the forts. Near the forts where British authority is more generally felt, men know that they are secured in the quiet possession of whatsoever they have lawfully acquired; and, moreover, contact with civilisation has resulted not only in the introduction of a certain taste for the comforts of Europeans, but also in an imitation of some of their habits and customs. Hence in the towns on the seaside there are to be found numbers of natives of Africa who dwell in large and well-built houses, comfortably and tastefully furnished. And it is not the educated native merchants of the higher class only who live comfortably. A number of educated natives, occupying subordinate positions as clerks, overseers, factors, and the like, are lodged at least as well as the same class of men in England. Nor are these tastes indulged in only by those who have received the benefits of education; for we see in all the principal seaside towns some very excellent houses of two stories, having several spacious, neat, and well-furnished apartments, which are occupied by natives who cannot read or write, but who, having acquired wealth, prefer to lay it out in this way. In the interior, men who from small beginnings have acquired riches by their industry or their good luck generally hoard their money, or, at all events, the greater part of it. They do not care for European modes of living. They do not buy couches, mirrors, knives, forks, spoons, mahogany tables, lamps, pictures, &c., &c.

On occasions of state most of the native chiefs of the interior display much barbaric splendour, which the chiefs on the seaside do not; yet the private residences of the interior chiefs are by no means to be compared with the dwellings of many poor and subordinate chiefs on the beach. We do not speak of course of Ashantee, but of those provinces called the Protected Territory, which lie between the seaside and the kingdom of Ashantee. In these countries there is much oppression and extortion, and all sorts of rascality are still going on. Wherever the authorities have great power, wherever in fact the Government, be it British, or Dutch, or African, is strong, there the property, life, and liberty of individuals are felt to be secure. In very many parts of the Protected Territory there is no powerful native Government, and the British have no authorised agent to check disorders. In such districts the place of Government is supplied by what are called Pynins, or elders, who very often have no other means of subsistence that what they derive from suits tried before them. Such tribunals are very frequently nothing more than agencies for extortion and oppression. In many, nay, most parts of Fantee they abound, and from their unrighteous decrees it is not always that the injured have the opportunity of appealing to the British Courts on the seaside. Much injustice is therefore perpetrated, and the victims are often those persons who are known to have acquired large sums of money by their own exertions, originally perhaps slaves, pawns, or at least strangers to the place. Such men, therefore, are in many instances afraid to make a display of their wealth, fearing lest their riches should bring upon them the jealousy and envy of their neighbours, and be the means of involving them in trouble."

Amongst these people, too, civil wars are constantly springing up. During the past year a system of petty warfare among the natives has been general along this coast, as appears frequently by the paper from which I have quoted the foregoing. At Quittah, at Ahguay, and in the interior countries of Dinkera and Akim, there have been contests. At Anamaboe, which is an important town, situated on the sea-side, nine miles to the eastward of Cape Coast, and where a considerable gold traffic with Ashantee is now carried on, a disturbance broke out last year between two companies, on the subject of one carrying a flag, of which the other claimed a patent right. In the principal towns of the Gold Coast the inhabitants are divided into companies, like our clubs in England; and these companies have their flags and captains. On native ceremonials, such as funerals and driving the devil out of town, these companies turn out in grand parade, but generally wind up with a row, which most frequently terminates with a pitched battle on some day appointed. Even if the affair above alluded to had not been settled by the intervention in time of magisterial authority, it is not at all probable there would have been any bloodshed; for the Africans prefer palavering to fighting, and a debate on the subject of a war is with them a thing of high and mighty consequence. My readers may be assured that this civil war business is the same all over the coast; the only difference being, that there is no honest "Heralder" like that at Cape Coast to record their conflicts. In the Bight of Biafra district, at all events, there is never a change from palm-oil and palavers throughout the year.

When we read such a paragraph as the following, referring to missions on the Gold Coast at the end of 1859, does it not strike the reader that there must be something strangely anomalous in the condition of this people?

"On the 31st December last there were on the Gold and Slave Coasts of Africa, 36 Wesleyan mission schools, 18 chapels, 24 preaching places. The number of scholars at that date was 1082 boys and 315 girls. There were 74 day-school teachers, 5 catechists, 33 local preachers, 1869 full and accredited members, 208 on trial for full membership, and the number of attendants on public worship was about 8300. During the year there had been 51 marriages, 127 baptisms of adults, and 122 baptisms of infants."

If I am asked to show the condition of the native African, notwithstanding all the benefits of missionary teaching, I do it in the words of the missionaries themselves. I find in the *African* newspaper of March 30th last, extracted from the *Cavalla Messenger*, an account of a mission convocation at Cape Palmas, at which amongst other things the following statement was made :—" The reports seemed to indicate a dead silence everywhere ; nothing like a revival of religion, but, on the contrary, a dreadful stirring up of the power of Satan. *The people are apparently becoming worse and worse.* Remarks were made by several persons, in which the little success of the Gospel lately was greatly deplored."

It would not be fair to infer from this that a like failure has been the result on all parts of the coast ; and yet we can see here, in the places of which this chapter treats, evidence that the following excellent practical plan is bearing but little fruit :—

" It has been the practice of the Basel Society, according to the precedent of the Moravian Brethren, to supply all their African stations with lay missionaries, who strive to train the native converts to industrious habits, and to teach them how to employ in the service of God and

men, the energies with which they have been
endowed, and the still undeveloped wealth of
their country. Workshops have been set up at
Christiansborg, Abokoby, Abude, and Akropong,
in which wood-sawyers, carpenters, joiners, coopers, shingle-makers, bricklayers, blacksmiths, lock-
smiths, shoemakers, and tailors are trained; and
although it is not to be expected that negroes
will soon be able to dispense with European su-
pervision and instruction in their trades, yet
their progress hitherto has been encouraging,
and their assistance has been of incalculable value in a country where no tradesmen are procurable, and where constant exposure to the sun
is almost certain death to Europeans. Nor is
the adoption of an improved system of agriculture of less importance, whilst the natives grow
with as little trouble as possible their most necessary provisions, and, to save labour, select
every year a new piece of ground, and give up
the rest to the inroads of the bush, to become the
hot-beds of fever and the haunts of all sorts of
noxious animals and vermin. Regular plantations,
of greater or smaller extent, have been laid out at
Akropong, Abude, Abokoby, and Gyadam, to
train an improved class of farmers. These attempts have proved that, under proper manage-

ment, the produce of the land may be increased tenfold, and that many resources for home-consumption as well as export have as yet been scarcely touched upon. With similar intentions a factory has been established at Christiansborg, with prospects of advantage both to the mission and the people."

The following is an abstract of the commercial operations in this part of Africa, carried on in 1858, which I have been kindly permitted to copy from the records at the Colonial Office :—

GOLD COAST, 1858.

COUNTRIES.	IMPORTS.	EXPORTS.
United Kingdom . .	£76,835 17 9	£118,553 6 5
United States . . .	31,122 12 0	20,421 5 6½
British Colonies . .	.. ..	.. ..
Foreign Countries—		
France	6,012 11 3	11,103 7 6
Holland	4,857 6 8	4,057 16 6
Portugal	1,435 11 2	.. ..
Other Countries . .	2,193 0 0	.. ..
	£122,456 18 10	£154,135 15 11½

" *Population.*—There is no means of ascertaining the population of the Gold Coast territory— judging from the poll-tax returns of 1852 to 1853, it would appear to be 151,346, omitting the Axim country, which, however, would not be more than 5,000 additional. The chief of the village has generally a number of Krooms, or smaller villages, dependent on him, at the head of each of which is a Captain, whose duty it is to march before the chief in war time. The chief agricultural productions of the Gold Coast are yams, Indian corn, banians, plantains, and cassava—males and females being alike agriculturists. Even in fishing at the sea-side with hand-nets flung from their canoes, they keep the barter and traffic principle. The fish caught are brought into the interior, and there exchanged for agricultural produce, which is again bartered by the people in the town. Cotton is coming up in the Volta river, under the auspices of the Rev. E. Freeman—but palm-oil is very small. Connected with Wesleyan missions there are twenty-eight chapels on this part of the coast, attended by an aggregate congregation of 5,600. A public free school for boys and girls is held within the walls of the Castle. This is under the superintendence of the Colonial Chaplain, and the books are supplied by Government. No industrial schools are here, more than anywhere else on the coast."

CHAPTER X.

Of the River Niger and Belzoni's Exploration in Benin—General
Scenery at the mouths of **rivers** falling into the Gulf of Guinea—
Similar to that of Eastern Africa, described by Captain Burton
—Author's Opinions on the Commercial operations up the Niger
after Pleiad's Expedition of 1854—Memorial presented to Lord
Palmerston in beginning of last year—Its Arguments, and the
Assent of Government to them—**Causes of Attacks by the Na-
tives** upon Steamers sent up by Mr. **Laird**—Commercial Opera-
tions recorded by that Gentleman during the past three **years**—
His Present Contract with **the** Government and its Proceedings
—Impossibility of establishing **a** Profitable trade up that River
without Government Help—A **Gun-boat**, War-steamers, and
Tug-steamer required—Sir John Bowring's opinion of the Negro
—Plans in reference to the Niger—Mr. Jameson's Views.

WE may imagine ourselves within hail of the
miasmatous banks of the historical Niger, when
arriving at the mouth of the musquito-infested
Benin. What the enterprising Belzoni could
have told us of the dark secrets of this unknown
kingdom must ever lie hid with his ashes, which

repose in the neighbourhood of its capital.

Coasting along by the mouths of the many rivers that debouch into the Gulf of Guinea, the eye of the voyager rests upon nothing more attractive than a continuation of scenes such as those described by Captain Burton in Eastern Africa, and which are sketched forth by Earl de Grey and Ripon in last year's address to the Royal Geographical Society, as of "a fever-stricken country, that is skirted by a wide low-lying belt of overwhelming vegetation, dank, monotonous, and gloomy, while it reeks with fetid miasma."

Let us flit over the marshy grounds that border the Niger's many mouths, and leave the mangrove swamps to the oysters and crocodiles, whilst we travel, with the progress of civilization and the development of commerce, up the Quorra to Central Africa.

It would be but a dish of *crambe repetita* to detail all the early explorations and progresses made up this river since the discovery of its mouth by the brothers Lander in 1831. In my account* of our Niger expedition of 1854, I have given

* Published by Longman & Co. of Paternoster Row, and forming vols 91 and 92 of "Traveller's Library."

a brief sketch of these ; and as the views which
I then expressed, in a report to Mr. Laird, have
undergone no change since that time, I record
them here, as they have not before been made
public by me :—

"S. S. Pleiad, Clarence Cove,
"November 20th, 1854.

"Sir,—Before I place in your hands my journal of our voyage up the Niger—Tshadda,
Binué—with a report on the position and prospects of trade along their courses—which I have
in contemplation to prepare on my passage home
—I trust you will not consider out of place a few
observations I take the liberty of making to you
now, connected with the report.

"The account of our trading produce will, I
have no doubt, be forwarded to you by Captain
Taylor. Of ivory, the chief article, 4258lbs. were
purchased by me on our passage up and down;
and 278lbs. by Mr. Crawford, during a stay of
six weeks at the confluence. The cause of such
a small quantity being bought will be explained
to you hereafter. All inquiries after copper ore
have failed in discovering the locality where it
is procured. I have with me a few specimens of
copper rings and brass ornaments manufactured
at Kano—the ' London' of Sudan—but the peo-

ple at Rogan Koto, and Hamarrua, where they were obtained, say that the metal of which they are made of is brought from the Hanssa country. At Gandike, they report that lead has been dug out of the ground at a distance of about six feet from the surface; but the piece which was given to me was evidently molten, and cast in an earthen mould. We have about 60lbs. of lead ore, in its primitive crystals, as it was excavated at a place called Afooro, about twenty miles from the river port of Anyashi, on the road thence to Wukari. Perhaps the few geological specimens which I have collected will indicate more than I have been able to ascertain of correct information. No quartz was met with, save a little on a small island, nearly opposite Mount Sterling.

" If a plea of justification were needed for my remarks, I think I have it in the fact of our crew of sixty-six hands being here to-day in nearly as good condition as when the 'Pleiad' left Clarence on the 8th of July. The preservation of their health, despite of a few severe cases of fever we had on board, may be chiefly attributed to the following causes :—

" *First.*—To our having entered the river at the least unhealthy season of the year, when the water is rising.

"*Second.*—To my having induced all the Europeans to take quinine solution* daily, without making any fuss for its palpable necessity.

"*Third.*—To our not being required to stow green wood in the bunkers, in consequence of having iron canoes for its conveyance.

"*Fourth.*—To attending to the health of the ship's crew, by having all the water drunk on board passed through the boiler before it was filtered—dry-scraping the deck instead of washing it—and passing some of Sir Wm. Burnett's zinc solution down the bath floor twice a-week—taking care to have the bilge water pumped out daily.

"*And last*—though not the least in consequence —keeping up the hilarity of all on board by the Kroomens' nightly dance to the music of a drum, kindly lent to me by Governor Lynslager.

"I quite agree with your remarks in one of your letters of instruction to Captain Taylor, that, 'without assistance from Government, no steamer can pay in the river trade;' and I believe, moreover, that, in the present condition of the country, 'no trade can be established without the

* The form of quinine wine used on this and subsequent occasions by me is prepared by Wm. Bailey & Sons, of Horsely Fields Chemical Works, Wolverhampton, and put up for shipment in cases containing one, two, or three dozen pint bottles.

assistance of Government.'   From Oddokodo up to Dagbo the country has been laid waste by the Fellatahs, and not a vestige of human habitation shews the place where the former town once stood.   Only three or four months past they murdered the king of Pandah (Fundah), burned the town of Ikeriko, and drove the king of Opotingiah (Potinka) to take refuge at Abasha, on the opposite side of the river, and the limit of the Egarrah country.   Yimmaha, Oketta and Oruko (indeed all the towns of the Igbarra and Bassa countries) have been plundered by them—some burnt—and many of the inhabitants slaughtered, more carried into slavery, and the remaining survivors driven to seek refuge in other than their native localities.   Nearly all the islands we passed in the portion of the Tshadda referred to were tenanted by refugees from these towns, whose exertions for common subsistence must meantime be suspended, for they know not at what moment, on returning to their native districts, the attack may be repeated.   The Fellatahs, mounted on well-trained steeds, and with poisoned arrows, poisoned javelins, and Hanssa swords, are ever giving way to an instinctive thirst for human blood, or urged by ambition for extent of territory, which I believe to be as much their impelling **influences as** any truculent fanaticism for the propagation of the Mahomedan creed..

" **Now,** as the **Attah of** Egarrah **has,** in the course **of my** conversation with **him,** expressed **his desire** to have **a** British settlement in his dominion, and commerce introduced thereby, **I** would propose that the next voyagers up **this river** should **be** empowered to treat for **a** piece of land at Iddah, **or a** few miles higher, upon equally ele- vated ground, opposite Ototouro, where Abukko's people are located. Here is an opening which might be followed up **by** our Government to this extent. Drs. Overweg and Barth have con- cluded a treaty with the Sheikh of Bornu, **who** expressed his desire **to see a squadron of** European boats on Lake Tshad, and guaranteed **to substitute** commercial traffic with the nations **of** Europe for the slave-trade. Between Egarrah **and the Bornu** kingdom it is nearly all Fellatah territory; and from a great part of Bornu com- munication **may** be opened by means of the Konadagu **river,** passing Bossa, to any estab- lishment on Lake Tshad. So that, on ami- cable terms with **the** Fellatahs—received with open arms by establishments protected by native **military** forces, and having a government similar to that of Sierra Leone and Cape Coast— the industrial resources of Central Africa will soon become developed, and the riches of the vast continent be poured down to us by the continuous streams of the Binué, the Tshadda, and the Niger.

"To turn the attention of the people of Africa to the cultivation of their soil, to teach them how, by industry, their slaves may be made to produce to them more substantial comforts than can be procured by selling them, ought to be our object in the first instance. Mawkish philanthropists may object to this as being an encouragement of domestic slavery. It is no encouragement. It is, at the most, a toleration of it for a good purpose. And of two evils, choose the least, hoping and working for the good time to come, when the slaves, by their industry, may liberate themselves and become sharers in the prosperity of their fatherland. Of their certainty to do this, I have assurance in a fact communicated to me by the Rev. Mr. Crowther, that several hundred slaves have so emancipated themselves at Abbeokuta. You may perhaps consider my suggestions as visionary, or the expectation of Government aid towards their accomplishment as hopeless. Granted that they are, I nevertheless conceive it to be my duty to urge their serious consideration on you. You are now at the head of a machinery which I conceive to be the best calculated to carry out such a plan—I mean the African Steam Navigation Company; and the following is an outline of what I would suggest :—

"In the first place, to have an understanding with the Fellatah Sultan at Sokatu, to secure from him the exercise of his influence over his extensive dominions, and chiefly to prevent the ravages of his people throughout the countries on the northern bank of the Tshadda. Whether this will need a demonstration of *your* moral force[*] or not, the Fellatah marauding must be put an end to before any commercial step can be taken with a prospect of success. Meantime, to purchase a piece of territory in the neighbourhood of Iddah, where a portion of a West Indian regiment should be established, sufficient in number to protect the traders, native as well as European.

"A small steamer, say the 'Pleiad,' with some improvements that I shall hereafter mention, would answer for a commencement; and it would not only strike terror into the minds of the natives below Aboh, by the dread of its power, but fortify those above by the certainty of its protection. A

---

[*] Mr Laird, in his evidence before a committee of the House of Commons, gave it as his opinion on one occasion that "moral force in Western Africa meant a 24-pounder with a British seaman behind it."

canoe stationed at Aboh, rendered doubly necessary because the interception of the palm-oil traffic
between this and the Bonny, Brass, and Benin
rivers must be the main object of trading
farther up; another at the confluence; besides
that at Iddah, a settlement near Apokko, on one
of the Dagbo hills; and, if farther up, at Anyashi,
the river port of Wukari, the capital of the
Kororoofa kingdom. From this place communication may be made by native canoes to Gan-
diko, Zhibu, and Hamarrua. Very little coal
would be required for a steamer, as the people
are certain to have wood cut when they are sure
of a market for it.

"There is no 'break in the navigation of the
Tshadda,' such as you supposed to be the cause
of the interruption of traffic upon it; but the inhabitants high up dwell in districts thirty or
forty miles asunder, and are not in friendly relations with one another.

"The steamer should go backwards and for-
wards, to and from the mouth of the river, and
the canoes and trading establishments, to deliver
produce and return with goods, making a trip
once a year, in August and September, as far as
the river port of Zola and Hamarrua. Owing
to a strong current of five and six knots, and the

absence of eddies in many parts of the river above Ojogo, canoes are not applicable for navigation so high up; and where they are used, they should have a very different sort of propellers from the flattened soup ladles used as paddles for those of the 'Pleiad.'

"From Dagbo to Ojogo, a distance of at least forty miles, is a range of country, with a rich loamy soil, where cotton and coffee can be produced in abundance, and where a *bonâ fide* model garden could be established, under the superintendence of men brought from Sierra Leone. Not such a model garden as that which was located on the rocky ground at Mount Sterling, nor one sufficient to realize such predictions as those of Sir George Stephens, in his pamphlet on the Niger trade, in being able to clear its own expenses after a three years' cultivation of the Delta; but one that may be the beginning of a good work, which will be the best practical lesson for the Fellatahs.

"And if the Government do not step in to put an end to the lawlessness of the Fellatahs, all ideas of a successful trade with the Niger-Tshadda-Binué countries may be given up. There can be no neutrality on the subject. Our Government, which has unfurled the British banner as the ægis of civilization and

Christianity over the world, has still a weighty debt on her shoulders to the vast continent of Africa. I cannot be accused of any attempt at declamation when I assert that the forty millions of money spent in West Indian emancipation have been little alleviation to the miseries caused by the fact that the inhuman slave traffic had been legalized amongst us for nearly two centuries—that the voice of humanity and religion, the glory and honour of our empire, and the practically commercial character of our country, demanded it. If the Government commenced the work, I have very little doubt that in a few years hence private enterprize will do the rest : British influence will be extended; pillage will cease; with its cessation will flow into Central Africa all the blessings of civilization, which otherwise centuries could not introduce; the trade will pay ; and the industrial resources of the country will become at length developed, to the peace and comfort of its inhabitants, and to the commercial prosperity of Great Britain.

" I have the honor to remain, sir, your obedient servant,

" THOMAS J. HUTCHINSON.

" To Macgregor Laird, Esq.,
    " 3, Mincing Lane, London."

In March of last year, a deputation consisting of Sir T. D. Acland, Bart., Lord Viscount Middleton, Lord Calthorpe, with several other gentlemen, presented a memorial to Lord Palmerston, on the national importance of steam navigation upon the river Niger, for the encouragement and protection of lawful commerce, and the more effectual suppression of the slave-trade.

This memorial was a repetition of a similar one presented to his Lordship in the month of August, 1855, after the return of the S.S. "Pleiad," from her exploring expedition of the preceding year. To their former application the Government had not acceded till 1857, when a contract was entered into with Macgregor Laird, Esq., to keep a small steamer on the river Niger for **five** years, for the purposes specified in the memorial, as well as for those of geographical exploration.

The memorialists pointed to the fact of an annual sum of money being voted by the British parliament for the expenses of a steamer towards the encouragment **and** protection of commerce in Gambia—of aid afforded to Dr. Livingstone for his further exploration of Eastern Africa—and of subsidies advanced for opening the navigation of the rivers of India, very justly submitting these as precedents in favour of their request.

They mention the fact of the vessels sent up by Mr. Laird, between 1857 and 1860, having been attacked by marauding tribes of the Delta, " who are deeply interested in opposing legitimate commerce, for the sake of an illicit slave-trade." Three of these vessels were attacked, but not by any persons having an interest in the slave-trade. This is one of the errors of a slave-trade theory; for such traffic in the Bight of Biafra is like that recorded at Angola by Dr. Livingstone, "a thing spoken of in the past tense." It was the palm-oil native brokers, who dwell between the districts where that article is manufactured, and the British receiving-ships at the mouth of Brass river, by whom these several attacks were made.

Further, they presented a statement, made by Macgregor Laird, Esq., shewing the prospects of an increasing trade up the Niger, after an experience of three years, by which it appeared that three factories had been established above the Delta of the Niger, viz., at Aboh, Onitsha, and at theconfluence of the Niger and Tshadda.

Mr. Laird further records :—

"At these permanent stations the produce of the country has been collected and prepared for shipment by my European and African agents, and it is satisfactory to state that their lives and property have been protected by the different tribes in whose territory they are located, and in no instance have they been subjected to insult or injury.

"A free passage was offered to Missionaries of all denominations of the African race, and the Church Missionary and Wesleyan Missionary Societies have established Schools and Churches at each of these stations, to the great and marked improvement of the people.

"The value of produce collected at these stations, and brought down the river, shows a gradual increase—

"In 1857, it realized in Liverpool . . £1800
,, 1858,   ,,   ,,   2750
,, 1859,   ,,   ,,   8000 to 9000.

In the last year cotton of quality equal to that of the Southern States of America has been brought down, and as it is grown extensively on both banks of the river, it will form a staple article of export.

"Though these sums show that the existing trade cannot support a steam-vessel upon the river, the rate of increase holds out a fair prospect of its doing so in the course of another three or four years. The great drawback is the hostility of the tribes in the Delta, where the

river is divided into narrow and tortuous chan-
nels, where the natives are armed with cannon
as well as musketry, and where they are encouraged and stimulated to prevent steamers
ascending by the chiefs and slave-traders on the
coast."

The Government, the memorialists, or Mr.
Laird, do not seem to notice the fact that these
muskets and cannon, with powder and shot, were
sold to the people who used them, and sold, too,
by the advocates of the extension of legitimate
commerce as the best means for putting down
the slave-trade.

The Government granted in part the application
of the memorialists, and the following explanation
of Mr. Laird's regulations is extracted from the
Cotton Supply Reporter, of August 10th in last
year :—

"3, Mincing Lane, London, 14th June, 1860.

"DEAR SIR,—I have entered into an agreement
with Her Majesty's Government to keep up a
communication by steamers between the mouth
of the River Niger and its confluence with the
Chadda, for three years, commencing from the
1st August next.

"I engage to make, if not prevented by un-
foreseen accidents, or the hostility of the natives

in the Delta, three voyages annually—two as high as the confluence and one to Onitsha, and to keep a floating depot at the mouth of the river, which will be visited by the mail-packet monthly.

"It is my wish to make this arrangement available to liberated Africans returning to their native countries on the banks of the Niger and Chadda; and in order to do so, I propose to charge a fixed rate of ten dollars per head for deck passengers of the negro race, finding their own provisions, to all parts between the mouth of the river and the confluence, and to take goods for them at the rate of five pounds per ton weight or measurement for the river freight, and to arrange with the African Mail Company to take passengers and goods from any part of the coast, at their printed rates of freight and passage money, in addition to the above. By this arrangement, the passage money from Sierra Leone to the Niger would be twenty dollars, from Lagos fifteen dollars; so that one payment should clear passengers or goods.

" Passengers can only be received under the conditions specified in the clause marked in the table of fares by the African mail-packets annexed. Each adult passenger will be allowed to take 28lbs. of personal luggage free of freight.

"I think the best plan to encourage this return of liberated Africans and their descendants, would be for the Church Missionary Society to form a committee of natives of the countries bordering on the Niger, resident at Sierra Leone and Lagos —to select such applicants as they deem suitable —to send out and report to them, either personally or by letter, on the advantages and disadvantages of such a return to the interior ; and if any assistance is given intended emigrants, it should be confined to paying their passage money ; and I object strongly to any being invited to go until accounts are received of the safe passage of the steamer through the Delta, and the permanent pacification of that district, which I hope will be accomplished this season.

" All persons settling on the banks of the Niger must clearly understand that they do so at their own risk, both of person and property; that they must conform to the laws of the country in which they locate themselves; and that the British Government does not undertake to protect them : in this respect they will be exactly in the position of those liberated Africans who have settled at Abbeokuta and other parts of the Yoruba country.

" I have no doubt Mr. Crowther will send full

reports, on his arrival at Onitsha, of the prospects for emigrants returning to Central Africa by the Niger, to his brethren in Sierra Leone and Lagos, and I would be guided greatly by his opinion.

"It is my intention to keep the 'Rainbow' constantly on the river; and I am in hopes that during the dry season it may be found navigable as high as Onitsha; and my agent will have orders to communicate with Her Majesty's Consul at Lagos full information as to the times when a departure will take place for the interior.

"I remain, dear sir, yours faithfully,

"MACGREGOR LAIRD."

There have been so many theories advanced about the best mode of civilizing the negro, as well as of aiding him in the development of his country's wealth, and so many of these have failed to accomplish the ends for which they were proposed, that I confess I have no plan to offer.

Of one thing, however, I must confess myself convinced—still to adhere to the principle which I enunciated six years ago—of the impossibility of effecting anything permanently advantageous in the Niger trade without the aid of Government in the beginning. Cash, capital, and companies are very good things in most parts of the world, but what is their power when opposed to marauding bushmen and treacherous savages?

There is no middle course in dealing with such people as those to be met with in the Delta of the Niger.

It seems to me an indispensable preliminary, for the establishment of healthy commercial operations up that river, that Government should have a gun-boat permanently attached to the service there for at least five years—that its first visit should be to the town from whence the shots were fired that killed the men in the "Rainbow" steamer—that notice should be given to the inhabitants to clear out in so many hours—and that its huts should then be levelled to the ground. This cannot be considered severe when it is remembered that no lives would be sacrificed, and that the building materials to construct new houses can be gathered from the bush in a few hours. The "moral force" impression would be made, and the presence of the gun-boat once a-year would keep this impression, as it were, stereotyped. In the meantime, and during many months of each season, the vessel might be cruising about for the benefit of her crew's health. To facilitate the operations of traders, be they natives or Europeans, I would likewise suggest that the Government should establish a steamer, say such a one as the colonial steamer " Dover," at Gambia, to tow up and down ships engaged in trading. The development of trade in its present condition cannot compensate any private individual for the expense of building and maintaining a steamer. This vessel should be commanded by a merchant sailing-master, paid by Government, and bound in a heavy penalty not to trade himself. A steamer is necessary to tow up all vessels against the current of the Niger, which is always running; and the experience of all the steamers that have gone out since 1854 (including the " Pleiad ") demonstrates the inexpediency of having Government and commercial operations under one and the same management, more especially when carried on in one and the same ship.

This tug, although armed, ought likewise to be fitted up in a different manner from the steamers of former expeditions. I do not allude to the disputed question of screw and paddle-wheels, about which I do not presume to judge, but to an essential matter connected with the safety of the lives of all on board—the necessity, namely, of a high bulwark of metal around the ship's side, to protect the men on deck from being shot down as the two poor fellows were in the S.S. "Rainbow."

The passenger traffic of native emigrants and missionaries from Sierra Leone ought to be confined to such vessel.

The men who theorize on the certainty of anti-slave-trade treaties and the cessation of the slave-trade leading to the development of Africa's industrial resources, seem to me to be as much special reasoners in the matter as Mr. Jameson in his pamphlet, inferring that the palm-oil trade became developed in a larger increasing ratio when its production was concurrent with the slave-export. The two conditions have no relation to one another—except on the *post hoc ergo propter hoc* principle. We require to go deeper into the social condition of the African races to find out why for the last twenty years the palm-oil produce in all the rivers has been at a comparative standstill. We should study the lax industry which is such a prominent characteristic of the Ethiopian race; and, above all, we should inquire how much their domestic life, their superstitious sacrifices, and their civil contentions have to do with the stagnation of their commerce. To my own knowledge, intestine broils, chiefly with the interior tribes, have tended so to reduce the amount of palm-oil produce in Bonny, as to make the proceeds of 1859 three thousand tons less than those of 1856.

In addressing the audience of the Mechanics' Institute at Manchester, during the past year, Sir John Bowring observed :—" He looked with some doubt and hesitation at the powers of Africa. He had lived among the blacks, and did not find in them the elements of industry to which he should look for a large production." A generalization of this kind might be regarded with distrust, did it not emanate from a man with large powers of observation, and were it not confirmed by what I have remarked. Let me not be misunderstood. I condemn no man's idea about what he thinks the best means of civilizing the African, or of investing his capital to profitable account. An eminent barrister, Sir J. Stephen, I believe, once advanced a plan for draining the Delta of the Niger, and converting its reclaimed acres into a model garden. I do not censure this. But I claim the right of entertaining a doubt as to its possibility, when I know that white men *could not* accomplish such a work, as its execution would take them off in death by thousands ; and I know equally well that black men *would not* do it, whatever reward they were offered. This is entirely apart from the possibility of accomplishing such a work by any human means, in which I confess I have no faith.

The plan proposed a few years back, by some gentleman in London, whose name I forget—" to cultivate the Sahara, and render England independent of the world for her cotton, coffee, tea and sugar "—may have appeared to its author very feasible. His design was to establish a joint-stock company, and to commence operations by constructing an aqueduct from the Senegal river to lake Tshad, or more probably *vice versâ*. Shrubs were to be planted—the ground of the desert was to be watered with watering-pots —and meteorology was expected to induce some change of climate out there that was to cause rain to fall—and thus, making the desert productive, to render England independent of the world."

On Mr. Jameson's proposal to form a company for the development of the Central African trade through the Cross river to the Niger, I have a few observations to make.

Without reference to the malarious swamps on the banks, he seems not to be aware of the obstacles existing up the Cross river, similar to those on the Delta of the Niger and at Bonny —the ferocity of the natives towards one another, and the probability of their extending this spirit to those Europeans with whom they may come in contact. The tribe occupying the island of Bosan, in the centre of the stream, have not permitted those of the Akoono-Koono district to pass by, for more than twelve years, with their palm-oil produce ; and thus a yearly damage to a great extent is done to the market at Old Kalabar.

The great mistake in the plans for civilizing the negro seems to be that the designers forget that it is next to impossible to apply any one mode of action to all tribes, and that it is **inexpediency** to endeavour to assimilate their undeveloped ideas to ours, instead of bringing our higher reasoning faculties to the development and improvement **of theirs.** However sensible and **true** may be the observation **of Captain Allen***—" that no undertaking formed by private individuals **for** purposes purely commercial can prosper in the interior of Africa "—nevertheless **the** plan of including a bazaar, with a government **house, hospital,** and barracks, seems to me to border **much** on the

* " Expedition to the Niger." Bentley, 1848, vol., ii., page 434.

chimerical. Our knowledge of the peculiarities of each tribe should teach us that a like mode of conduct is not applicable to all.

To develop the industrial resources of Africa, by teaching her children how to cultivate cotton and coffee, and to increase the manufacture of palm-oil, seems to me the first step. It is a question worth the consideration of the legislative councils of our colonies in Western Africa, if the encouragement of the pawning system* would forward this object; but if private or Government enterprise can do nothing better towards the civilization of Africa, than what it has done up to this time—namely, making rum and guns and powder our chief articles of export in exchange for native produce—they cannot hope that the barbarous tribes of Ethiopia will be much more advanced in comfort or civilization a century hence than they are at the present time.

* *Vide* Chapter I.

CHAPTER XI.

Despotic Government in the Palm-oil Rivers—Pilotage and Trading Comeys at Brass, New Kalabar, and Bonny—Commencement of Troubles in Bonny on the Dethronement of King Pepple—New Articles to Treaty in January, 1854, constituting Dappo King—Abolition of Trading made imperative on the part of the Governing Head in Bonny—Prohibition of Chopping Oil, or of going to War—Establishment of **Quadruple Regency**—Causes of the Inefficiency **of such a Form of Government** —Proved by the Experience of Five **Years—No Foundation for** King Pepple's Claims on the British Government for Indemnity —**Fact of his** Dethronement emanating from his own People— British Authorities having no Power to nominate or reinstate a **King in an African Neutral** Territory—Letter to the Bonny **Supercargoes.**

T HE principles of native government, which exist amongst all the tribes on the banks of the palm-oil rivers, are purely despotic.

At Brass the governing power is divided between Keyah, head of the Obullumabry district, nephew of the late King Boy, and Orishima, a nephew of the late King Jacket,

who holds the reins over the Bassambry territory.

The trade regulations enjoin the payment of sixteen pieces of cloth, or eighty bars of other merchandize, for the pilotage of vessels entering and proceeding up this river; and for vessels leaving the river twenty pieces of cloth, or a hundred bars of other merchandize.

The "comey" for vessels coming here for trading purposes is at the rate of one puncheon's worth of palm-oil, reduced to British goods, paid for each mast carried by a ship.

Besides this, there exists another comey in the shape of a bar levied by the supercargo on every puncheon of palm-oil brought for sale. This is of course out of the property of the man who owns the palm-oil, and is expected to be levied in behoof of the monarch by the British trader.

Amongst these governing heads there does not exist the same open daring spirit of defiant opposition to British influence which we recog-nize in Dahomey, Ashantee, and elsewhere. As in Bonny and Kalabar, a spirit of commercial elevation is rising here amongst certain men, which exercises the same commanding influ-ence in the councils of the people that the almighty dollar does in other parts of the world. For example, Keya and Orishima are held with a sort of curb by the native palm-oil traders, who urge them in "palaver" debates to expend their comey in settling disputes that may in any way tend to intercept the communication with the interior palm-oil markets of the Brass brokers. The house of Gun, which divided the sovereignty with Boy for some time after the death of its head, kept the latter in check, till Keya, on the sudden death of Amanga (a descendant of Gun's), came in to be undisputed ruler.

By one of the provisions of their native code for the regulation of trading with white men, it is enacted, "that long detentions having heretofore occurred in trade, and much angry feeling having been **excited in the natives'** minds from the destruction by white men (in their ignorance of the superstitions and customs of the country) of a certain species of boa-constrictor that visits the cask-houses, and which is 'ju-ju' or sacred to the Brass men, it is hereby forbidden to all British subjects **to** destroy or harm **any of these** reptiles on their premises, to give notice **to the** chief man in Twa, who is to come and remove it away."

The chiefs of Brass district are the only ones in either the Bight of Benin or of Biafra with whom no anti-slave-trade treaty has been entered into. Nevertheless, no foreign export of slaves is carried on from this any more than from the other rivers, whose chiefs have been paid by our Government an indemnity for its suppression.

Up New Kalabar river King Amacree may be said to be the undisputed reigning head, although held in check socially by the superstitious tomfoolery of a ju-ju king, named Akoko (the death of one of these potentates is recorded elsewhere); and commercially by a family named Barboy, who are first-class traders, and believed by some persons to have a presumptive right to the monarchy of New Kalabar.

The adoption of the principle of free-trade in these places would appear to me very unjust, inasmuch as the native brokers are obliged to pay comey at all the native towns by which they pass in conveying palm-oil from the interior markets. In all the rivers of the Bights, however, the subject of the abolition of " comey " has been mooted from time to time.

In New Kalabar and Bonny, as well as at Brass, there existed for a considerable time what was styled the "Bar comey." This was a customs duty, independent of the ordinary port dues. The trader who was entitled to receive this comey was one to whose family sway the other native traders were subservient; and it was levied at the rate of one bar per puncheon for all the oil going on board any ship. To ensure accuracy in the payment of this duty, a small boy was generally placed in the vessel to keep tally.

It was frequently collected by the supercargo for the native trader to whom it was due; and occasionally the supercargo made a contract in the gross for an amount of about five puncheons worth of palm oil as the total of the trading voyage.

It was the commencement of a troublesome crisis in the social and commercial history of Bonny when King Dappo was constituted as the legitimate successor to the deposed king Pepple, The clauses of this nomination act were agreed to in Bonny Equity Court House, on 23rd January, 1854, and ratified by Consul Beecroft, in presence of Lieut. C. H. Young, commanding H.M.S.S. "Antelope," and a number of native traders. The very first article embodies ideas directly opposed to all principles of African government. It pro-

hibits the new king from trading directly, or indirectly (by giving trust to Bonny men); it al-
lows to him for his support two-thirds of the
comey of every ship coming to trade in the
river, applying the other third to meet the ex-
igencies of the country; each party also con-
tributing sufficient for the support of Pepple out
of their shares, provided he is not possessed of
sufficient means of his own. By one of its provisions it allots a puncheon of oil as a reward to
any person who shall give information respecting
any breach, on the part of his majesty, of the
agreement by which he is bound not to trade—
thus placing him under the constant surveillance
of spies who are paid for giving information
touching his delinquencies.

Seizing oil for debts, and the imprisonment of
traders for the same reason, were abolished by
these regulations.

The other clauses of this code ordained that
the king or chief should not go to war
with neighbouring tribes without informing
the supercargoes of the reason and necessity
for so doing; and that he should pay his
debts before beginning any aggressive warfare: of course an exception was made in case of
a war for self-defence. The headmen, officers,

and slaves of the deposed king were allowed to trade, whilst Yanibo and Ishaca—two adherents of Pepple's house—were from that time forward to be considered chiefs of Bonny, and to take their place accordingly.

Twelve months passed away, and showed the transitory nature of empire in Bonny, as in other parts of the world. During that year king Dappo died, and Consul Beecroft also was called to his last account.

Dappo having left no successor, save an infant, it was considered necessary for the orderly government of the country to constitute a regency; and accordingly this form of executive, though somewhat after the model of the provisional government in France, was ordained, pursuant to the **following** declaration :—

" Whereas, in consequence of the death of king Dappo, **of** this river, it has become necessary to establish **a** regency until an heir shall become of age, for the government of the country, and the protection of British interests—and for the fulfilment of the existing treaties, slave-trade and commercial—we do hereby nominate, appoint, and empower the undermentioned chiefs to act as and constitute that regency, viz :—

" ANNE PEPPLE.   CAPTAIN HART.
ADA ALLISON.   MANILLA PEPPLE.

" The last of these four chiefs, Manilla Pepple, in all cases consulting with Bannego and Oko Jumbo, two gentlemen of the river.

"We, therefore, empower these chiefs, constituting that regency, to act as may be required of them for the good government of the country; and that all British subjects will abide by the requests or decisions of such regency, and refer all matters or questions of dispute to them.

" Given under our hands, on board Her Britannic Majesty's Ship 'Philomel,' lying in the river Bonny, this 11th day of September, 1855.

" J. W. B. Lynslager,
" Acting British Consul, Bight of Biafra.

" John McD. Skene,
" Commander of H.B.M.'s Steam-vessel ' Philomel,'
and Senior Officer, Bights Division."

The experience of five years has taught the British as well as the native traders that this government has been no more than a mockery and delusion, its paternal care of the country, and its protective guardianship over British life and property, being alike deceptive. The four Regents, so styled, were the representative heads of four houses, which never lived in amity or unanimity; they had their little jealousies of trade as well as their domestic social bickerings; they took the comey, but never joined in concert to expend it for obtaining peace in their own immediate circle, or in the interior country markets; consequently civil war was ever rife around and about them, as there existed in the Bonny territory no strong-handed man like Pepple to put down such disturbances, leading to an immense loss of British property, by the mastery of physical force. For, after all, it is sad to be obliged to confess that despotism is the only form of government which is calculated to preserve law and order in the present social degradation of the native Africans.

Even the mobocracy, who obliged the Regents to do as they pleased, became at length anxious for Pepple's return. Combined as they were of so many comflicting parties, representing the four houses, they distrusted one another, and consequently were afraid of making unanimous appeal. A civil war in the town of Bonny, which had occurred just after Dappo's death, and which had obliged Yaniba and Itschaca to seek for shelter at Fernando Po, may have been a moral force impediment. Dappo's son was only three years old when his father died; and as a long time would intervene before he could assume the government of the country, the people wished for Pepple's return.

But although **all** Pepple's followers were exterminated in the last civil war, **and** although during his reign the majority of the inhabitants acknowledged Dappo to have been the **lawful heir** to the throne, **they** privately urged the supercargoes to apply to me, to aid in Pepple's return.

It will be observed that this application, coming as if from the supercargoes themselves, could not have the **support of Her Majesty's** government.   I pointed out to them, according to the additional articles to the commercial treaty with Bonny, signed on **the 23rd** of January, 1854, in presence of Consul Beecroft and Commander Young, that the native chiefs and traders were the only persons whose names were signed to that document—that they had exercised their national prerogative to depose Pepple and elect Dappo as king—and that it was their prescriptive right to do so.   I likewise gave it as my opinion to the supercargoes, that no British subjects, whether they bear **Her** Majesty's commission or **not,** have authority to supersede, nominate, or reinstate an **African** potentate at the head of his tribe **or** country in any place outside British territory, **without** the consent of the people who are his constituents.   The law of nations defined by Montesquieu to be "founded upon justice, equity, convenience, and the reason of the thing," is directly opposed to our taking upon ourselves any such prerogative as a benefit to our commercial interests. Were we to take it upon ourselves to nominate Pepple as king, and did scenes of bloodshed ensue, such as those of late occurrence, the consequences to our trade, as well as to our feelings of humanity, would be disastrous.

Supposing such calamitous occurrences did not result, no French or American trader coming here need obey the ordinance of a man placed in power by British authority. There were other trifling contingencies, too, that seemed to put out of question the possibility of Pepple's returning to assume the position of a governing monarch; namely, that he owned no canoes, possessed no house or property in Bonny, and had not one single adherent of his family at that place.

I deem it my duty to explain here the want of foundation in Pepple's claims on the British Government for compensation, with reference to the fact of his being deposed from the sovereignty.

Pepple applied to Mr. Beecroft,* after he had

* Vide Journal, enclosure No 1, in Slave-trade 48, February 20th, 1854; Class B, April 1st to March 31st, 1855.

been deposed, requesting that he might be taken to Fernando Po, to be there under his protection.

In his letter to Mr. Beecroft, dated Clarence, 7th of June, 1854, he writes :—

"Your being Her Majesty's representative here led me throw myself into your hands, to come to Fernando Po;" and a letter from all the chiefs and traders in the river Bonny, which was written to Mr. Beecroft previous to his visit in Her Majesty's ship "Antelope," 19th of January, 1854, announced : "We accordingly declared him no longer king."* Consequently Mr. Beecroft had nothing to do with removing him from his sovereignty. His proceeding to Sierra Leone from Ascension, and from Sierra Leone to England, was neither carried out nor sanctioned through the instrumentality or with the consent of Her Majesty's Government; therefore, sending him back again to Bonny, even if he should comply with the wishes of his people (conveyed indirectly through the British supercargoes), is a matter in which all those most nearly concerned should take the primary steps of providing for the expense of the voyage, of securing peace to his country, and of assuring protection to British interests.

* Vide enclosure No. 2, in Slave-trade 48, *ut ante.*

I subjoin a letter of thanks which I presumed to give five years ago to the Bonny supercargoes, joined with some opinions on their trading transactions. I do this because the principles contained therein are equally applicable to other trading communities :—

> "British Consulate, Fernando Po,
> "April 24th, 1856.

"To the Chairman and Members of the
Court of Equity, Bonny.

"Gentlemen,—Your kind and courteous letter, placed in my hand as I was about to leave Bonny in H.M.S.S. 'Bloodhound,' on the 10th inst., I had not the opportunity to reply to and thank you for till now.

"Believe me when I assure you that, although I cannot feel conscious of meriting, in the slightest degree, the high compliments paid to me in that letter, the reception of such an honour from the representatives of the merchant princes of Liverpool will ever be duly appreciated by me. My duty to my Government and my country cannot fail to be kept before my mind by such approbation ; and when I remember the source whence it comes from—'gentlemen who are first among the first' of African traders—the pleasure and gratification of it are doubly enhanced.

"Although yet but a neophyte in consular duties, and much the junior in years of the majority of members of your court, I trust you will not consider I am overstepping the bounds of my duty in giving you my opinion of some matters relative to your Equity Court.

"I wish the Bonny Equity Court to be considered the model after which institutions of its kind are formed in the Bight of Biafra. There are many reasons why this ought to be so, and which are unnecessary for me to explain now. In order to keep it worthy of imitation, it should be a Court of Justice, in the amplest meaning of the word; and it ought to be an institution for the protection of your own interests as traders, for the generation and nurture of amity amongst your body, as well as for the endeavour to establish a feeling of confidence between the native traders and yourselves in commercial matters. I say commercial matters, because I believe that a great deal of injury may arise from the supercargoes meddling in any way in the social laws, prejudices, or customs of the natives.

"When you remember that thirty years ago fairs were held in Bonny for the sale of slaves once or twice a-week—and when you know that, from July 1854 to July 1855, above sixteen thousand tons of oil have been sent from this and New Kalabar rivers to Liverpool, you will consider that, in such a short space of time, it is very hard to expect of the people the growth of their knowledge in the *morale* of civilization to proceed *pari passu* with that of their nascent consciousness as to how advantageous to their country's interests are becoming their relations with Great Britain. This is their first-acquired learning; and you know as well as I do that civilization is in no part of the world the growth of a single day. Moreover, you are aware, as I have recognized it on my late visit to Bonny, that the slaves—men of that class which was formerly the market commodity there—are growing up to know that they have as much liberty to trade as the head men.

"Knowledge such as this will, I have no doubt, eventually cause revolutions in the principal African kingdoms; and you will find it cannot be for your interests in the slightest degree to interfere with any of the social struggles that such a changing condition of affairs is likely to lead to, mixed up as they will doubtless be with their ancient follies, superstitions, and brutalities.

"I would not presume to write to you thus, but that I feel confident you will take my opinions as they are intended—not as implying the presumption of offering advice, but as mere grounds for your own cogitation and reflection.

"I quite agree with you that nothing would conduce so materially to the prosperity of the Bight of Biafra trade as a man-of-war placed here at my disposal for frequent visits to the rivers within my jurisdiction. I am sending your letter home to Lord Clarendon; and I have every confidence that when the war is terminated, and his lordship can turn his attention to Africa, the condition of this part of the world will not be neglected.

"Accept each of you individually my best wishes for your health, happiness, and prosperity; and believe me, gentlemen, your obedient servant,

"Thos. J. Hutchinson,
"H.B.M.'s Consul."

CHAPTER XII.

Commercial Dealings in the Palm-oil Rivers—The Natives' Distrust of European Traders—Rev. **James** Martineau on the Cycle of Credit — Indiscriminate **Trust** given by the Supercargoes at Old Kalabar—Letter of Sir **J.** Emerson Tennant to African Merchants at Liverpool—Limited Trust Recommended, commensurate **with** the Annual **Produce of the** River—Suggestion of adopting the Hulk System—Opinion **of Government on** the **Arbitrary** Conduct of Supercargoes in **Old Kalabar—Advice given to** the Supercargoes of their Trust being a mere Speculation—**System** of Chopping Oil—Adoption **of** Native Laws **for Recovery** of Debts—Present Code of Commercial regulations up the Old Kalabar—Author's Attempt to improve them —With Copy of Advice **to** Supercargoes. .

ALL men **who take an interest in the commercial** probity of the British nation will **regret to see** such a paragraph **as** the following, endorsed by one who has reason **to** know its truth :—

" Next to the abolition of the marts for slaves in **Cuba,** we believe that legitimate commerce, carried **on by** honest agents, and on an equitable system, is the one thing needful to extirpate the heinous practice of bartering human beings. Before this can be introduced, however, a complete change must come over the spirit of modern commercial enterprise with the African coast. Trade, as now carried on to that region, is not conducted on the principles of fair dealing, if we are to credit the accounts which reach us from those who are on the spot, and have abundant opportunity of judging. Hence has risen a spirit of distrust on the part of the African traders towards Europeans, which, though it may not, and in fact does not stop trade, considerably impedes its development, and operates prejudicially in other respects. In no direction does it do this more than in causing the coast chiefs to prefer the old trade in slaves to any other, for at least they have an appreciation of the market value of a man, at any given time; whereas the market-value of a cask of palm-oil not only varies with the coming of every ship, but depends on the conscientiousness of the trader. We can assert, on authority, that were legitimate trading prosecuted on equitable principles, the coast trade would speedily augment to at least two-fold its present extent."*

The trust system has been the cause of all this

* *Anti-Slavery Reporter*, April 1st, 1856.

—a system having no foundation on any principles like those laid down in a "Discourse upon Commercial Morals," by the Rev. James Martineau, in which he says:—

"Credit is essentially a reliance upon character during the currency of a transaction; and with the cycle of the transaction it should ever be susceptible of close. Restrained within these limits, the mere existence of incomplete and unrealised transactions constitutes no offence against the apostle's precept, *provided the balance sheet which records them be at every moment unambiguously right*, and be reviewed at intervals too short for danger to creep in. This is the one point on which the question of *integrity* surely turns. And here it is that, to the eye of the mere outward observer, the modern notions of honour seem to be in danger of deplorable decline. There ought to be no difference on these questions between the invariable sentiment of the Christian moralist and the feeling of the man of business. *But in the rapid expansion of relations and the haste of human affairs practices slide insensibly into existence, and get a footing as usages, before any conscience has time to estimate them ; and when they have won the sanction of prescription, they soon shape consciences to suit them, and laugh at the moral critic as a simpleton, and hurry on to the crash of social retribution."*

The clash of retribution in financial losses has not yet come to all, though it has to some; and the continuance of this laxity of commercial principle has been productive of worse results to trade than I would venture to describe.

From the first day of my official connexion with the rivers in the Bight of Biafra—more especially with one, the Old Kalabar—I endeavoured to impress on the representatives of British merchants the wrong of their resorting to native law for the recovery of debts which in their extent so far outraged the cycle of healthy commerce. Common sense should have taught them, as well as the merchants at home, the difficulty of loading ten thousand tons of shipping—an amount of tonnage frequently there—in a river whose annual produce has never been known to exceed three thousand tons of palm-oil. The recommendation which I gave, with a view to check the growing spirit of discontent and distrust amongst them, is well conveyed in the following letter sent by the Board of Trade to the African Association at Liverpool, which I have received liberty from the Right Honourable the Lords' Committee of Privy Council for Trade to insert here :—

" Office of Committee of Privy-Council for Trade,
" Whitehall, 28th of May, 1857.

" SIR,—I am directed by the Lords of the Committee of Privy-Council for Trade to invite (through the instrumentality of your Association) the earnest attention of the merchants interested in the trade of the west coast of Africa to the state of things that exists there at the present moment; and to the danger that, if the trade carried on with the natives be not speedily placed on a more legitimate and sounder footing, the development of the resources of that region, which is now seriously retarded, may be ultimatelychecked, and a lucrative commerce, susceptible of infinite extension, may eventually decline, or be altogether withdrawn from European enterprise.

" Complaints are received by Her Britannic Majesty's Secretary of State, by nearly every mail from the African coast, against the arbitrary and unjust proceedings of the British supercargoes towards the native chiefs and traders—of violence to their persons, and the forcible detention of their goods; and there is reason to apprehend that, ruined by their share in their transactions, or disheartened and disgusted by an occupation in which they do not find ultimate advantage, these native dealers are occasionally driven to abandon peaceful and industrious pursuits, and betake themselves again to civil anarchy and the slave-trade.

"Without ascribing this discouragement wholly to one cause, my lords cannot doubt that it is attributable in a great degree to the system of excessive credits, on which, at the present, the barter with the African middle-traders is mainly carried on by the representatives of British houses in the Kalabar, Kameroons, and other rivers of Western Africa.

"To so great an extent is this acted upon, that Her Majesty's consul for the Bight of Biafra, writing to the Secretary of State on the 21st of February last, states that it has been represented to him that at that moment from nine to eleven thousand tons of palm-oil were due by the native traders in one single river, the Old Kalabar, where the annual produce does not exceed one third of that quantity. Thus, in a single district the entire produce of three prospective years would be absorbed to discharge the obligations of one.

"This alone is a serious consideration in the case of an uncivilized people unable to resist the temptation of excessive credit in the first instance; and afterwards impelled, rather than discharge engagements of such old standing, to convert their available goods to their own immediate profit, to the disregard of their creditors' claims.

" But to this dishonest course the natives feel themselves impelled by another consideration, which, however indefensible in itself, is still sufficient in their eyes to justify evasion.

"The prices at which European articles are pressed upon them in the first instance are unnecessarily exorbitant, in order to admit of a profit to the British adventurer, who thus intrusts his property to a native about to set off to the interior in search of African produce, with which, after a lapse of one or two years, he may or may not return to discharge his debts. The only security of which the supercargo can avail himself in such circumstances is to place so high a nominal value on the goods which he advances, as may protect his employers against partial default, and cover not only the risk but the actual cost of shipping long detained in the rivers to await the returns from the speculative investments, with all the incidental charges for interest of money, insurance, depreciation, commission, wages, and outlay on the crews. It is not to be wondered that the native debtor, aware of the disadvantageous terms on which he had originally contracted his engagement, on returning to the coast, and bringing with him the articles collected during his long circuit in the interior, should hesitate to deliver them to the creditor, and should yield to the bait of better terms offered by a rival European agent.

" Such a system of comparatively unlimited credits, by tempting the native into debt, fosters the tendency to dishonesty in him ; whilst the supercargo, for the assertion of his own right, finds himself in a condition to resort to force—and force which may appear ostensibly justifiable under such circumstances is apt to extend itself to other cases in which justice is less colourable; and the system degenerates into habitual fraud on the one hand, and systematic violence on the other. In such a struggle it must be obvious that legitimate trade cannot long endure ; and it has already been represented to Her Majesty's Government that civil commotions, which frequently agitate the coast and threaten destruction to European as well as to native life and property, are probably encouraged by men rendered desperate by unsuccessful dealings with Europeans, who hope to escape in the confusion ; and that such individuals eventually betake themselves to a life of turbulence and slaving.

"With a view to apply a check to the further growth of this system, it has been pressed on the Secretary of State for Foreign Affairs that it will be expedient to bring back the system of trading in the African rivers to a sounder and more legitimate condition, by calling the attention of those interested to the propriety of greatly contracting the present facilities of credit between their supercargoes and the natives dealers. The Consul of Biafra suggests, with this view, that in his opinion the best plan whereby the merchants of Liverpool embarked in the African trade can extricate themselves from the probability of serious losses is by instructing their supercargoes (and rendering it incumbent on them to obey these instructions), not to give out more than a certain amount of trust, in proportion to the yearly produce and the amount of tonnage in the rivers; and that they should make it a general rule, that where an amount of oil is brought to a ship for sale, at least *one-third* of it should be placed to the credit of the old account, and the remainder paid for in goods on delivery.

"Mr. Hutchinson is further of opinion, that 'to avoid competition between two agents of one

house, the *hulk system*, as adopted by Messrs. Horsfall, in Brass and Kalabar, Kameroons and Bonny, would be far the best ; because common
sense should teach that a single vessel on shore
would be a much more profitable investment
than sending out four vessels in charge of two
different supercargoes—if from no other reason
than the saving of expense of insurance, of officers' and seamen's wages, and of the wear and
tear of the ships.'   These recommendations, emanating from a gentleman of Mr. Hutchinson's experience and opportunities of observation, appear
to my lords eminently worthy of the attention of
the merchants interested in the African trade ;
and their adoption would probably remove one
source to which the evils adverted to are very distinctly to be traced.

"I have, at the same time, been instructed to
intimate that measures will be taken to control
the violent conduct so frequently exhibited by
supercargoes in the African rivers, that additional powers will be conferred for this purpose,
and that Her Majesty's Government will rely on
the great mercantile houses interested in the
development and permanent prosperity of the
African trade, to co-operate with them, and, by
their legitimate authority over their agents on

those rivers, to **put an end to those** practices which have hitherto prejudiced **lawful** commerce, and hereafter, if not checked, to be productive of still more serious evil.—I am, &c.,

(Signed)   " J. EMERSON TENNANT.

" The Secretary **to** the Association of Merchants
" Trading to the West of Africa, Liverpool."

On more than one occasion I have felt obliged to tell the British supercargoes in Old Kalabar, that " they did not seem to me to know that trade on all African rivers, where trust is given, can be regarded only as a speculation, inasmuch as there exists no international code of commerce between Great Britain and these countries, whereby they might be enabled **to** recover their debts by civil jurisdiction. The moral force of **a consul,** aided by the physical power of a man-of-war, could not be applied to this purpose. And where a supercargo, as was often the case, had recourse to a custom of the country in seizing one man's goods, or imprisoning one man's person, for **a** debt due **by** another, it **put** aside the possibility of a remonstrance **on the** consul's part for the payment **of** a debt. **For such a** step as this was but the precursor of lawlessness, in leading the other supercargoes (deprived for the time of the captured man's trade) to urge the native traders to reprisal."

This system of seizing, or, as it was entitled, "chopping," a trader or his palm-oil was a part of the Egbo institution. On no part of the coast was moral force more of a "farce" than up this river. To gather together the conflicting temperaments of the Kalabar supercargoes, and amalgamate them into unanimity of action, was a task more than Herculean. And as long as the system of unlimited trust continues to be followed—as long as recourse is had to native laws—whilst the merchants of England send an amount of tonnage quadrupling the annual amount of the country's produce—so long it will not be possible to make commerce in that river what honest trade ought to be everywhere. The existing statute, by which the by-laws and regulations for trading matters between the British supercargoes and the natives were settled, was agreed to at a conference held on board the ship "Africa," Captain Cuthbertson, lying off Duketown, Old Kalabar, on the 17th of April, 1852. It was ratified by Consul Beecroft, then on an official visit to the river in H.M.S.S. "Bloodhound." Amongst its provisions one is, that the "comey" (or custom bar), levied at the rate of twenty coppers per registered ton, be paid in the proportion of two-thirds to King Eyo, and one-third to King Duke Ephraim—the former being the head potentate of Creektown, as well as the most extensive trader in the country, and the latter being chief over Duketown.

The fourth article of this statute, which enjoins that compulsory trust be abolished, and that supercargoes be allowed to purchase oil if brought alongside, was perfectly useless; as well on account of the large amount of trust which stood in the hands of the native traders, as from the fact that the new arrivals in the river found it impossible to buy oil without giving credit. If a native trader were courageous enough to venture to a ship with the view of selling his oil, it was sure to be " chopped " in its progress before arriving at its original destination. This system led to mutual distrust amongst the supercargoes, the most prominent symptom of which was, that the treaty made by Consul Beecroft was broken in some of its most important provisions before the vessel which bore him had crossed the river bar on her return to Fernando Po.

The fifteenth article, which provided that " should any person take trust from any vessel, and be unable to pay his debts, his house and

property should be forfeited and sold by the king
and duke," was equally unavailing; for each trader
being in debt to several supercargoes, of course
none would be satisfied to let the house and property of a man be sold for the payment of a single
contract.

When I visited this river in September, 1856,
on board H.M.S.S. " Myrmidon," I tried to make
stronger the ties of friendship between the native
and British traders, by suggesting a few additions
to their by-laws, and proposing that they should
open an equity court for mutual protection and
the cultivation of mutual amenities.   At this
time several natives of Kalabar, who had been
formerly sold out of this country as slaves, and
who had been emancipated as well as educated at
Sierra Leone, were sent down here by the Rev. Mr.
Jones of the Fouraboh Grammar School, no doubt
in the praiseworthy hope that, returning to the
" Jerusalem of their younger days," they would
spread the blessings of civilization and Christianity over the pagan land of their birth.   The
manner in which these men commenced this work
was by assisting the native traders to ship oil for
England in the mail steamer, although this oil
had been bought and paid for from the cargoes
of vessels then in the river.

To try and obviate such a practice, of palpable injustice and injury to British property, it was deemed expedient to insert the following as a provision in the new code:—

"*Article* 12.—That no man can be recognised as a legitimate trader in the country unless he pay, through the court, a comey of twenty thousand coppers per annum for the privileges of purchasing and shipping oil, and that persons who may attempt trading without paying such comey shall be liable to have their oil seized as smuggled produce and delivered to the supercargo next in rotation to leave the river, he giving to the king an acknowledgment in book or books for debts to the like amount due to him."

On the face of it this may seem to be protecting a monopoly; but it will appear nothing of the kind when the reader comes to consider the immense amount of British property that was out on trust—amounting at this time to more than two-and-a-half years annual produce of the country. Moreover, the protective comey did not exceed in amount what two vessels of five hundred tons each would be obliged to pay at any time.

The supercargoes wrote to me a letter of thanks for the regulations which I then instituted, and which may be seen by those curious in the matter, in Hertslet's "Commercial and Slave-Trade Treaties, Laws, &c." * After some personal compliments they expressed themselves as confident that, under the government of the Equity Court, their trading connexions with the natives would soon assume a more healthy condition than before.

To this I replied as follows:—

"British Consulate, Fernando Po,
"October 16th, 1856.

" To the Supercargoes of Old Kalabar River.

"GENTLEMEN,—Your letter of 4th October gives me more pleasure from the sentiments it expresses of your confidence in the establishment of the Equity Court, than from the high and unmerited compliments you pay to myself. True, I have been longer acquainted with the peculiarities of your trade than with those of any other river in Western Africa ; and therefore I should feel doubly interested in the prosperity of your commercial dealings with the native traders.

" I trust you will not be offended with me for saying, that ever since my first visit to the Old Kalabar river in 1850, I have lamented the defi-

* Vol. x., page 686.

ciency of commercial morality which I saw existing between the supercargoes and the natives. I know very well that the present body of supercargoes ought not to be blamed for by-laws and regulations that were framed and put into practice by their predecessors; and although I believe that reform of old abuses cannot be effected in a day, I give it to you candidly as my opinion, that the establishment of an Equity Court such as that you have just formed seems to me to be the most effectual means of generating a feeling of confidence between your body and the natives, and a more healthy condition of amity between yourselves than has hitherto existed.

"And let me assure you, as a point of my belief, that without simultaneous and sympathetic action in trading matters things will always be at odds and ends amongst you. I do not desire to see men unanimous in their private tastes and habits; for, without differences of sentiments and sensations, the world would not go round so harmoniously as it does.

"For examples in commercial unanimity look at the corn exchanges, the stock exchanges, the whole series of mercantile communities at home, and you will see that they are governed as well as kept in prosperity by the unanimity of their members. Let it not be said that in the infantile trade of Africa the elements of discord are your upholding prop; for depend upon it, these elements have not an invigorating or enduring power.

" The pecular position in which you are placed, having so many thousand pounds worth of goods out on trust with the natives, has induced me to assent to a few provisions in the code of bye-laws, for the government of your Equity Court, that I would not otherwise have sanctioned; but I trust that time will do away with the necessity of these (Articles 18 and 22); and it is my firm conviction that you will find yourselves in a more independent position, and your merchants' property less liable to be sacrificed, if you do not permit the natives to take credit from you to such a large amount as they have hitherto done.

"The same advice as I have given to the Bonny supercargoes, not to meddle with the superstitions or domestic broils of the natives, I give to you. On all matters in which the brutality of Egbo law interferes with your commerce, I would advise you to appeal to me; for trading can never assume prosperity in any country where such an abominable institution exists ; and it is my duty to protect you from its evil influence. Were there no other reason for my opposition to it than the fact that a man tried and condemned by Egbo is doomed to have all the property and slaves in his possession (whether they be his own or not) divided as a prey amongst its high-priests, I would deem it an obligation on me to oppose its codes. But when I see that Egbo affords no protection to British life or property, and that it is a system maintained to keep the slave population in subjection by the grossest brutality, I am equally justified in setting my face against it.

"As many of your best and most honest traders are of the latter class—slaves—you will be glad to hear that I have received instructions from Her Majesty's principal Secretary of State for Foreign Affairs, to insist strongly, in the name of Her Majesty's Government, on the discontinuance of the barbarous custom of permitting a masked man to go about the town on Egbo days, with liberty to whip all the slaves, men, women, and children, whom he may meet.

" I shall watch with interest and attention over the growth of the ' more healthy condition ' of trading matters which you anticipate from the

Equity Court; and shall at all times be willing to give you my assistance, by 'every lawful means,' in securing you and the merchants whom you represent from loss by the dishonesty of the natives.—I am, gentlemen, &c.,

"THOS. J. HUTCHINSON,

"H.B.M. Consul."

During the short existence of the Equity Court it brought to light the fact that, at the commencement of the year 1857, goods for debts of eleven thousand tons of palm-oil were out on trust with the natives. At the then quotation of palm-oil—48*l.* per ton—this made a debit of 528,000*l.*, more than half a million of money. Out of the foregoing amount there were due, at the same time, by King Eyo, over and above six hundred puncheons, or about four hundred tons of the article, to the different trading vessels at the time in the river. These ships were nine in number, capable in the aggregate of carrying home 7832 tons of palm-oil, and the yearly average of the Old Kalabar country has for a long time ranged from three to four thousand tons per annum, rarely, if ever, exceeding the latter.

The difficulty of having these debts cleared off was aggravated by many causes.

The growing antagonism between the slave

and free class, generated by the fact of some of the former becoming independent traders, and trying to evade the naturally despotic as well as consequently jealous character of the latter, became a powerful barrier of opposition to mutual confidence amongst the natives; whilst a like spirit of reciprocal distrust between the British supercargoes, however it may have been engendered, was certainly fostered and strengthened by some merchants sending out two trading vessels, each under the guidance and management of a separate and independent trader.

The advice contained in Sir J. Emerson Tennant's letter was as little heeded as that in mine. Merchants sent out their supercargoes with fresh consignment of goods, and still the same system was persevered in, without any effort, by reasoning with the natives, to have the long due debts discharged. Indeed, the rivalry between British traders in this river was extended to such an outrageous length, that at one time during the last year more than eight thousand tons of shipping were stationed there.

Such was the condition of affairs, needing a Queen's Order in Council, at the end of the year 1860.

Before leaving the Old Kalabar district, I

may record the existence in it of a curious fact in domestic therapeutics, which I omitted to notice in my former work on Western Africa. From a time so far back that there is no record of its origin—indeed, perhaps, long before Franklin obtained electricity from the clouds—the women have been accustomed to use the electric fish as a remedial agent, by putting two or three of them into a tub of cold water, and then immersing therein a child affected with fits or colic. I need scarcely add that the contact of the child with the electric influence is always secured by the aid of the person administering the bath.

Dr. Wilson of Edinburgh, who read a paper on the subject in the Natural History section of the British Association, in Dublin, during the meeting of August, 1857, believes it to be of the same genus as the Silurus or Malapterurus of the Nile.

The following superstition must strike all students of nature as an illustration of the wide prevalence of certain established customs among savage as well as civilized communities. Amongst the Efik tribe, who are the residents here, there exists a practice of cooking food and leaving it on the table of a fabric called the " devil house," which is erected near the grave of a man or woman. The food is placed there in calabashes, and it is believed that the spirit of the deceased, with those of the butchered serfs who are her or his fellow-travellers, frequently come to partake of it in their journey to the world of spirits, whither they are supposed to be travelling.

From recent explorations made amongst the Fiji Islanders, in the Pacific Ocean, by Dr. Berthold Seeman,* it appears that an exactly similar custom exists among the aboriginal Fijians, whose ethnology is not yet decided, as different opinions are set forth upon it by various authors.

Dr. Seeman writes, that "the path led through numerous taro, banana, and yam plantations, and close to an altar made of sticks and native cloth, on which food for the spirits of the dead was placed. The mass of Fijians will have it that these offerings are consumed by the spirits of their departed friends and relations, who are supposed to have great supernatural influence."

It is a melancholy reflection that a somewhat similar analogy, in their anthropophagic tendencies, exists between the Fijians and many of the West African tribes.

* Vide *Athenæum*, No. 1735, Jan. 26, 1861, p. 120.

CHAPTER XIII.

HER MAJESTY's Order in Council for conferring magisterial authority on West African Consuls is on the same model as that passed (present the Queen's Most Excellent Majesty) at Buckingham Palace, 19th of June, 1844, which was intended to confer on Her Majesty's Consular officers in the Ottoman dominions jurisdiction in criminal cases.

The chief difference being, that the African order includes civil cases (which had been previously provided for in the Grand Turk's dominions), and likewise makes ordinances for the protection of Kroomen, as well as other natives of Africa.

In the memorandum for the guidance of Her Majesty's consuls in the Levant, with reference to the exercise of jurisdiction under the Order in Council, dated Foreign Office, July the 2nd, 1844, and signed by the Earl of Aberdeen, then Secretary of State for Foreign Affairs, it is laid down :—" The right of British consular officers to exercise any jurisdiction in Turkey in matters which, in other countries, come exclusively under the control of the local magistracy, depends originally on the extent to which that right has been conceded by the Sultan of Turkey to the British crown ; and, therefore, the right is strictly limited to the terms in which the concession is made."

Mr. Tuson, in his British Manual, amongst remarks on the duties of a consul generally, proceeds to observe : " It may be as well to state that it is an acknowledged right, founded upon international law, that all offences against the marine laws of the country, committed on board any vessel belonging to such nation, when in a foreign port, are considered crimes against the law of the country to which the ship belongs, as the vessel's deck is considered the territory of the country she appertains to. This will not, however, hold good in the case of offences against persons belonging to the state in whose harbour the vessel happens to be anchored, as then it assumes quite a different aspect, for it becomes one against the law of that land, and can be punished accordingly."

In the present state of political government up the rivers in the Bight of Biafra, it is scarcely possible to acquire by treaty any right from the rulers there. They do not understand what is meant or desired by an Order in Council. They consider our Queen has power (or ought to have it) to make laws for the government, and, if necessary, the punishment of her subjects in any part of the world. Consequently they will not sign a treaty, whose meaning they cannot understand or appreciate, save so far as they know it has no signification of a direct monetary advantage. King Amakree confessed to me that he did not know how he could give me more power than my Queen was fit to give : not being able to read the treaty, he suspected its containing something insidious, but frankly agreed to sign any "book" if he were paid for it, as he had been **paid** for his anti-slave-trade treaty.

In Bonny, as I have explained elsewhere, the government is in the hands of a quadruple regency, the heads of four factions, each of whom is suspicious of the other: these men are in fact the governed instead of the governors, being dictated to in every act of their executive authority by their family mobs. To impress upon the minds of these people any idea of such an international treaty as is required in the case of the Queen's Order in Council I found to be an impossibility; each party, owning a plurality of cliques, misrepresented, so **far as they could** understand, the objects which I had in view; and some of them even went the length of stating their objections to be grounded on the dread that our government wanted to do with Bonny what the French had done at Gaboon.

In Kameroons, where there are six petty chiefs, each holding sway over his own particular district, a similar condition of social distrust is in existence. One chief is afraid to do anything, in the matter of "putting his hand to book," unless it be done by all, and in the presence of all.

The perpetual civil feuds existing amongst these men render it frequently impracticable to get all of them together on board a man-of-war for any purpose.

When they do go each is under the care, guidance, and *soi-disant* protection of his own particular supercargo friend ; hence may be inferred the difficulty of getting these men to sign any such treaty as that in question.

The Brass chiefs, Keya and Orishima, never go on board a man-of-war ; for their abiding places, Bassambry and Obullamabry, both forming the capital of Nimbe country, are more than forty miles above the reach of ordinary navigation.

In Old Kalabar the two chiefs Eyo and Archibong have signed the treaty for the Order in Council. I believe their having done so is, in a great measure, due to their not being so influenced by the supercargoes here as are the chiefs in the other rivers.

No better principle could be laid down, in reference to executive administration on the coast of Western Africa, than that which is expressed in the following extract from the report of a select committee on consular services and appointments :—" A latitude of discretion and an exercise of authority may be entrusted to consuls established in a country where the customs and religion are more or less antagonistic to those of European civilization—and where the weakness of the rulers is unable to secure a full protection to life and property, which would be altogether superfluous and unadvisable in the case of those who are resident amongst a well-regulated community."

There is an important truth in the following principle of international law, laid down by Mr. Cobden in his letter to the Sheffield Foreign Affairs Committee, a few years ago, with reference to what is styled " the maritime supremacy of England ":—"If our supremacy be only that of arms by sea or land, we should at once take the Chinese or Russian monarchy for our model and our guide. The supremacy to rule the waves with an arbitrary power, or to make laws for those amongst whom laws had hitherto been unknown, is not one that our Government should advocate, or our country sanction, in the nineteenth century. Australia and Africa may need our protection. It should only be given to them by demonstrating our moral superiority—by communicating a knowledge of our industrial arts, as well as manufactures. England, foremost in the ranks of progress, need fear no international competition against her in this; but at the same time all her codes, which she, or her representatives, are called on to sanction between savage tribes and her government, should be founded on the eternal laws of truth and justice."

It is a melancholy reflection that neither British agents nor native tribes in Western Africa can be impressed with the sentiments of Christian humanity enunciated in the foregoing remarks.

The Orders in Council connected with China and the Ottoman Empire, and that proposed for Western Africa, are all after similar models, giving to the consuls three courses of proceeding:—first, a summary decision; second, a decision with the assistance of assessors chosen from the British community; third, a recourse to the supreme courts—for China at Hong Kong, for the Levant and Turkey at Malta, and for Western Africa at Sierra Leone.

I hope I shall not be accused of tautology in my mode of expression, when I state that up all the rivers in the Bight of Biafra—as, I believe, in all the rivers of Western Africa—the moral force of a consul, without the moral influence which the presence of a man-of-war alone can bestow, is a moral farce, as regards his authority and power;

therefore the Order in Council, which is the subject of the present chapter, needs very serious consideration as to the most effectual mode of carrying it **out**.

Let us cursorily run through its provisions. It is **founded on** an act of Parliament of the 6th and 7th year of Her Majesty's reign, cap. 94, intituled " An act to remove doubts as to the exercise of power and jurisdiction by Her Majesty **within** divers countries and places out of Her Majesty's dominions, and to render the same more effectual."

That act, amongst other things, provides that " it is and shall be lawful for Her Majesty to hold, exercise, and enjoy any power or jurisdiction which Her Majesty now hath, or may **at** any other time have, within any country or **place out of Her** Majesty's dominions, in the same and as ample a manner as if Her Majesty had acquired such power and jurisdiction by the cession or conquest of territory."

The first paragraph of the Order in Council provides that Her Majesty's consuls appointed to reside in any territory or place on the west coast of Africa, shall **have** full power and authority **to** carry into effect, and enforce by fine or imprisonment, as hereinafter provided, the observance of the stipulations of any treaty, or of regulations appendant to any treaty, between our Government and the native chiefs, or any European Government.

The consul is further authorized to make and enforce, by fine or imprisonment, rules and regulations for the observance of the stipulations of such treaties, and for the peace, order, and good government of Her Majesty's subjects being within such territory or place.

So that here, *in limine*, we can see the indispensability of a man-of-war, with accompanying executive authority, to levy fines and enforce imprisonment on natives as well as British subjects. The "rules and regulations for the observance of the stipulations of such treaties" must vary with the peculiarities of commercial transactions in each river.

The second paragraph, with reference to affixing in the consul's office the rules and regulations applicable to palm-oil traders in Brass, New Kalabar, Bonny, Old Kalabar, and Kameroons, seems to me practically of little value. By this paragraph it is also provided that a printed copy of such regulations, certified under the hand of the consul to be a true copy thereof, shall be taken as conclusive evidence of the existence of such regulations; that no penalty can be incurred for any breach of such rules till they shall have been one month posted up in the consul's office; and that the allowance or disallowance of all similar regulations to be law shall depend upon the approbation or disapprobation of Her Majesty's principal Secretary of State for Foreign Affairs.

By paragraph the third a consul is empowered, upon the complaint of any party, to summon a British subject before him, for disregarding and infringing any rules or regulations for the observance of the stipulations of treaties; and to award a penalty, not exceeding a hundred pounds, or three months' imprisonment.

The paragraph succeeding this provides that, in a case where the period of imprisonment is likely to exceed one month, the consul is authorized to summon two British subjects of good repute to sit with him as assessors; and to do this, of course, before he has heard the charge.

The remainder of this paragraph provides that in the event of the assessors, or either of them, dissenting from the conviction of the party charged, or from the penalty of fine or imprisonment, the consul shall take note of the dissent, with its grounds, and shall require good and sufficient security for the appearance of the party convicted at a future time, in order to undergo his sentence or receive his discharge, pursuant to the final decision of Her Majesty's principal Secretary of State for Foreign Affairs.

It will be, in many cases, out of a consul's power to enforce obedience to the latter stipulation; as, for instance, where a supercargo may have a ship loaded ready to start for England, from which he may never return. Moreover, a grand difficulty stands in the way of carrying out this provision, viz., that the only British subjects of good repute available as assessors are the supercargoes themselves.

The three paragraphs succeeding the last are on the point of civil suits against British subjects, either by native Africans, or by the subjects of the government where the consul resides, or by a subject or citizen of any foreign state in amity with Her Majesty. A consul's decision, in such cases, may be impugned, by giving notice, within fifteen days, of appeal to the supreme court of Sierra Leone. On this appeal, all the documents produced before him, and no other, must be forwarded by the consul to that supreme court, he at the same time obtaining from the protesting party security that he will be satisfied to abide by the final decision of said supreme court, and that he will be accountable for all costs, should there be a failure of such appeal.

Civil suits instituted by British subjects against natives can be heard and determined only provided the natives will submit to the consul's jurisdiction. Civil suits between British subjects are disposed of in like manner, giving a similar liberty of appeal to the supreme court at Sierra Leone.

In all cases, whether civil or criminal, the said supreme court has authority to admit further legal evidence than that which had been brought forward on the investigation before the consul, if it can be established that the evidence now forthcoming was not available at the time the aforesaid investigation took place.

The examination of witnesses on oath, the issue of compulsory orders for the attendance of British subjects to give evidence, and the settlement of suits and contentions by amicable agreement, with power to order the apprehension of

British subjects charged with crimes or offences, and to compel other British subjects to appear as witnesses—are then provided for.

* The fifteenth paragraph authorises a consul, in the case of an individual who proves refractory after having been twice sentenced for crimes, and for whose future good behaviour proper security cannot be advanced, to send him out of the place, or territory, on board a man-of-war or British vessel, as a distressed British subject, unless he is able and willing to defray for himself the expense of his passage.

The moral force bearing of this paragraph would seem to me to have a very salutary effect *in prospectu.*

Passing over several intervening paragraphs, which refer chiefly to matters of discipline, I come to the thirty-third, one of the most important of the whole, for the protection of Kroomen. By this it is provided that all masters of British ships shall make an agreement in writing with these men, specifying the date of hiring, the rate of wages, the allowance of provisions, the period of engagement, and the place of discharge. A copy of this agreement is to be given to the head man of the Kroomen, and another to the consul at the first place he touches at, if there be one there. All such agreements are to be ready for inspection by any consul, or commander of Her Majesty's Navy.

The foregoing paragraph gives to the Kroomen the same protection as is accorded to British seamen by the Merchants' Shipping Act of 1854.

Effectually to carry out the provisions of this Order in Council, more especially in a district like that of the Bight of Biafra, whose jurisdiction ranges from Cape Formosa to Cape St. John, a coast distance of more than four hundred miles, the constant presence of a man-of-war steamer is perfectly indispensable.

It is neither my province nor my duty to make more observations than I have already made on the parts of this Order in Council referring to fines and imprisonments, or to the possibility of the consul, in the present condition of affairs in Western Africa, enforcing his decisions against British subjects in any suit; but I must record my opinion here, that the rules and regulations for trade require very serious deliberation. Hitherto the opinions and principles of the supercargoes have been followed; and when it is recollected that no two of these men are ever unanimous upon any subject, it may be inferred what a lack of principle is exhibited in their application of the whole body of existing regulations.

CHAPTER XIV.

To Batanga—Reputed Non-existence of Slavery amongst the Ba-
pooka and Banaka Tribes—Provoking Calms and Preposterous
Currents in the Bight of Biafra—View in the Roadstead of Ba-
tanga—The Waterfall at Lobei River—The Canoes and their
Fishing Occupants—Canoe Racing on the Rolling Billows—
Universality of Pipe-smoking here—A Visit to King William
—Description of His Majesty, his Uniform and his Menage—
General Appearance of the Beaux and Belles of Batanga—De-
scription of the Chief Koluctoo's Seven Wives—Walk along
shore to the Waterfall—Beauty of the scene and its Accessories
—Information about Interior Tribes.

BEING disposed to take a look at one of the outlets
bordering that unexplored district of central
Africa which lies between Darfur, Adamawa, and
Kororoofa, with other localities visited by Dr.
Barth, and the districts of Congo, Angola, Loanda, with the Mokololo explored by Dr. Livingstone, I chose Batanga for my visit. The extensive interior *terra incognita* of that region is
described, in Mr. Arrowsmith's sketch of Central

Africa prefixed to the first volume of Dr. Barth's Travels, as " inhabited by independent pagan tribes."

Previous information respecting the Batanga part of the coast makes me desirous to ask from geographical and topographical authorities permission to divide the Bight of Biafra into two segments—the one extending from Cape Formosa to Rumby Point, on the western side of the base of Kameroons mountain; and the other reaching from that to Cape St. John.   One of my chief reasons for this is, because the former districts are known to me and to everybody out here as the swampy, malarious localities whence, in the olden times, slaves constituted the principal exports, as palm-oil is in the present; whereas the latter reach of shore is represented as being diversified by high mountains rising in its interior—having no swamps, no malaria, producing a little palm oil, and, from the single spot of Batanga alone, yielding above forty tons of ivory per year.

Although the maps do not say so, there are two Batanga territories.   Little Batanga, the most northern and westerly, is, with a river of that name, included within the greater part of the territory enclosed within the Bight of Panavia.   Big

Batanga comprises the territory on the coast extending from Cape Gara-jam to the river Campo, a distance of about forty-three miles. Both of these districts are inhabited by the Bapooka and Banâkâ tribes; and it seems an additional justification (were such a thing necessary) for my desire to know something about them, from my own personal observation, that, as I am informed, no domestic slavery exists amongst them, and that they have never been known to sell any slaves for exportation.

Whoever says to the contrary, I maintain that there is no benefit to be derived from one's complaining on board a sailing ship in the Bight of Biafra, although calms, in combination with preposterous currents, will sometimes make the most philosophic person in the world wish all kinds of bad luck to the clerk of the weather. Here am I on board a little schooner—such a clipper that even a breeze no stronger than that emitted by a parlour bellows would make her "walk the waters like a thing of life"—here am I on board this little craft for twenty-six hours, under the lee of the island of Fernando Po, her stem at one time pointing to Cape Vidal, and now with stern towards it, trending in the direction of Cape Horatio ; then disdaining both, and swinging lazily towards Kameroons river, on the African continent; yet never moving one single yard in the direction which I desire to go, namely, to Big Batanga, in lat. 2° 53′ N., long. 9° 53′ E.

But the longest calm will have an end; and so the land wind at night enables us to creep away. In twenty-four hours after starting we had dropped anchor in the roadstead, and the view from the ship's deck was such a one as dispelled all our ideas of the unhealthiness of the African coast.

At a distance of what appears about ten miles interior to the harbour of Batanga is the Naanga mountain, which is marked down in the Admiralty chart * as one thousand seven hundred and seven feet above the level of the sea, but to which no name is given. Considerable elevations—some of pinnacled or sugar loaf, and others of table-land formation—rise all round, as far as the eye can reach; whilst falling in three different streams, appears the white foam of the tumbling cataract of Lobei river, known as the waterfall of Batanga. Viewed from the sea, it has an extremely picturesque and refreshing aspect; for we observe two large sheets of

* Sheet 20 of West Coast of Africa Charts, between Fernando Po and Cape Lopez.

water, separated by lofty trees and clumps of rock, from one of which, as it falls, a smoky spray is constantly rising. A towering vegetation and great black boulders are seen stretching to a considerable distance to the westward, amongst which the waters, dashed into showers of spray, come rumbling down over a large bed of rubbly stones; the course of the stream gradually declining from the centre of the fall, and thereby making a semi-arched shelving, till it trickles out at the extreme end, only a few feet higher than the river's bed below. Between our vessel and the shore, numerous black streaks on the water, each having a dot in its centre, soon appeared distinctly as small canoes, the dots representing the negro occupants, each of whom had a string in his hand, which, with the country-made hook affixed to its end, bespoke its owner's occupation of fishing.

The appearance of these canoes, as well as the agility of their tenants, is very remarkable. The former are not more than from six to eight feet in length, fourteen to sixteen inches in width, and from four to six inches in depth. When fishing the man sits on the canoe as we sit on horseback, his leg at either side being the guiding and propelling power. The line, with its beardless hook, having a dead shrimp for a bait, is "played" up and down with one hand, whilst with the other he now and then seizes a large wooden ladle and bales out the boat with a rapidity of motion that at first sight seems really ludicrous. The canoes, being made of light wood, are carried to and from the sea on the shoulders of their owners, as is done by the natives of Ossamaree, up the river Niger.*

During my few days stay at Batanga, I observed that from the more serious and industrial occupation of fishing they would turn to racing on the tops of the surging billows which broke on the sea shore ; at one spot more particularly, which, owing to the presence of an extensive reef, seemed to be the very place for a continuous swell of several hundred yards in length. Four or six of them go out steadily, dodging the rollers as they come on, and mounting atop of them with the nimbleness and security of ducks. Reaching the outermost roller, they turn the canoes stems shoreward with a single stroke of the paddle, and mounted on the top of the wave, they are borne towards the shore, steering with the paddle alone. By a peculiar action of

* Vide Author's Narrative of Niger, Tshadda, Binue Exploration, page 171. London : Longman, Brown, and Co., 1855.

this, which tends to elevate the stern of the canoe so that it will receive the full impulsive force of the advancing **billow, on** they come, carried along with all its impetuous rapidity. **Sometimes the** steerer loses the balance of his guiding power; the canoe **is turned** over; **its** occupant is washed out, and **the light** little piece of wood gives **a few** lofty jumps from wave to wave, reminding one of a horse at a steeple-chase, that, having thrown his rider, takes it into his head (or rather his heels) to gallop about the country, and jump over ditches on his own account.

Yet, despite of these immersions, no one is ever drowned, as they are capital swimmers—indeed, like the majority **of** the coast negroes, they may be reckoned amphibious.

In their piscatorial excursions, it sometimes happens **that a prowling shark,** tempted to pursue the fish which the fisherman is hauling on the line, comes within sight of the larger bait of the negro **leg,** and chops **it** off without remorse. A case of this kind had happened a very short time before the period of my visit, and the poor victim had died; but this did not diminish the number of canoes riding the waves, nor render one **of** the canoe occupants less energetic or daring than **before.**

These canoe labours constitute the whole of the work done here by the males. Digging, delving, and planting the ground, as well as carrying ivory from the interior, are the occupations of the sex who are considered the weaker in civilized countries, but who in all African states, whether slavery exists there or not, are obliged to be " the hewers of wood and drawers of water "—the laborious serfs on whom every hard and burdensome duty is devolved.

When on shore I saw one young woman, evidently on a journey, carrying a large bundle of plantains on her back, the weight of which she bore by means of a withe of country twine, that encircled her forehead, and pressed tightly against it; whilst her husband, or master, or owner, as the case might be, walked by her side, swaggering a stick, and smoking a pipe, as if these two operations were the only duties required of him.

Every one in Batanga—except perhaps the sucking baby—smokes from a black pipe. As a man or woman walks by the piazza of the trade store where, resting on my portable bed, I am sheltering myself from the rays of the noon-day sun, he or she stops to gaze at me, and then, proceeding along, gives a strong suck to, and an equally vigorous whiff from, the pipe, with an air which seems to imply their consciousness that smoking tobacco is the *ne plus ultra* of negro enjoyment.

Whilst waiting for the sun to descend a little lower, in order that I might have an agreeable walk of about three miles to the waterfall, I learned that the palace of His Majesty King William was not far away, and so I sent him word that I purposed doing myself the honour of waiting on him as soon as he was ready.

This I found to be the etiquette. In about an hour after I was told he was waiting for me, and so I proceeded to the royal residence, not with any flourish of trumpets, or beating of drums, or prancing of steeds, but with the simple attendance of a brawny negro, who volunteered to hold my large umbrella over my head.

I had not very far to walk—through over-shading plantain leaves, and between huts—till I saw a large red banner stretched over the street from the top of one house to another, on which the name of King William was printed in white letters each a foot long. Under the right end of the flag, and at the door of a small house, was seated an old man, with grey hair, dressed in white trowsers, a blue cloth cap with a gold band, and a light frock coat. This I was told was King William. As he stood up to receive me, I saw his upper garment was a white plush livery coat, with scarlet lappets to the pockets, and bright brass buttons, bearing the effigy of some horned animal's head, with its mouth wide open and its tongue thrust out, as if it had just spurted forth its accompanying motto of *Peius letho deliquium.*

I hope those who have a reverence for the labours of Sir Bernard Burke, and for heraldry in general, will not be offended at this vulgar description of the armorial bearings in question; nor with my literal translation of the motto, as "Death before dishonor." But there did really appear to me something so comically grotesque in the *tableau vivant* before me bearing the title of royalty, that it excited my merriment. More especially when the king, on introducing me into his house, shewed me all his valuable property, which consisted of several large deal trunks, containing within them a quantity of second-hand livery, looking-glasses, jugs, mugs, as well as other varieties of crockery-ware, cloth, guns, large brass pans entitled Neptunes, pipes, and such like articles of *virtu.* Not a chair, table, or bed was visible anywhere. Some of the women had stools to sit upon, and nothing more like a throne was the seat occupied by **His** Majesty.

Our conference being ended, a **few turns** through the town showed me little **more** than their **low-roofed huts and** luxuriant plantain trees. **The** houses very much resemble those of Kameroons, in their rectangular bearing to **each other:** the streets are wide and straight. The only glimpse of social life which one can obtain in walking these streets, is that of women in groups of twos or threes stretched on mats **outside a** door here and there, each lady having a servant occupied in the exploration of her hair—for what purpose may be guessed! Large glass beads, white or green, woven into all kinds of fantastic patterns, on the heads, and **small seed** beads, made into fanciful cinctures, round the necks, constitute the chief ornaments **of the** belles and beaux of Batanga.

On my **way** back from my ramble I met, and was introduced to, a man named Koluctoo, a chief of the Benjembi country—between Batanga and Campo—who was accompanied **by seven** of his wives. The appearance of these ladies presented nothing so remarkable as its **variety.** One of them was distinguished by a ring **of small** beads hanging from the central cartilage of her nose; another had brass rod-wire wound round her legs from ankles to knees; a third was adorned with a piece of some green leaf thrust through a large hole that had been perforated in the lobe of her right ear. The fourth had her hair dressed up into a ridge extending from the base of the skull to the forehead, and resembling in its fashion the helmet of a dragoon; the barber's art had made up the hair of the fifth in the semblance of an ebony cone; whilst to the sixth the African perruquier had devoted more labour, and consequently more science, in plaiting it. Amongst this lady's wool was here and there a flat cake, with a greasy look, the nature of which for some time puzzled me. The seventh, who was the oldest of all, and, therefore, the first as regarded position, wore two plain copper rings round her ankles; she had an ornament on her forehead, which at first seemed a slice of sausage, but which I was informed was of the same material as that on the head of number six, namely, goat's fat, enclosed in a piece of mucous membrane. This lady was vigorously smoking a pipe of native manufacture.

As the cool time of day approached, I turned my steps in the direction of the Lobei river, to see the waterfall. The road lay along the hard sand of the beach, save hère and there, where masses of rock jutting into the surf obliged the traveller to seek a pathway behind them, or across their summits.

Yet these rocks, down to the water's edge, had upon them sufficient earth to nourish large trees and parasitic plants, as well as flowers, from none of which was there the slightest emanation of heavy odour, such as is generally characteristic of African bush. Tall guinea grass grew about in many places—of course away from the sea-beach —and as I walked on, there was not a single mangrove plant discernible. This absence of the malaria-producing mangrove, which I know does *not* exist for several miles on either side of Batanga sea-shore, might be likely to induce one to form a good opinion of the sanitary condition of the place, were we not aware that the same plant is not found at Elmina, Cape Coast, Akkra, and other Gold Coast districts (save at the very mouths of their few rivers)—localities which certainly have not the reputation of being the least unhealthy parts of the western coast.

Little charm as there is in the surrounding scenery of sand, rock, sea, and wild bush, the walk is an extremely agreeable one; and for a considerable time before arriving at Point Lobei, we become aware of our approach to a waterfall by what gives an additional interest to every step — namely, the peculiar booming sound of the river rolling over a considerable descent.

Every one is acquainted with the surging noise which the waves make when breaking on the sea-shore. That noise had been sounding in my ears for an hour and a half, as I walked along the beach. Yet, as I approached the fall, the solemn thunder made by its waters caused that of the sea to appear in contrast like a hissing scream. The mouth of the Lo-bei river appeared very rough, having no doubt a shallow bar, and being now under the influences of a strong sea-breeze ; but we rounded its southernmost point, and, after a further walk of a few hundred yards, I saw the waterfall in all its beauty before me.

I must confess that I have never viewed in Africa a scene so eminently picturesque, and so deserving the pencil of a painter, as this cataract and its surrounding scenery. At the bottom of the left side fall, which is divided in its centre by a buttress of stone, is a ledge of rocks, stretching three-fourths of the way across, on which several naked negro children, each with a fishing-rod in its hand, are standing. To the right of this is a lofty clump of rock, rising higher than the bed of the river, and, therefore, dividing the fall into two parts, between which are a few trickling streams, that seem pushed aside from the main ones, as if they were poor relations compelled to find a way for themselves. Each of these falls is about thirty feet in width; and behind the lofty clump of rock just mentioned, arises a towering red wood tree, sixty feet in height at the very lowest computation. There is then another elevated rock, backed by a higher tree; and a quantity of surrounding shrubbery separates the main torrents from a number of smaller ones, spreading over an extent of a few hundred feet, and gradually shelving downwards to the extreme end of the river's right side. The whole stream forms a tranquil lake at the bottom, on which were a number of small red canoes, whose occupants were fishing in the same style as those already described in the roadstead of Batanga. Stretching away to the point called Ndunga, on the right side of the river, is a number of bombax and red wood trees, on some of which parasitic creepers mount to their very summits; whilst gardens of plantains, and the brown huts of the negroes on the Lobei side, lend an additional attraction to the savage beauty of the scene, which it is impossible to convey on paper.

But, above and beyond all, my senses were wrapt by the unceasing thunder of the falling water, which one cannot help recognizing as—

> "The voice of the great Creator,
> That speaks in that mighty tone."

In the rainy season the quantity of water descending is of course much more copious, but I question if even then it has a more beautiful aspect than that which it presented on the evening of my visit.

The trade which is carried on here by British merchants is managed through black interpreters and store-keepers, all of whom are natives of Gaboon.

In strolling along the beach one morning for the pleasure of the cool air, and the benefit of what was to be seen, I met one of those gentry, whose air of seeming independence at once attracted me. I asked him to sit down on a rock hard by; and we entered into conversation. Very soon I learned that he had been in England, where his chief point of education was in what its adepts style " the noble and manly art of self-defence." He questioned me about the present condition of a number of pugilists in England, whose names he gave; and I have no doubt that I fell very low in his estimation by confessing to him that I had never even heard of the existence of the "fancy men" in question.

As he was about to walk away, seeing no doubt that I did not possess a sympathetic spirit, I directed his attention to a large crowd of women, who had gathered near us on the beach, having with them many bundles of yams as well as of young living plantain trees, and asked him what they were about to do? He replied, with quite a haughty air, that they were the gardeners of Batanga, who were waiting for a canoe to take them and the produce up the coast, where the gentlemen had gardens "all the same as the Bristol gentlemen have their country places at Chepstow."

Of course after this I did not oppose his departure; for I saw at once that his assumed refinement would incline him to regard with contempt what I will confess was my main object in first addressing him—namely, the attainment of some information about the people and countries interior to Batanga. Such information it is impossible to obtain from the people themselves, because they have some suspicion of the object of a white man's inquiries, under the dread that he may penetrate to the interior and injure the trade.

A ramble to the town of King John, who had no more likely or unlikely semblance of royalty about him than a very old and very bad black beaver hat, with a piece of printed calico round his loins, gave me an opportunity of meeting with another of these Gaboon factors, from whom I picked a few pieces of information, most of which seemed to me to be probably near the truth.

The mountain Náánga, already mentioned, was described as having a large lake in its neighbourhood, called Etibu. Interior to the mountain are the Boola and Gumbe countries—from which the ivory is brought down to Batanga and Gaboon by a tribe of reputed Bushmen, known as the Dauberi, or Diberi. Beyond or around the Boola and Gumbe districts no tribe, except the Bowela and the Bani, is known of—the latter of whom ride horses, and wear monkey skins, having likewise long hair, which, fashioned into three or four plaits, is allowed to fall down on their backs. Some of them, wearing the long plaited hair, have been seen at Batanga.

Can these be the Bati of Dr. Barth ? *

* Vide chapter xviii.

CHAPTER XV.

Further Information about the Tribes and Countries Interior **to** Batanga—Of the Fabulous Green Bird reputed to feed on Elephants' Eyes—Country whence Ivory comes—The Rev. Mr. Wilson's Account of the Banaka Tribe—He records nothing of the Absence of Slavery amongst them—Countries between Batanga and Cape St. John—Corisco Islands and their Aborigines —The Benga Tribe—American Mission at Corisco—Corisco Boats—Entrance to Gaboon River—The French Establishments there—Tribes of the Mpongwes, Shekanis, Bakeles, **and** Pangwes —**Ascent** of this River by Governor Beecroft in 1846—Natural products **of the** Country—The Rev. Mr. Mackay on the exploration **of the** Rivers Nazareth and Fernan Vas.

Contiguous to the Bani country is a large lake called **Njong,** or Ndong, so large that, with our limited horizon, it is impossible to obtain a complete view across it.

May this be the Ndob of the Rev. Mr. Anderson ? *

Near this lake, and not **far** from Bani, my in-

* Vide chapter xviii.

formant told me of the existence of a bird, named the Newjande, which had been described to him, and which measured five fathoms, *i.e.* thirty feet, from the tip of one wing to the tip of the other. Its beak is a fathom, or six feet long. No man dares to go near it, and no gun is fit to kill it. Its favorite food is obtained by killing the elephant, whose eyes it devours. On inquiring the colour of this bird's plumage, the answer I received—namely, that its feathers were *green !*—made me shut my note-book with a "mental reservation" as to the ignorance of Baron Cuvier.

The greater portion of the ivory conveyed down here is brought from the Gumbee country. The old days of elephant hunting are gone by, these princes of the forest being now slaughtered by powder and ball, and by pit-falls.

No palm-trees are visible along the coast here, save a few of the cocoa species : but up the rivers Little Benito and Campo a small quantity of palm-oil is manufactured.

Of the Banaka tribe, which inhabits Batanga and the neighbourhood, a very interesting description is given in the Rev. Mr. Wilson's work on Western Africa :—*

* " Western Africa : its History, Condition and Prospects. By the Rev. J. Leighton Wilson, eighteen years a missionary in Africa, &c."

" The Banaka people occupy a district of country twenty-five miles in length, half-way between the Kameroon River and the Bay of Corisco, and have as many villages as they occupy miles of sea-coast. As a people, they differ in many important respects from all the other tribes in this section of the country.

" It is only recently that they descended from the mountainous regions of the interior; and while they still bear all the marks of the better health which belongs to these higher elevations, they also exhibit strong traces of the true savage condition in which they have been brought up.

" Their complexion is a shade lighter than those living on either side of them, and their general appearance reminds one much more strongly of the Kaffirs of the Cape of Good Hope than any sea-coast natives within the tropics. Their language is but imperfectly understood, as yet, by any of the neighbouring tribes ; and as none of them speak the English with any degree of ease, very little reliable information has been obtained in relation to the particular part of the country they formerly inhabited, or what induced them to come down to the sea-coast.

" Their language, so far as it is understood,

shows that they belong to the same great family which have spread themselves over the whole of the southern half of Africa ; but whether they are more nearly related to the tribes on the eastern or western coast of the continent, remains to be proved.

"They seem to be simple-hearted and peaceably disposed, and as yet have acquired but few of the tricks of their more experienced brethren in the same region.   It will require very little intercourse with the civilized world, however, to make them perfect adepts in all the petty villanies of the maritime tribes, provided that intercourse is not regulated by the principles of sound religion.

" Foreign vessels have had no trade with them until within the last fifteen years.   Previous to that time they had no relish for ardent spirits, and it was with difficulty that any of them could be induced to taste of it in the first instance. But those days of happy ignorance are gone; that taste has been acquired, and nowhere is rum now in greater demand.   How very important is it that the influences of Christianity should be thrown around these people before they are carried away by this fearful temptation !

" They are as simple and primitive in their

customs and habits as any people in the world. In their forest homes they had no covering for their bodies, but a narrow strip of cloth made out of the inner bark of a forest tree. More recently they use the cotton cloth which they receive from vessels in exchange for their ivory, but still in very scant measure. Their women disfigure their faces very much by making large holes in their ears, and through the cartilaginous parts of the nose. Weights are attached to make the hole large enough to pass the finger through. Pieces of fat meat are frequently worn in these holes, but whether for ornament or fragrance is not known. I inquired of one of them why she did it, and received the laconic answer, " My husband likes it."

" In their intercourse with white men they are peaceable and forbearing. But among themselves they have some stringent laws, which are enforced with unsparing severity. Theft and adultery are punished with death, and it matters not what may be the character or rank of the offender.

" Passing along the beach on one occasion, my attention was called to a half-consumed human carcass hanging from the limb of a tree; and upon inquiry I learned that it was the wife of one of the principal men of the place, who had been hung for stealing a bunch of plantains. The corpse was left hanging by the roadside as a public warning.

"Their habitations are the merest huts, and are almost concealed from view by the luxuriant banana trees with which they are always surrounded. The huts of some of the wealthier men are raised on scaffolds, eight or ten feet above the ground, and are entered by climbing up a ladder, which is drawn up at nights. Birds and animals are carved on their doors and window-shutters, and often with a good deal of taste.

" Although they have not been living long on the sea-board, they have become the most noted canoemen on the whole coast. They have two kinds of canoes: one is made of cork wood, very small, and intended to carry only one person; the other is made of very hard wood, is small and tapering at both ends, but is large enough to carry thirty or forty persons.

"The small canoe does not weigh more than eight or ten pounds, and is too narrow for an ordinary sized person to be seated in it.

" A saddle or bridge is laid across the middle, not more than two inches wide, but several inches higher than the sides of the canoe, as a seat. They use very light paddles, but send it over the roughest sea without danger, and with almost incredible velocity. While propelling with both hands they will use one foot to bale the water out of the canoe. When they would rest their arms, one leg is thrown out on either side of the canoe, and it is propelled with the feet almost as fast as with a paddle. They will dash with perfect safety over a surf that would swamp almost any boat that could be made. I have often seen them revolve around a ship, sailing at the rate of five or six knots an hour, half-a-dozen times in the course of half an hour. When tired of running around the ship, a man will climb up her side with one hand, and haul up his canoe with the other.

"In the larger canoe, they perform voyages of fifty or a hundred miles. Sometimes half a dozen of these canoes set out together, and go as far as the Gabun or Cape Lopez. When they go in such large troops, and quarter themselves upon a single person, to be entertained for several weeks, it is felt to be a severe visitation; and the Gabun traders sometimes give them the dodge, notwithstanding all the honour implied by such a visit."

It appears to me strange that the Rev. Mr. Wilson does not mention a word about the absence of slavery amongst these people. If my information about its non-existence be correct, it makes one's reflections sadder in cogitating over the condition of these untutored Africans. The absence, in their superstitious rites, of such cruelty as exists amongst the tribes of Kalabar, Bonny, and Brass, may be advanced as evidence of their moral superiority; but when one looks at the lack of industrial pursuits among these people, the question starts up—"Can the Ethiop change his skin?"—or his nature either?

Between the Batanga country and Cape St. John are some small streams besides the rivers Campo and Benito. Itemo is the native name of Campo river, and the countries on both sides of it are entitled the Egara. The Beku tribe, of whom nothing is known save the name, are found in this territory. Eeienje is the country through which the Benito runs, and Eyo is the name by which the river is designated amongst the aborigines on its banks. The people are likewise called Eeiengis, and are of course—like all known to the Batanga Banaka—"Bushmen."

As we pass the mouth of Benito river and voyage towards Cape St. John, extensive mountainous ranges are visible in the interior, none, however, presenting an appearence that would lead me to identify them as Saddle Hill, Table Hill, or the Seven Hills (one of whose sharp peaks are recorded as 2,786 feet high), described in the chart before mentioned. The Bapooka tribe are in this part of the country. We pass Bilovë and Beninje points before we reach Ninje, which is the native name of Cape St. John.

It is unnecessary for me to mention here, that all the names by which these parts of the coast are known were given to them by the early Portuguese and Spanish geographical explorers.

Interior to Ninje point, and abutting into Corisco Bay, is another point called Malenga. Between these two points is a small river named Agei, by which communication may be made nearly to the base of Mitre Hill, mentioned in the chart as 3,940 feet high. In that direction there is also a line of rock, containing a large quantity of quartz, described to me by a gentleman who had some of it in his possession, and who had been for several years in Australia, as exactly resembling that which he had seen containing gold at the diggings.

The Bay of Corisco is a large basin of water,

situated between Cape St. John and Cape Esterias. It contains four or five islands, only two of which—Corisco and Big Eloby—are inhabited. The people are the Benga tribe. Into this bay the rivers Muni and Danger debouch. Their mouths are several miles apart, but no person is aware of their intercommunication, or inosculation with each other, in the interior. The population of Corisco does not exceed two thousand. For many years an American Mission, sent out by the Presbyterian Board of Foreign Missions, has been established here, whose chief, the Rev. James L. Mackay, has reduced their language to writing, and translated into it much of the Gospel. This gentleman, in company with the Rev. Mr. Clements, has explored more than a hundred miles of country across the Sierra del Crystal range of mountains, which lie in the direction between Corisco and Gaboon. The neighbourhood of these mountains seems to be the stronghold of the Pangwe tribe, of whom I shall hear something at Gaboon.

The natives of Corisco are artificers of very large boats, which they scoop, in canoe fashion, out of the single trunk of a tree. Some of these canoes are from thirty to thirty-six feet in length, about five feet in beam, and four in depth. They are propelled by oars as well as by sails, and are generally schooner-rigged. As we were passing **Corisco Bay,** one of them came alongside our ship; and, from my conversation with its occupants, I found that its owner had been away to Ninje Point (Cape St. **John) on** some "women palaver"—the *causa teterrima belli* since the world was created. Although not interested in hearing the particulars, I nevertheless gained some information on a *Gradus ad Parnassum* style of aristocracy that exists amongst the tribes hereabouts.

The Mpongwes of Gaboon hold the first position; the Bengas of Corisco the next; and the Bapookas, with the Banakas, the lowest. Thus, a Bapooka or Banaka **man** would not presume to buy **a wife** from his superior of Corisco or Gaboon; but those of the latter places will buy from the **former.** In the present case, the Benga man had, some time previously, bought and paid a high price for his wife. She, not satisfied with her lord and master, returned to the home of her fathers; and it was on a mission to claim her recovery that my informant was now engaged. He had to advance an additional sum of money, and to bide his time for **the performance** of certain formulæ of heathen tomfoolery (but whether of the John Doe or Richard Roe class I could not say), ere she was given up to him.

Rounding Cape Esterias, we passed by its innermost corner, entitled Point Joinville, and found ourselves in the river Gaboon. It may be needless for me to state that up this river the French have a considerable establishment;—a guard-ship; a military and civil department, with a hospital, contained in Fort d'Aumale; a convent of religious sisters; and a mission, at the head of which is a bishop, Monseigneur de Bessieu. From De Kerhollet's " Manuel de la Navigation à la Cote Occidentale d'Afrique,"* I learn :—" Le fleuve ou l'estuaire du Gubào, dont nous avons francisé l'orthographe, et que les indigènes appellent Mpongwho, est devenu Français depuis 1843 ; époque à laquelle d'après les ordres de M. Bouet Willaumez, alors gouverneur du Senegal, le capitaine de frégate de Monleon, commandant le brick, ' Le Zebre,' y établit un comptoir fortifié sous le nom de Fort d'Aumale. Les deux rives du fleuve avaient été précédemment cedés à la France par des traités passés par Monsieur le Capitaine de vaisseau Bouet Willaumez, avec les differents rois des populations voisines. Ce

* Tome 2, p. 518.

Comptoir n'offrit aucune difficulté d'établissement, mais nécessita des nombreux travaux de defriche- ment, et de mouvements de terrain."

In the neighbourhood of Cape Esterias we pass by, on entering the river, a creek called Guergay, up which is to be found a tribe named the Bulous, who speak a different language from the Mpongwes. The latter are the aborigines of the districts on both sides of the river, to a distance of about thirty miles into the interior. Their chief towns in the neighbourhood of the French station are those of King Qua Ben and King Glass. Near the latter is an American mission station, with which the Rev. Mr. Wilson was connected for many years. From twenty to thirty miles higher up, on the other side of the river, are two other large towns, entitled King William's and King George's Towns. On Konig Island, about twenty miles from the mouth of the river, a number of these people are also located. Contiguous to Fort d'Aumale a very pretty garden was laid out, a few years ago, by Mons. Bouet, then commandant of the Comptoir. It bears, how- ever, the appearance of impairment in its arrangements now, which everything in Africa gradually assumes, despite of the best care-taking. There is also here a pretty little Père la Chaise;

and the bishop has a considerable quantity of land under cultivation. There is a breakwater at the pier, which is very useful. About half a dozen French merchants have stores in the neighbourhood of the Comptoir. We find one réstaurant, kept by a French widow; and the establishments of the English merchants—four in number—are located higher up, in the neighbourhood of Glass Town.

The Shekanis, the Bakeles, and the Pangwes are the tribes known as occupying the interior countries up the river. Petty warfares, joined to, if not having their origin in, the foreign slave-trade, have reduced the first of these (Mr. Wilson says) to a mere handful of people. The Bakeles, one of the many migratory tribes of Africa, coming from no one knows where, usurped and held possession of the territories formerly owned by the Shekanis. They, however, are now being put to the rout by the Pangwes, who, though not heard of till late years on the Gaboon side of the Sierra del Crystal range of mountains, are coming step by step down the river's banks, and settling there. The reason which they give for their inroads is that their produce did not realize the amount which they expected, much of which they deemed themselves to have been deprived of through the roguery of the **Shekanis** and **Bakeles**. The Pangwes are reported, **upon** good authority, to be cannibals. **Leaving their** anthropophagy aside, **there appear so many** other points of resemblance between them and the Felatahs, that I am disposed to extract the interesting description given of them by the Rev. Mr. Wilson* :—

" The Pangwes, in some respects, are very remarkable people ; among savages, I do not know that I have ever met men of nobler or more imposing bearing. Their form is indicative of strength and energy, rather than grace or beauty. Their stature is of medium size, but compact and well-proportioned ; and their gait is alike manly and independent. The complexion of both males and females is two shades lighter than that of the maritime people ; and their features, though decidedly African, are comparatively regular. But their hair, and the mode in which it is worn, is, perhaps, the most striking characteristic about their appearance. It is softer than the usual negro hair, and is usually plaited into four braids, two of which are worn in front, and two pass over the shoulders, and not unfrequently reach more than half-way down the back. At the

* Op. Cit., p. 303.

same time, their bodies are smeared over with a red ointment, which heightens the singularity of their appearance to a very remarkable degree. They wear no clothing, except a narrow strip of bark cloth between their legs. Their legs and arms are decorated with rings of brass or ivory. A broad-bladed knife or dirk, in a sheath of snake or guana skin, is attached to a leather thong tied around the middle. A hatchet of peculiar shape is carried on the shoulders; and the men are seldom seen walking out without a bundle of long spears in one hand. White pound beads are very much admired. Broad belts of them are worn around the arms and legs, and they are worked into the hair so as to form a complete bead wig.

"They are remarkably expert in throwing the spear. In their wars they use cross-bows and poisoned arrows, and have shields made out of the skin of the elephant. They show a good deal of mechanical ingenuity in casting copper rings, and in manufacturing knives and other implements of war. It is said they melt their own iron, which is true, unless it is found in a native state, which seems to be the more common opinion at the present day. That which is used by the Pangwes is regarded as much superior to the trade iron brought to the coast; so much so, that they will not use the latter at all. It is not only used for the manufacture of instruments, but is the circulating medium through the Pangwe country. Strips of iron, in size and shape like the blade of a horse-phleme, and tied up in bundles of eight or ten pieces, are the real currency of the country, by which the price of every other article is regulated. They are the only people in Western Africa I have ever known who had a circulating medium.*

"They cultivate the soil to some extent. Yams, cocoa, Indian corn, plantains, beans, and a few other articles, are raised in sufficient quantities for their own consumption. They are much addicted to hunting, and excel all others in killing the elephant, which they prize both for its tusks and its flesh. The habit of contending with this monster of the woods, involving so much peril of life as it does, has done much, without doubt, to develop their energy, and to make them just the men of the dauntless intrepidity which they seem to be."

* The Yorubas have long had a circulating medium of cowries. The Filatahs, up the Niger, have likewise a currency similar to that described by Mr. Wilson in connexion with the Pangwes. At page 254 of my "Impressions of Western Africa," it will be seen that these *are not* the only people in Western Africa possessing a circulating medium.

An ascent of this river was made in March, 1846, by Governor Beecroft, in the S.S. "Ethiope." The steamer did not go farther than from sixty to seventy miles up the stream; and Dr. King's report on this voyage comes to the conclusion that, "from this ascent, it has been ascertained that the river is of no importance as a highway into interior Africa."

To the former products of ivory, red wood, and bees-wax, coming from the Gaboon country, India-rubber has been lately added; but the industrial products of the adjoining districts are not likely to make Gaboon a position of high commercial importance.

Nevertheless, since the names of Livingstone, Barth, Burton, Speke, and Bowen stand out on the roll of successful African explorers, without the aid of rivers or steam-boats, I consider it my duty to point out that a journey straight across the continent from Batanga, Corisco, or Gaboon, would enable the traveller to discover the peculiarities of those "independent Pagan tribes" before mentioned, and finally to emerge at a point nearly opposite to Aden in the Red Sea. This would be a route considerably northward of the track recorded by Mr. Macqueen,* as having been

* Vide Proceedings of the Royal Geographical Society, vol. 3, No. 2, p. 362.

taken by Silva Porto, a Portuguese trader, who effected three several journeys from Benguela, emerging at Mozambique. Such an enterprise might likewise lead to information as to the in-country courses of the Kameroons, Gaboon, Congo, and Nazareth, as well as many others of the comparatively unknown rivers of Western Africa.

On the subject of the exploration of this neighbourhood, I extract the following from a letter written to me by the Rev. James Mackey, of Corisco:—" Whilst your Government is doing so much to open up this continent to commerce and Missionary efforts, and seems to be willing to do so much more, I wish you would direct their attention to this part of the coast-interior; for here is a vast unknown region. The Muni, Mundah, and Gaboon rivers are all shut. They all rise in the mountains, at perhaps no more than a hundred and fifty miles to two hundred miles from the sea, and are navigable scarcely half that distance, on account of falls in the mountains. But my impression is that the Nazareth, which falls into the sea just north of Cape Lopez, extends far into the interior. This river has, I think, been much overlooked. It has several mouths. It is united by a kind of network of waters with the Mexias and Fernan Vas, the latter of which is forty miles or more south of the principal embouchure of the river. I was once, several years ago, at the mouth of the main stream, and supposed, from its appearance, that it was not large; but I learned from the Rev. Mr. Walker, of the Gaboon Mission, who entered the river in a boat and ascended over a day's journey, that the stream is both large and strong—the current not stemmed by the tide, and an immense quantity of water discharged by it. It is probable there are falls at a hundred or a hundred and fifty miles from its mouth, as the same range of mountains which is to the eastward of us (*i.e.*, of Corisco) passes, I believe, at about that distance from the Nazareth mouth."

CHAPTER XVI.

THE subject of the French voluntary emigration system might seem a very ticklish one for any person in my position to descant upon, were I not fortified, at the beginning, by being enabled to record thereon the opinion of one of the heads of Her Majesty's Government. The Right Honorable the Earl of Malmesbury, in one of his despatches to Mr. Howard, Her Majesty's Minister Plenipotentiary at Lisbon, on the affair of the "Charles et Georges," expresses the views of the Government with an independence equally evident in all his Lordship's correspondence with reference to that matter. From the Foreign Office, at date of October 15th, 1858, his Lordship says :—"You are aware that Her Majesty's Government have never altered their opinion as to the analogous nature of the French scheme for exporting negroes with that of the avowed Slave-trade." *

I may advance, as one of my chief reasons for putting together some evidence touching this emigration, the dread that many persons may be labouring under the same uncertainty about it as the Emperor of France confesses himself to be in a despatch dated St. Cloud, 30th October, 1858, and addressed to his cousin the Prince Napoleon :—

"Mais quant au principe de l'engagement des noirs mes idées sont loin d'être fixées. Si, en effet, des travailleurs recrutés sur la cote d'Afrique n'ont pas leur libre arbitre, et si cet enrôlement n'est autre chose qu'un Traité déguisé, je n'en

---

* Vide Despatch 41, at page 46 of 'Further papers relating to the case of the 'Charles et Georges.' Presented to both Houses of Parliament, by command of Her Majesty, 1859." London, Harrison & Sons.

veux á aucun prix. Car ce n'est pas moi qui proté-
gerai nulle part des entreprises contraires au pro-
grès, à l'humanité, et à la civilization,"

It may be observed that Count Walewski
" utterly repudiates the idea that the proceedings for obtaining free negro labour gave any
encouragement to the traffic in slaves ; and that
he was prepared to uphold this assertion
against all who dispute it."

But I would like the noble Count to prove
how the so-called voluntary emigration system
adopted by his nation can be regarded merely as a
system for obtaining free labour, when there are
palpable facts contradicting the assertion which
Count Walewski is prepared to uphold against all
who dispute it.

The first and most important is one known to
all who are acquainted with Africa, that, of the
two classes of slaves and freemen of which its
population consists, the freemen *will* *not* emigrate, the *slaves cannot!*

Love for their native homes and affection for
their families are two of the strongest characteristics of the negro tribe. Hear one of these
chiefs giving utterance to his sentiments—one of
the class who are free to emigrate:—*

* Denham and Clapperton's Narrative of Travels and Discoveries in Northern and Central Africa, p. 264.

"Zahr, with his followers, after looking at me with an earnestness that was distressing to me for a considerable time, at length gained confidence enough to ask some questions, commencing as usual with 'What brought you here? They say your country is more than a moon from Tripoli.' I replied, 'To see by whom the country was inhabited, and whether it had lakes and rivers and mountains like ours.' He then inquired, 'And have you been three years from your home? Are not your eyes dimmed with straining to the North, where your thoughts must ever be? Oh, you are men, men indeed! Why, if my eyes do not see the wife and children of my heart for ten days, when they should be closed in sleep, they are flowing in tears.' "

Hear, too, the sad though rhapsodical wailing of the Kroomen (all of whom are free to emigrate) on their being engaged in 1856 by a Monsieur Chevalier :—

"Oh! sad it is to us. We are a weak and ignorant race of creatures, have no power of ourselves to go to French Guiana, and bring our men from far to see what they are doing— whether are sold to different parts of the world.

"Oh! my friend, how shall we find out our

men? We beg of you with the pleasure of your heart to assist us in this matter. Please, oh go there, for we willing to do anything for you; had we money, we would to pay or reward you, we would have done it; as England is the most powerful nation on the globe, we apply to you for assistance among these Kroos. There are three youngsters belonging to the Mission School, one is married, his wife and child. Please, oh please, we want our men to come home. Mothers' hearts is aching for her children with wishful hearts. Many eyes looking upon this wide Atlantic Ocean, and longing for their sons to come home, but in vain. As you are the people of God, feel for us, and may the Almighty bless and preserve you in your labours. Amen.

"Signed by the hands of the principal kings and chiefs.

" Saml. Boyd,

"King's Secretary, Fish Town, Cape Palmas.

" To the British Consul at Fernando Po."

No man with a spark of feeling can read the finale of this pathetic appeal, wanting the " men to come home," and depicting " mothers' hearts aching for her children," without feeling doubtful of the propriety of describing such a system as that which called it forth as one of "voluntary emigration."

The disastrous affair of the "Regina Cœli," in the early part of 1858, afforded very manifest evidence of the sense in which Count Walewski's system of free negro labour was understood.

The account given of this affair by Mr. Blyden, of Monrovia, is contained in the following words, which I extract from an American Magazine, the *Anglo-African:*—

"In the early part of April last (1858), the 'Regina Cœli,' a French ship engaged in the enlistment of labourers, as above stated, was lying at anchor off Manna, with two or three hundred emigrants on board, among whom, in consequence of some of their number being manacled, considerable dissatisfaction prevailed. During the absence of the captain on one occasion a quarrel broke out between the cook and one of the emigrants; the cook struck the emigrant; the latter retaliated, when a scuffle ensued, in which other emigrants took part. This attracted the attention of the rest of the crew, who, coming to the assistance of the cook, violently beat the emigrants, killing several of them. By this time those emigrants who had

been confined below were unshackled, and, join-
ing in the fracas, killed in retaliation all the
crew, save one man, who fled aloft, and pro-
tested most earnestly his freedom from any
participation in the matter. The emigrants,
recognizing his innocence, spared his life, but
ordered him ashore forthwith, with which order
he readily complied.

"The surviving emigrants, having now sole
charge of the vessel, awaited the arrival of the
captain, to despatch him as soon as he touched
the deck; whilst he, learning their intention,
did not venture aboard, but sought and obtained
aid from the Liberian authorities, at Cape Mount,
to keep the exasperated savages from stranding
his vessel. Meanwhile the English mail-steamer
'Ethiope' arriving at Monrovia, her captain
was prevailed upon to proceed to the rescue of
the 'Regina Cœli.' He did so, and safely towed
her into Monrovia Roads. The emigrants all
made their escape."

From the same writer, and in the same paper,
we glean the following fact, affording further
evidence of the result of this system :—

"Nearly coincident with the above circum-
stance, and perhaps, in some measure, the result
of it, was another of similar character in the

interior of Liberia.   One or two native chiefs, it appears, had collected a number of persons, and were conveying them, manacled, to the coast, for the purpose of supplying the emigrant vessels. On their way they stopped with their human load to pass the night at a native town.   During the night one of the captives, having worked himself loose, untied the others, when a revolt took place, in which the prisoners killed their kidnappers, and made their escape."

Further evidence on the spontaneous will of the Africans to emigrate is afforded by Commodore Wise*—not from hearsay testimony, but from facts of which he had visible proof before him. His letter is dated H. M. S. S. "Vesuvius," St. Paul de Loando, September 5th, 1858 :—"All attempts at disguising the real nature of the French emigration scheme have been lately given up.   It is now a common occurrence to observe these unfortunate negroes brought in from the interior in twos and threes to the French factory, secured by ropes to the forked end of a wooden pole encircling their necks, their hands strongly bound, and thus dragged along by their owners, whilst a third negro hastens their movements by the lash.

* Vide Blue Book, Slave Trade, Class A, 1859, p. 190.

"At Loango the voluntary free emigrants are now guarded in the same manner as slaves. Many of them have attempted to escape; and in order to prevent any chances of such an attempt proving successful, the French agents make it a practice to secure these unfortunate negroes to irons in gangs of twos and threes; they may be thus observed every morning, when brought down to wash in the lagoon, at the foot of the barracoon."

The affair of the " Charles et Georges," on the east coast of Africa, being nearly simultaneous in its occurrence with that of the " Regina Cœli" on the west coast, let us take wings in our "labour of love," and transport ourselves to the neighbourhood of Mozambique, to ascertain if they manage the system more humanely there.

We may save ourselves the journey, however, as on the desk before us lies a blue book,* from which can be extracted a morceau from a despatch of Consul M'Leod's, in which he describes the circumstances usually attending the removal of emigrants from the coast of Africa, to supply a ship waiting for her voluntary passengers at the island of Madagascar. The voyage is made in a dhow belonging to an Arab named Kallifan, and

* Slave Trade, Class B, 1859, p. 13.

their port of departure is somewhere in the neighbourhood of Zanzibar. "During the voyage they
receive just sufficient uncooked rice or beans, with
a little water, to keep them alive, and are left day
and night without any covering whatever, and
surrounded by their own excrement. Their
destination is some port not likely to be visited
by any of Her Majesty's cruisers ; and arrived
there, the only improvement in their condition
is a full allowance of water. Should it happen
that, by stress of weather, the ship that is to
take them is retarded in her arrival, their sufferings are much increased ; and when the poor
creatures do at last get on board the French
ship, the sudden change to an ample diet produces sickness and sometimes death. The captain of a French vessel says that, on one occasion,
when he landed at Europa Island to get some
turtle, he found upwards of a hundred negroes
lying on the beach, without any protection
against the sun or rain. They were guarded by
some armed Arabs, and were waiting the arrival
of a vessel to take them to Bourbon. Their
provisions were nearly exhausted, and if by any
accident the vessel should be retarded, it is easy
to conceive what their fate would be. As these
dhows are for the most part old and unseaworthy,

and they often lose their way, there can be no doubt that numbers of the negroes die of starvation."

I hope it will not be suspected that I have ever been engaged in the cattle trade, from my confession that I am able to testify to having frequently seen pigs put on board steamers for transhipment from Ireland to England; and that I have observed, even in summer, that they were protected from casual inclemencies of the weather, and not "left a day and night without any covering whatever," as is the custom with negroes who voluntarily emigrate from Zanzibar to the islands of Bourbon or Réunion.

Having seen so much of the humanity side of the question, let us now look at it in a commercial point of view. I cannot say whether it is a peculiarity of the climate or not, but one does often see philanthropy and trade on the west coast of Africa as nearly related as the Siamese twins.

Although a blue book is not exactly the kind of book with which we are likely to try and wile away the time in a shady arbour on a Summer's day, some startling facts may be occasionally gleaned from these interesting annuals.

In one before me I see that Consul Lawless of Martinique states to Lord Clarendon the fact that "with the emigrant, on arriving at Martinique, is produced a receipt of his for two hundred francs (*i.e.*, 8*l.*) expended in procuring his ransom."

Consul Lawless further says, "I am unable to inform your Lordship whether the above mentioned sum of 200 francs is really disbursed by Messrs. Regis for the emigrant."

This information I am happy to supply to his Lordship and Consul Lawless, from a record in my own journal, which will prove that the Messrs. Regis actually do not expend this sum in procuring the emigrant's ransom.

At Gaboon, as well as at Loando—both of which places supply Messrs. Regis with emigrants—the following prices are paid for them:—

	Invoice Price.				Net Value in Gaboon.		
	£	s.	d.		£	s.	d.
1 Gun - - -	0	10	0	..	1	0	0
1 Keg of Powder -	0	12	0	..	1	4	0
8 Single pcs of Chill or Romals - -	1	4	0	..	2	8	0
2 Shorts (half doz.) -	0	17	0	..	1	14	0
2 Gals. of Rum -	0	5	0	..	0	10	0
1 Matchet, 1 Iron bar, and a few trifles amounting say to -	0	3	6	..	0	7	0
	3	11	6	..	7	3	0

The head man gets a dash of about six shillings worth for each negro he succeeds in bringing to the voluntary market.

Turning a single leaf backward in my annual, I read a sketch by the same respectable Consul (Lawless), a sketch which is too vivid and too interesting in any way to curtail:—

"I have now to state to your Lordship the conditions, of a pecuniary nature, subject to which the services of immigrants are secured to the Colony, and the proportionate part of the expenses of their introduction, which the Government and the proprietors support. In accordance with the terms of their contract with the Home Government, Messrs. Regis are entitled to receive from the Colony, for each adult labourer landed at Martinique, after such labourer has been indented to the proprietor to whom he is allotted by the Administration, a sum of 500 francs, viz., 200 francs, being the amount of their stated disbursements for the immigrants' use in Africa (I shall presently explain to your Lordship the nature of this disbursement), and 300 francs, the premium given them as compensation for their pains and trouble by the Government.

" From the sum of 500 francs a deduction of

3 per cent. is made for the benefit of the Naval Pension Fund (*Caisse des Invalides de la Marine.*) The first-mentioned sum of 200 francs is repaid the Government by the proprietor **before** he receives the immigrants allotted to him, together with a sum of 30 francs, which is termed 'registration fees,' on taking up the indenture of each immigrant. Of the remaining 300 francs so advanced in the first instance by the Government, the proprietor is obliged to reimburse a further sum of 200 francs, in three equal payments, to be made in each twelve, twenty-four, and thirty-six months; he is also required to pay a 'proportional duty' (*droit proportionnel*) of six francs per annum, in half-yearly instalments, being a tax at the rate of 5 per cent. on the yearly wages of one engaged labourer.

"This tax, as well as the registration fees, is, however, appropriated to the increase of the Immigration Fund. In case of the immigrant's death within the period of his engagement, the proportional duty ceases; but not the obligation to complete the reimbursement of the 200 francs, which must be paid regardless of that contingency. But, on the other hand, the proprietor is entitled to receive out of the immigrant's wages the 200 francs which Messrs. Regis are reputed to have paid for his use in Africa; and deduction of 3 francs per month is made from each adult immigrant's salary, until this sum of 500, I mean 200, francs is paid.

"Your Lordship will remark from the foregoing details that the 500 francs allowed to Messrs. Regis for each adult immigrant are, in point of fact, supplied as follows :—

"100 francs by the Government, 200 francs by the proprietor, and 200 francs by the immigrant.

"And the total cost to the proprietors to secure the industrial services of the latter for ten years, amounts to but 290 francs, viz.;—

	Francs.
Paid in cash	200
„ in three instalments .	200
Registration Fees . . .	30
Proportional tax . . .	60
	490
Less the amount which he recovers from the immigrant .	200
	290

"According to the engagement subscribed to in Africa by the immigrant, which is the same document that is afterwards transferred to the proprietor here by Messrs. Regis, the term of the immigrants' obligatory stay in Martinique is for ten full years, which are not to be held completed until he has worked ten times 312 days. During this time he is to be provided with lodgings, medical attendance, and two suits of clothing. His rations consist of salt-fish, rice, and cassava flour, in the usual proportions given to the native agricultural labourers, and his wages at the rate of twelve francs per month, of twenty-six working days; only one-half of his earnings are paid to him monthly, and the other half at the expiration of the year, when his account on the register of the estate is made out in his presence before the Juge de Paix, and due deductions are made for sickness and absences. For each day's absence without leave, or from sickness occasioned by his own excesses, the immigrant forfeits one day's pay actually earned, in addition to the days so lost. It may, therefore, be computed that an average actual residence of twelve years will be necessary to entitle the immigrant to his 'repatriement,' which even then he can claim only in case of his having made a monthly deposit of the tenth part of his wages in the Immigration Chest."

I wish particularly to point the attention of

those who consider a " repatriement " possible to the last part of the foregoing extract, from which it appears that an immigrant can only claim the right of being sent back to his country in case of his having made a monthly deposit of the tenth part of his wages in the Immigration Chest."

With reference to the affair of the " Charles et Georges," the correspondence on which was the occasion of eliciting Count Walewski's famous repudiation noticed at the commencement of this chapter, it appears, from incontestable evidence, that all the negroes found in that vessel, when she was captured by the Portuguese man-of-war " Zambesi," declared that they had been brought there against their will. Some of them had been stolen or kidnapped from their owners at Mozambique ; whilst the delegate from Réunion, who was on board in the character of a government officer, could produce no evidence of a single man having volunteered his services.

The history of this matter from beginning to end, divested of its official mystification, appears to me very simple, and may be briefly told.

By a Portaria, or decree, of the Marine and Colonial Department of Portugal, bearing date 27th of February, 1856, it appears that the Portuguese Government does not allow the hiring, or otherwise taking away from its African possessions, of any negro labourers. The exportation of negroes from the African colonial dependencies of Portugal is not only considered contraband by the treaty of 1815, but is made by their own laws an act of piracy in the Portuguese territory.

On the 20th November, 1857, a circular had been addressed to all the Governors of districts by the Governor-general of Mozambique, with the view of preventing the exportation of colonists from the ports of that province—a thing which had been in operation in connexion with the provisions of the voluntary emigration law sanctioned by the French Government in 1852.

Let us bear in mind that this circular primarily appeared before the public in the official bulletin of Mozambique, of December 19th, 1857, on the very first day of which month was dated the report of the commission appointed by the Governor-general of Mozambique to investigate the circumstances under which the barque "Charles et Georges" was captured on the coast of Quintungonha by the Portuguese man-of-war "Zambesi," which report condemned the vessel and her crew to the penalties enacted in the decree of 10th December, 1836.

When we investigate the reason of this ship, captain, and crew being mulcted for contravention of law, of course our first inquiry is into the particulars of their offence.

The fact comes out that she had been anchored for several days previous to the 20th November in the port of Canducia, having with her, as an executive officer, a delegate from the administration of the French island of Réunion, and that she had got on board 110 negroes, fifty-nine of whom were embarked at Quintungonha, none of them as volunteers, for they had been sold to the captain ; and some of them had been stolen from their masters, a few of whom belonged to the city of Mozambique.*

On the day succeeding the date borne by the circular of prohibition, out comes the Portuguese man-of-war "Zambesi" from Mozambique, and captures the "Charles et Georges." The latter was brought into Mozambique, tried by a commission instituted for the purpose, and condemned as a slaver. Captain Rouxel, the master, was condemned to two years' imprisonment in irons—a sentence which he escaped by appealing to the court of Relagao, at Lisbon,

---

* From the *Journal de Commercio* of Lisbon, of February 24th, 1859.

whither he accompanied his vessel to have the appeal tried.

Thereupon appears the French representative at Lisbon, the Marquis de Lisle, and makes a plea to the effect that the " Charles et Georges " had sailed from Réunion before the prohibition of the 20th of November was known there—a thing not at all improbable, when we remember she was captured at Canducia, and brought to Mozambique on the 26th of the same month ; that the men were hired as emigrants, and were free to act as they pleased—even to return to their country after their period of five years of servitude was completed. The latter part of this, meaning ten years instead of five, and bearing upon the repatriement fund, is perfectly intelligible as it stands.

These facts being proved by papers of agreement, it comes out on the evidence before the commission that the papers were all forged, and the emigrants deposed to the fact that they had been sold or kidnapped—at all events, handed over to the captain against their will.

Meantime the affair, although only one of a cargo of negroes, was beginning to assume a serious aspect. Our Government did everything possible to throw oil upon the troubled waters, and bring the affair to a peaceable conclusion, but without success.

A council was held at Paris, presided over by the Emperor, on the 2nd of October, in the year following, and it was determined to demand the release of the " Charles et Georges," with indemnity for her unjust and illegal capture. The reason advanced for making this demand imperative was, because "she was a French ship, having a government delegate on board, authorized to hire labourers ; and her condemnation as a slaver was tantamount to connecting the imperial government with the traffic in slaves, therefore derogatory to the honour of France."

The demand was made by the Marquis de Lisle on the part of France, and refused by the Marquis de Soule on the part of Portugal.

Hence two vessels of war were dispatched to the Tagus, to frighten the Portuguese ; and on the 26th of the same month a squadron of four men-of-war—two of which had meantime put in to Lisbon for coals on their homeward voyage— steamed out of the Tagus, the steamer "Caligny" towing the " Charles et Georges.".

Passing by the charges of informality made against the judge at Mozambique, of having omitted to refer (as it seems he ought to have done) the proceedings to the superior court at Loanda for their approbation—as well as an accusation brought against the Mozambique governor, of having allowed two other ships on the same mission to escape—namely, the " Marie Caroline" and the " Marie Stella," whilst he seized the " Charles et Georges—it appears to me that no unprejudiced person can come to any other conclusion on the subject than that the matter from beginning to end reflects no credit on either the Portuguese or French government.

The commander of the U.S. ship "Dale"* having read over the papers, which were shown to him on board one of these emigrant ships, comes to the conclusion that, "from the degraded condition of the natives of the coast, I cannot but believe that this action of the French government will result in their benefit"—a conclusion, to my thinking, rather premature, seeing it was educed from an examination of papers instead of passengers.

No one ever wrote more truly than the Earl of Malmesbury did in his correspondence, addressing Earl Cowley, Her Majesty's minister, in the following words :—" Experience will doubtless

* *Vide* " Correspondence with the United States' Government on the question of right of Visit," p. 29. Par. Papers.   Harrison, London.

prove to them " (the French government) " that it " (negro emigration) " must give rise to international disputes, massacres of the French crews, retaliatory cruelties to the negroes, and a general encouragement to the illegal slave-trade all over the world."*

That it has given rise to internecine wars in Africa is known from the testimony of Mr. Blyden, already quoted; of the Rev. Mr. Townsend, Church of England missionary at Abbeokuta ; and of Doctor Livingstone.   That the horrors of the middle passage endured by these poor emigrants equal those recorded of *bonâ fide* slave-trade voyages, may be inferred from the fact that the French steamer " Stella," which left Longuebonne, near Kabenda, on the south-west coast of Africa, with a cargo of 950 voluntary emigrants, arrived at Guadaloupe, after a thirty days' voyage, with only 647—one-third of the whole lot having perished, at the rate of ten per day.

I have too strong a faith in the humanity and intelligence of the French Emperor, government, and people, to believe they would sanction such a system as this were they aware of the existence of such horrors in connection with it as I have deemed it my duty here to record.   On the part

* Foreign Office, October 30th, 1858.

of His Imperial Majesty more especially, the strongest evidence has been given of his opposition to it by the "Convention ratified between Her Majesty Queen Victoria and the Emperor of the French, relative to the emigration of labourers from India to the colony of Réunion." This treaty was signed at Paris on July 25th, 1860, and ratified in the course of the following month by the plenipotentiaries of the respective nations, namely, Earl Cowley and Monsieur de Thouvenel.

The provisions of this convention are of very great importance, and seem calculated to do away with all the abominations of the first-mentioned system.

Although coolies are not definitely mentioned, they are nevertheless the tribe of emigrants for whom these regulations are instituted.

Agents chosen by each government, and holding the same position as consuls, have to superintend the proper organization of the emigration.

It is the agent's duty first "to satisfy himself that the emigrant is not a British subject, or, if a British subject, that his engagement is voluntary, that he has a perfect knowledge of the nature of his contract, of the place of his destination, of the probable length of his voyage, and of the different advantages connected with his engagement."

The two most important articles in this convention are the provisions "that the duration of the emigrant's engagement shall not be more than five years;" and that, "in the distribution of labourers, no husband shall be separated from his wife, nor any father or mother from their children under fifteen years of age."

A code of such regulations as these is pretty certain to crown the energy of the French merchants in their West Indian colonies with more success than any plan which bears sorrow to the Africans, however unconscious they may be of its agency.

CHAPTER XVII.

Of Fernando Po under its new Regime—Governor Don Chacon, and his Proclamation of 1858—Alarm caused to the Residents of Clarence (now Santa Isabella) by that Proclamation—Their Remonstrance against its Provisions—Failure of these Remonstrances—The Commencement of Spanish Work in Colonization —Mortality amongst the Colonists—Its Causes—Clearing the Bush—Ascent to the Peak of Fernando Po—The Queen of Spain's Decree concerning her Possessions in the Gulf of Guinea —Example of Fertility in Fernando Po—The Aborigines the greatest Obstacle to the Development of the Island's Cultivation —Their Natural Indolence and Social Habits—Sketch of an Aboriginal Wedding—Sensible Evidence of Approach to a Fernandian Town—*Cuisine* at the King's Residence—Dress of the Bride and the Bridegroom—The Nepées, or Professional Singers—Matter of their Epithalamium—The Mothers being Boonanas, or Bishops performing the Marriage Ceremony—Peculiarity of the Mode of Celebration—Savage Dance in the middle of the Ceremony—Procession to the Bridegroom's House— Natural Politeness—Nuptial Offerings—Banquet after the Ceremony.

IN the year 1858 the Spanish Government seemed determined to do something effective, by laying claim to its possession in the Gulf of

Guinea. Fernando Po was visited in the month of May of that year by a Spanish war steamer, the "Vasco Nunez de Balboa," whose commander soon made known the object of his visit, by issuing the following proclamation :—

"Commander Don Carlos Chacon, knight of the military order of St. Hermenegilda, captain of frigate in the Spanish Navy, commander of Her Catholic Majesty's squadron in the islands of Fernando Po, Anno Bon, and Corisco, governor-general of all the said islands, makes known to all—

" 1st. The religion of this colony is that of the Roman Catholic Church, as the only one of the kingdom of Spain, with the exclusion of any other; and no other religious profession is tolerated or allowed but that made by the missionaries of the aforesaid Catholic religion ; and no school allowed.

" 2nd. Those who profess any other religion which is not the Catholic should confine their worship within their own private houses or families, and limit it to the members thereof.

" 3rd. Mr. Lynslager is appointed lieutenant-governor in the colony, until the resolution of Her Majesty the Queen of Spain is known.

" 4th. All the other by-laws and regulations

for the good government and order of this colony, which are not contrary to that enacted this day, will remain in full vigour till further ordering.

"Given under my hand and seal, on board H.C.M. vessel 'Balboa,' this 27th of May, 1858.

"(Signed)   CARLOS CHACON."

It is not my business or duty to cast any imputation or disparagement on the Spaniards for their first proclamation at Fernando Po. I merely record the fact that it fell like a bombshell amongst the inhabitants at Clarence, who had been since 1843 under the religious superintendence of Baptist missionaries, and who since their first settlement here, under Captain Owen, in 1827, had considered themselves under the protection of Her Britannic Majesty's Government, and therefore entitled to perfect liberty of religious worship, in whatever form they wished to make the profession of their faith.

A remonstrance was at once made by the Baptists against this proclamation, as being contrary "to that liberty of worship decreed and allowed by Don J. I. de Lerena, Captain in the Spanish Navy, and Commander of the brig 'Nervion,' in the year 1841, and confirmed by the Spanish Consul-General (the Chevalier Guillemard), in the year 1846." This remonstrance further entreated that the execution of the foregoing decree should be delayed till a final appeal could be made to the Queen of Spain.

It was shown that, by a conveyance from the West African Company to the Baptist missionaries, dated 13th June, 1843, there were assigned to " William Brodie Gurney, his heirs, executors, &c., all that the factory, plantation, and settlement, called or known by the name of Clarence, situate and being in the island of Fernando Po, on the west coast of Africa, or howsoever else the same is or may be called, known, or described, and all messuages, dwelling-houses, tenements, factories, sheds, huts, stores, warehouses, outbuildings, yards, gardens, land, hereditaments, and appurtenances whatsoever thereunto belonging, and therewith had, held, used, occupied, or enjoyed. And all the cleared and other land and ground lying and being around the said factory or settlement, or held with or as part of the same, as the same is now or was late in the tenure or occupation of the said African company, or their agents."

A legal form, to which the Spanish Governor paid no attention, as he did not recognize the authority of the West African Company to make any such conveyance.

His reply, therefore, very courteously stated his inability to comply with the request ; but at the same time expressed his readiness to forward their memorial to the Queen of Spain.

The only conclusion arrived at was, that the Baptist missionary and his family, consisting of wife and two daughters, left the island, and emigrated to a place in Amboise Bay, on the continent, to which they gave the name of Victoria. Two or three—certainly not more—families of the negro members of their church went with them.

Accompanying Don Carlos Chacon there came four Jesuit priests, his secretary, a lieutenant in the navy, a commissariat officer, and a custom-house clerk. Soon after the steamer in which he came arrived the transport "Santa Maria," with a number of emigrants—some women and children.

With the exception of the government staff, and the Jesuit Padres, the remainder of those who came passed a miserable wet season. No houses had been prepared for them, and they were therefore obliged to pick up lodgings where they could, the only places in which accommodation was procurable being the huts of the negro residents, all of which had earthen floors—a **very** unhealthy thing **for** Europeans in any part of Africa, especially in the wet season.

Rapidly succeeding the proclamation came **the** change of the name of the chief town, Clarence, to St. Isabel, **and Spanish** titles to all the streets were posted up on boards at the corners. **A** hospital was erected near Point William, and wherever there was an available spot for the purpose a staff was fixed in the ground, and **the** Spanish flag hoisted thereon.

In the month **of** August, 1859, the war frigate "Ferrolana" arrived in St. Isabel harbour, having on board His Excellency Brigadier Don Jose de la Gandera, who had come to relieve Don Carlos Chacon. He was accompanied by his family. With **him** came likewise 150 soldiers, many women and children, a staff of executive officers, and a regimental band.

On the first day of his landing under a salute from the Spanish and British men-of-war in the harbour, the following Royal Decree was read at the Government-house, in presence of the staff in their uniform, and **of** nearly all the inhabitants of the town :—

" ROYAL DECREE.

" According to what has been proposed to us

by our Council of Ministers, we have decreed as follows :—

"Art. 1. The Minister of War and Colonies will adopt necessary measures to colonize the islands of Fernando Po, Annobon, Corisco, and their dependencies.

"Art. 2. There will be appointed to that station by the Minister of Marine those vessels of war which other necessities of the State can spare. The way in which this service is to be performed will be established beforehand by the Ministers of Marine and Colonies.

"Art. 3. There will be also appointed to the said dominions the military forces which the Minister of War may consider necessary; allowing the commanders, officers, and soldiers those advantages considered convenient by the Minister of War and Colonies. For the necessities of these forces, and for those of the inhabitants in general, there will be sent to the dominions of the Bight of Guinea the number of military physicians and surgeons considered necessary by the Minister of War.

"Art. 4. A General of Brigade, or at least a Colonel, will be appointed Governor of Fernando Po and the adjacent islands, with an allowance of six thousand dollars a year.   The Governor first appointed to this post has a right to promotion after three years' residence in the country, or before that time if he distinguishes himself by his services.

" Art. 5. The Governor of Fernando Po, Annobon, Corisco, and their dependencies, is responsible for the tranquillity of the islands under his government; therefore, besides the authority given to him by this decree, and that he may further receive, we invest him with the discretional power which the nature of the country or the urgency of unexpected events may require.

" Art. 6. The military and naval forces are under the command of the Governor. With respect to the last named, the power allowed by the general regulations of the Admiralty to the viceroys of the Indies are also granted to him.

" Art. 7. Should absence, sickness, or any other motive prevent the Governor from acting, he will be represented, in cases relative to the government, by the highest military commander.

" Art. 8. In the cases before said the receiver will take charge of the administrative affairs; but should any alterations be necessary, he will be obliged to consult the council, according to the 18th Article.

" Art. 9. A barrister will be appointed as Secretary to the Governor, with an allowance of three thousand dollars a year; and also a clerk, with an allowance of one thousand dollars per annum.

" Art. 10. In order that the Governor may be rightly informed of the necessities of these islands, a functionary will be appointed under his orders, entitled the Special Delegate of Public Works. This functionary will have an allowance of two thousand dollars a year, and one thousand more for his expenses; and will be obliged to study the quality of the soil, its productions, the currents of the waters, to survey the country, and to perform any other commissions which the Governor may entrust to him.

"Art. 11. For the administration and collection of the rents and taxes established, and those that may be established in future, a Receiver with three thousand dollars, and a Comptroller with fifteen hundred, a year, are appointed.

"Art. 12. A Judge is appointed, with an allowance of three thousand dollars, whose duty is to assist in all matters relative to the administration of justice.

"Art. 13. From the sentences of the Judge, an appeal may be made to the Council, constituted in court, with the assistance of the Governor; in such cases the Secretary will fulfil the duties of Reporter, and the Judge will be unable to assist.

"Art. 14. A public notary is appointed, with an allowance of fifteen hundred dollars, and is not permitted to receive fees.

"Art. 15. An Interpreter is appointed, with an annual allowance of two thousand dollars, who must possess the necessary qualifications, in at least the English, French, and Portuguese languages.

"Art. 16. In order that the clearing out of lands, &c., may be effected in the manner most advantageous to the country, and most conducive to the public health, a civil engineer is appointed to superintend these works, with an annual allowance of two thousand dollars, and one thousand for necessary expenses.

"Art. 17. The Governor is allowed 2000 dollars, annually, for representation expenses.

"Art. 18. The Governor in Council, with the approval of the Receiver, may dispose of 25,000 dollars a year, for the improvement of the islands.

"Art. 19. The mission of the Jesuits, sent to Fernando Po, and the adjacent islands, may dispose of six thousand dollars a year. The

Superior of the Mission must render an account of its investment to the Governor, who will remit the same to the Minister of the Colonies.

" Art. 20. The Superior of the Mission, the Receiver, the Judge, and the Secretary, form the Council of the Governor, but whatever may be the opinion of the said Council, the responsibility of the resolutions made in it will always fall upon the Governor, excepting in cases provided for in the 13th Article. When the Commander of the Naval Forces is on shore he will be admitted into Council, and take precedence after the Governor. This Council must meet for matters of importance, but the Governor may convoke it when he pleases

" Art. 21. With the advice of the Council, the Governor may grant lands to natives of our kingdom, or to national companies who may apply for such lands, either for purposes of cultivation, or for the establishment of factories or storehouses.

" Art. 22. As before said, with the advice of the Council the Governor may likewise grant lands to foreign individuals or companies who may apply for them, for the purpose above mentioned, but with the payment of an annual fee, to be regulated and established by the Government.

" Art. 23. Before granting the said lands, the Governor will select those necessary for the building of the church, barracks, hospital, &c. With respect to those necessary for the naval dependencies, the Governor and Commander of the Naval Forces will agree.

" Art. 24. All cultivated lands will be free of contribution or taxes during five years.

" Art. 25. The Governor in our name will grant to the owners of these lands the title of possession.

" Art. 26. Of such lands as have been conceded to this day by the Governor, the grant is confirmed, and titles of possession will be given to the owners.

" Art. 27. The owners of lands already granted, or that may be granted in future, in the islands of Fernando Po, Annobon, Corisco, and their dependencies, will lose all right of possession, if such lands are not cultivated or built upon within two years after their respective confirmation or concession.

" Art. 28. The duties of five per cent. for importation, and two and a half for exportation, will be continued. Anchorage duties of twenty-five reals, for vessels above twenty tons and less than fifty; of fifty reals for those above fifty and less than three hundred and fifty; and of one hundred reals for those that guage from three hundred and fifty to seven hundred tons above the last guaging. Vessels under twenty tons are free of anchorage.

" Art. 29. All bonded goods or merchandise are free of duties for importation or exportation, but will pay one per cent. for storehouse expenses.

" Art. 30. A gratuitous passage to Fernando Po, and the adjacent islands, will be granted by the Government to all natives of our dominions applying for the same.

" Art. 31. A sum of one million of reals is assigned to the Governor, for the assistance during the first year of the colonists to these islands; but with the indispensable condition, that colonists applying for such assistance shall be engaged in some art or occupation. Of the sums so expended, and others before mentioned, an account will be given to the Minister of the Colonies.

" Art. 32. The sum of two millions of reals is appointed for installation expenses.

" Art. 33. These sums, likewise those requisite for the support of the military and naval forces assigned to these islands, will be furnished from the revenues derived from the island of Cuba, and included in its budget.

" Art. 34. The Minister of Colonies will establish periodical communications between the Peninsula and the possessions in the Gulf of Guinea.

" Art. 35. A circular containing all the necessary information, for commerce in general, of the mercantile condition of the said islands, will be forwarded to the Governors of all the provinces of our kingdom.

" Art. 36. The Minister of Colonies will adopt the necessary measures for carrying the present decree into execution.

" Given at our palace the thirteenth of December, eighteen hundred and fifty-eight.

" Signed by the QUEEN.

" The Minister of War and Colonies,
" (Signed)   LEOPOLDO O'DONNELL."

Despite of all former experience, the colonists came out, or were sent out, as unprepared as ever to resist the deadly climate; and the consequence was, that, in a very short time, gaunt figures of men, women, and children might be seen crawling through the streets, with scarcely an evidence of life in their faces, save the expression of a sort of torpid carelessness as to how soon it might be their turn to drop off and die.

More than twenty per cent. of those who came out died in the space of five months; and the " Patino," screw steamer, carried back fifty of them to Cadiz, who looked, when they embarked, more like living skeletons of skin and bone than animated human beings.

His Excellency Brigadier Gandera began the work of bush-clearing very energetically. One hundred Kroomen were obtained from the Kru coast, and an area of from four to six miles around the town was cleared. But the bush sprung up with renewed vigour; for such is the fertility of the soil on this island, that I have known of Indian corn, planted on a Monday evening, making its appearance four inches above the ground on the following Wednesday morning—within a period of thirty-six hours.

Concurrent with the erection of spacious barracks under Governor Gandera's administration, an ascent to the highest peak of the island was effected by Señor Pellon—one of the Spanish Government officials, who was accompanied by

Mr. Gustav Mann, botanist to the Niger expedition in 1860. A considerable part of the journey up was effected by the aid of donkeys, a group of which had been brought some time previously from Teneriffe. At the very summit they found a huge crater, almost circular in its upper edge, of about sixty feet in circumference, and apparently about fifty feet deep.

Near this summit they found a jar, with a shred of cloth resembling a piece of an old flag. The former, on being brought back to town, was recognized by one of the inhabitants as the jar left there by Mr. Beecroft in his ascent of 1840. The temperature was found to be 39° Fahrenheit during the night; for a thermometer was left there, for which they returned on the following day. While they were up on the mountain a shower of hail descended. The vegetation was observed to be sparse, chiefly consisting of heaths and mosses. Between the last aboriginal town of Bassili and the highest peak they passed four native huts, and the highest one was not many hours' walk from the mountain's summit. Nearly all the vegetation about the top had been burned by the natives a few weeks before ; and this was done by these simple people in the hope of frightening away the white man, of whose ascent to the

top of the peak they have a great dread—
because, they say, white man gets too near their
original home,* and can bring down on them
any calamity. For example, if an epidemic
were to break out amongst them after such
a trip, they would attribute it to the white
man's evil spirit ; as they did some deaths which
occurred after Mr. Beecroft's ascent in 1840.

From this journey, however, some good resulted.
Mr. Mann procured for the Royal Botanic Gardens at Kew a number of the first tree-ferns that
have been sent to England from Western Africa.
By the observations of both the explorers, it
appears that a temperate and invigorating
atmosphere is found at some elevation, a cir-
cumstance which proves the existence of those
natural capacities for a sanatorium that would
render Fernando Po a health-restoring locale for
all invalids suffering from debility caused by the
miasmatous fevers of the continent.

The question of the Spaniards establishing
such a position, which would need the clearing
of a large quantity of colossal trees and bush—
the making of roads and the erection of houses
—is one that I presume neither to asseverate nor

* Vide page 201, " Impressions of Western Africa," where I
have mentioned that a Fernandian's idea of the origin of his tribe
is, that they came originally out of the crater at the mountain top.

to contradict. But against the probability that the soil of Fernando Po should be so cultivated as to produce remunerative profit from its natural resources, the greatest obstacle appears to me in the fact that the island occupied by from twenty to thirty thousand of the aboriginal Boobees, or Fernandians, the laziest and most worthless race of negroes to be met with anywhere in Africa. They are not warlike; but they have in former times shewn their antipathy to the Spaniards by poisoning the sources of the streams that supplied with water the towns of the early Spanish colonizers in 1780. Since then they seem to have in no wise become more humane or more civilized ; and although the Baptist missionaries have laboured with zeal amongst them for a period of seventeen years (from 1841 to 1858), the influences of their teaching have had no effect in christianizing, or civilizing, or even humanizing, a single individual of the tribe.

Of their social customs the most interesting appear to me those connected with their marriage ceremonies, to one of which I was witness in the end of the year 1857, which I will attempt to describe.

Although they keep no chronological records nor register of passing time, save that which the new moon gives them, they hold yearly festivities in the dry season, which they recognise as the beginning of a new year. These festivities are generally commenced in November, and continued during the two following months, being entitled "Lobos." They comprise dancing, singing, eating porcupine or gazelle chop, and drinking palm wine, fermented as well as unfermented.

During the " Lobo" period, weddings or " Boolas" are generally celebrated.

Having had an intimation from Boobokaa ("the man of many boxes"),* who is head king of Issapoo, that one of his daughters was about to be married, I took it for an invitation, and walked up to his town a few days before Christmas to be present at the ceremonial.

The first thing of which one is sensible, when approaching a Fernandian village, is the odour of Tola pomatum,† wafted by whatever little breeze may be able to find its way through the dense bushes. The next is the crowing of cocks. Indeed, the poultry tribe seem to be the only bipeds endowed with any activity in this island.

---

* The names of many of the Fernandian chiefs have significations of this kind, like those of the North American Indians. One king is named Bosotchee, which is the Fernandian for " thunder ;" another Borobabagne, which signifies " good deer's flesh."

† I have explained in my work, " Impressions of Western Africa," that Tola pomatum is a compound of ashes of palm oil, and the mashed leaves of an herb having a brownish scarlet hue.

At St. Isabel, the capital, some of these, who may be considered the watchful sentinels, crow at ten at night. The refrain is renewed at midnight, again at two o'clock in the morning, and at day-break the whole host of cock-a-doodle-doo-ers join in a universal chorus—perhaps to announce the coming forth of the rising sun.

On getting inside of the town our first object of attraction was the cooking going on in His Majesty's kitchen. Here a number of dead "Ipa" (porcupines) and "Litcha" (gazelles) were in readiness to be mingled up with palm oil, and several grubs writhing on skewers, probably to add piquancy to the dishes. These are called "Inchakee," being obtained from palm trees, and look at first sight like Brobdingnagian maggots. Instead of waiting to see the art of the Fernandian Soyer on these components, I congratulated myself on my ham sandwiches and brandy and water bottle safely stowed in my portmanteau, which one of the Kroomen carried on his back, and sat on my camp stool beneath the grateful shade of a palm tree to rest awhile.

Outside a small hut belonging to the mother of the bride expectant, I soon recognised the happy bridegroom, undergoing his toilet from the hands of his future wife's sister. A profusion of Tshibbu strings* being fastened round his body, as well as his legs and arms, the anointing lady, having a short black pipe in her mouth, proceeded to putty him over with Tola paste. He seemed not altogether joyous at the anticipation of his approaching happiness, but turned a sulky gaze now and then to a kidney-shaped piece of brown painted yam, which he held in his hand, and which had a parrot's red feather fixed on its convex side. This I was informed was called "Ntshoba," and is regarded as a protection against evil influence during the important day. Two skewer-looking hair pins, with heads of red and white glass beads, fastened his hat (which was nothing more than a dish of bamboo plaiting) to the hair of his head; and his toilet being complete, he and one of the bridesmen, as elaborately dressed as himself, attacked a mess of stewed flesh and palm oil placed before them, as eagerly as if they had not tasted food for a fortnight. In discussing this meal, they followed the primitive usage of "fingers before forks," only resting now and then to take a gulp of palm-wine out of a calabash which was hard

* Small pieces of Achatectonica shell, which represent the native currency in Fernando Po.

by, or to wipe their hands in napkins of cocoa-leaf, a process which, to say the least of it, added nothing to their washerwoman's bills at the end of the week.

But the bride! Here she comes! Led forth by her own, and her husband expectant's mother, each holding her by a hand, followed by two Nepées (professional singers) and half-a-dozen bridesmaids. Nothing short of a correct photograph could convey an idea of her appearance. Borne down by the weight of rings, wreaths, and girdles of "Tshibbu," the Tola pomatum gave her the appearance of an exhumed mummy, save her face, which was all white—not from excess of modesty [and here I may add, the negro race are reputed always to blush blue], but from being smeared over with a white paste, symbolical of purity.

As soon as she was outside the paling, her bridal attire was proceeded with, and the whole body was plastered over with white stuff. A veil of strings of Tshibbu shells, completely covering her face, and extending from the crown of her head to the chin, as well as on each side from ear to ear, was then thrown over her; over this was placed an enormous helmet made of cowhide; and any one with a spark of compassion in him could not help pitying that poor creature, standing for more than an hour under the broiling sun, with such a load on her, whilst the Nepées were celebrating her praises in an extempore epithalamium, and the bridegroom was completing his finery elsewhere.

One of the Nepées, who, for what I know, may have been the Grisi of Fernando Po, and who had walked eight miles that morning to assist professionally at the ceremony, commenced a solo celebration of the bride's virtues and qualifications. Whether any person of musical taste, who had listened to it, would have entitled the chaunt a combination of squeel, grunt, and howl, I cannot say; but that it produced satisfaction amongst the native audience was evident from the fact of the energetic chorussing of several assistant minstrels, who yelled out—"Hee—hee—jee—eh!" at the termination of any passage containing a sentiment that met with their approbation, the exclamation being synonymous with our "bravo."

The song, as translated to me, set forth the universal joy of nature at the festival which was approaching; amongst other matters, recording the existence of a race of wicked amphibious people who lived on the African continent, and who would doubtless attempt to come over to disturb the universal harmony ; but who, they knew, if they went into the water on that day, would be all remorselessly devoured by the sharks. It terminated with a recapitulation of the bride's attractive qualities, her beautiful form, figure, and good temper ; the latter a quality which I had no reason to doubt, as I did not enjoy the pleasure of the lady's acquaintance. But when the Nepéé wound up her praises by enumerating, amongst her other prepossessing attributes, "the sweet smell" proceeding from her, which was the cause of inducing a white man to come and witness the ceremony, I turned away with a shudder, of what kind you may guess, at this outrage on poetic license, and said to myself, "If Nepéé only knew the truth!"

The candidates for marriage having taken their positions side by side in the open air fronting the little house from which the bride elect had been led out by the two mothers, and where I was informed she had been closely immured for fifteen months previous, the ceremony commenced. The mothers were the officiating priests—an institution of natural simplicity, whose homely origin no one will dare to impugn. On these occasions the mother bishops are prophetically entitled " Boonanas," the Fernandian for grandmother. Five bridesmaids marshalled themselves alongside the bride postulant, each, in rotation, some inches lower than the other; the outside one being a mere infant in stature, and all having bunches of parrots' feathers on their heads, as well as holding a wand in their right hands. The mothers stood behind the " happy pair," and folded an arm of each round the body of the other—Nepées chaunting all the while, so that it was barely possible for my interpreter to catch the words by which they were formally soldered. A string of Tshibbu was fastened round both arms by the bridegroom's mother; she, at the same time, whispering to him advice to take care of this tender lamb, even though he had half-a-dozen wives before. The string was then unloosed. It was again fastened on by the bride's mother, who whispered into her daughter's ear her duty to attend to her husband's farm, tilling his yams and cassada, and the necessity of her being faithful to him. The ratification of their promise to fulfil these conditions was effected by passing a goblet of palm wine from mother to son (the bridegroom), from him to his bride, from her to her mother, each taking a sip as it went round. Then an indiscriminate dance and chaunt commenced; and the whole scene—the Tola paste laid on some faces so thickly, that one might imagine it was intended to affix something to them by means of it—the dangling musk-cat and monkey tails—the dish hats and parrots' feathers —the bunches of wild fern and strings of Tshibbu shells, fastened perhaps as nosegays to the ladies' persons—the white and red and yellow spots, painted under the eyes, and on the shoulders, and in any place where they could form objects of attraction—the *tout ensemble*, contrasted with the lofty bombax, beautiful palm, cocoa-nut, and other magnificent tropical trees around, presented a picture rarely witnessed by a European, and one calculated to excite varied reflections.

When fatigued with dancing, and when all the company, from the cracking of the Tola putty, looked as if they were about to fall into man's original element of clay, the six other wives and the Nepées walked away, followed by the bridegroom, with the bride and the bridesmaids after him—all marching down the pathway which led to the bridegroom's house.

Knowing the ceremonials were not yet finished, I followed the company for half a mile. As they went along, the former wives **of the** newly-married man sang, and jumped, and **wheeled** around, beckoning to the bride to come on; **who,** poor creature! with her helmet and her cinctures of shells—if nerves had been in fashion in Fernando Po—would have needed smelling-salts, or a douche of cold water, half-a-dozen times on her journey.

The outside palisading, in which was a faint attempt at a gate, was reached. **Here I** witnessed an act of natural politeness, which no disciples of Chesterfield or Mrs. General could rival. The old wives preceded the new bride on her way in through the outer enclosure, as if guiding her to her new home; but when they reached the inner palisading they all gave way to her, allowing her to precede them in her progress. Within this the ceremony was proceeded with, **the** bride standing with her back to the door, her husband's arm again embracing her, and hers round his body likewise. One of his children presented a huge brown painted yam, which she received, with a renewal of advice from her mother to attend to the cultivation of this esculent. Others of his children fixed epaulets of Tshibbu in their proper places; the bridegroom put four rings of the small shells on the middle finger of her right hand; another piece of advice, or lecture, was given to her son by the bridegroom's mother, and the ceremony was completed.

Before the feasting commenced, the bride and the bridegroom visited their parents and near relations to announce to them the fact that the ceremony was completed, and to claim their approbation.

All the friends from distant parts who had come to be present brought dishes with them. Some poor women, who had nothing better to give, carried bundles of fire-wood on their heads —a present which might appear ridiculous to anyone who did not remember the widow's mite, and its gracious acceptance.

When it was all over, I could not avoid admiring the strength of character of that young woman, who had gone through such a day's toil with such unshrinking fortitude; and I protest against being called "an old bachelor" for recording this sentiment.

Whether it was the hot sun, or what brother Jonathan would call "the loud smell," or a combination of both, that urged me not to think of waiting to partake of the banquet, I cannot say. At all events, I soon turned my back on the bridal party, and left them to enjoy —not their honeymoon, nor their treacle-moon, but their "Tola"-moon, without presuming, on the *de gustibus non disputandum* principle, to cast any imputation on their peculiar tastes.

CHAPTER XVIII.

WHEN the Baptist missionaries at Fernando Po found the first article of Don John Joseph de Lerena's proclamation set aside, namely, "to secure to every person or persons their liberty, their individual property, and their religion, so long as they continue to obey the laws of the colony," they at once resolved on transferring themselves to the mainland of Africa.

Accordingly, Amboise Bay, at the base of the Kameroon mountain, was selected for the purpose ; and their new settlement was at once dignified with the title of Victoria.

The Rev. Mr. Saker, the head of the Baptist mission, made a purchase from King William of Bimbia, of an extent of land reaching from a small stream of water flowing into Man-of War Bay to the point eastward of Aboobee, or Pirate Island—a coast distance of about eighty miles.

Before visiting this place, I had learned from the *Missionary Herald*, of November, 1858, that the name of Morton Bay was given by the colonists to the inner cove facing the settlement of Victoria, as well as to that on the beach. Here a market was held every third day, in which fish, plantains, yams, and fowls were to be purchased for the merest trifle.

The advantages set forth by the Rev. Mr. Saker and his congregation as possessed by the new settlement were, that it had no mangrove swamps — no musquitoes—that it was a site within reach of any temperature, to be attained by its residents on ascending the mountains—that there were two islands in the middle of the bay, Ambas or Ndami and Mondoleh — either being appropriate for a light-house ; and that there was a well-sheltered bay inside these islands, safe and capacious enough for a large portion of the British Navy to anchor in.

A river of fresh water flowed into the bay, fish was abundant in the harbour, and, greatest advantage of all, they could have what was denied to them in Fernando Po—freedom of religious worship.

An examination into the hydrographical benefits of the bay as an anchoring place, made by Commodore Wise, R.N., in H.M.S.S. "Vesuvius," during the year 1859, did not prove it to be anything like the description of it given by the enthusiastic missionaries. At one important point of the bay, described in the Rev. Mr. Saker's chart as having from four to six fathoms of water, it was found by Mr. Brown, Master R.N., who had charge of the soundings, to have only from six to nine feet.

There is no doubt that Amboise bay is the least unhealthy station on the west coast; but its iron-bound rocks, and the inaccessibility of its islands, would require an immense outlay of capital to make the neighbourhood habitable.

The Bimbia people, whose sovereign, King William, holds sway over all this neighbourhood, are of the Isebu tribe. The natives of the islands Ndami and Mondoleh profess to be a different race from the Bimbians, although speaking the same language. Of their genealogy, as of that of all African tribes, no accurate account can be obtained.

The Baquiri tribe are located above the Isebus, or Bimbians, on the Kameroon mountains. They are represented by their neighbours—with a reciprocal appreciation which seems universal here —as being savages. A tribe called Batohke dwell near to the Rumby Point, on the western side of the base of the mountain; whilst between the latter and Amboise Bay are the Jonghi, at a place not twenty miles from Fernando Po.

Around this interesting locality there seems to me a large field for the inquirer into African ethnology — a branch of knowledge in pursuit of which a larger amount of accessories is required than I have been able to obtain.

Nevertheless, I shall take this opportunity of stating here the result of some inquiries I have been making.

It will be recollected that a chart of Dr. Barth's explorations in Central Africa had been compiled, as well as published, under the superintendence of Mr. Petermann, before the Pleiad's expedition up the Niger-Tshadda-Binue, and therefore previous to the doctor's return to Europe. In that chart was mentioned a tribe called Bati, who were described as " Pagans, reputed to be of a white colour, and of beautiful shape—to live in houses made of clay—to wear clothes of their own making—and to exist in a country from which a mountain is visible to the S.W., and close to the sea."

From the position in which the Bati country was placed in Mr. Petermann's chart, there could be no doubt that Kameroons was the mountain referred to.

On my first official visit to the river Kameroons, in January 1856, I made inquiries from the British, as well as native traders, if such a race were known; and I received information that there was a people styled Bari, not Bati, who, instead of being white, were yellow-coloured; who were of fine shape, and who lived near the place indicated on the chart. Any information about their peculiarities of worship, dress, mode of living, trade, or agriculture, I found to be perfectly unattainable. I learned, however, that they were very warlike, as well as that they rode on horses; and I forwarded the result of my inquiries to Dr. Barth. He wrote to me, in reply, that he did not think the Bari and Bati were of the same tribe. "For," he added, "*r* and *t*, as far as I know, are never changed in these languages—not like *r* and *c*, *p* and *f*, *dh* and *l*, and others. Besides, I think the *a* in Bari is a long vowel, while in Bati it is short. I, therefore, must suppose these two tribes distinct; but they may live near together. Any information which you will be able to gather about that interesting corner behind the bay must evidently be of the highest importance; but a great difficulty will of course arrive, with regard to identifying the various tribes, as there is no doubt that the same tribe may be called by a very different name on the coast and in the interior. So I am almost sure that the Ding-ding, who are living in huts erected in the branches of large trees, will have quite another name; and the same is probably the case with the Tekar."

*   *   *   *   *

" Have you any communication with Duketown? I am uncertain with what country
round the bay I shall identify Mbafu, a district which has been visited by the predatory
excursions of the Fulbe, and which they represent as in continual intercourse with the Christians; it is near the sea-shore. . . . . . .

" Yours truly,

" H. BARTH."

Thinking I might obtain some information on
these matters from the Old Kalabar missionaries, I transmitted Dr. Barth's letter to the Rev.
W. Anderson, and subjoin his reply :—

" Duketown Mission House,
" Old Kalabar, July 22nd, 1856.

" MY DEAR SIR,—I have made diligent inquiry
among the Efik people in reference to the Ding-
ding, the Tekar, and the Mbafu.

" 1st—Ding-ding. Nothing seems known of
them here, or of any men living in trees. The
people laugh heartily when told of them, and say

Y

'they must be brother to the birds and monkeys.'

"2nd—Tekar. The people here know of no country of that name; 'suppose it no be the Ataka or Atakha or Ataga, who live somewhere beyond Akunakuna. None of the Ataka people are in Old Kalabar.'

"3rd—Mbafu. There is a people, or country, or both, far on the other side of Qua, called Mbafum. Some of them are sometimes brought as slaves to Old Kalabar.

"I have long wished to ascertain the position and distance from Old Kalabar of a country called here Mbrikum, Mburikum, or Mbudikum. Many of them are brought here as slaves. They are more liked in Old Kalabar than many brought from other countries. They are peaceable, honest, energetic; they represent their country as being three months' journey from Old Kalabar—as being destitute of large trees, and as being not far from some 'big watery,' on which ships are visible. Their country is much infested by men who 'wear trowsers and ride on horseback,'—I suppose some Moorish tribe—and who are called Tibare. They may be the Tilbe (Fulbe?) referred to by Dr. Barth.

*   *   *   *   *

" I observed that Dr. Barth has not found *r* and *t* interchangeable among the tribes he has visited. They are so in many Efik words. The word in question, if communicated to twenty Kalabarese, would forthwith be pronounced by the one-half Bati, and by the other Bari. In Efik we can say either. 'Ku wût owo,' *or* 'Ku wur owo,' (don't kill man); 'Enye okût osang,' *or* 'okur' osang (he sees way); 'Tat inna,' *or* 'Tar inna' (open the mouth); 'esit ayat (or ayar) enye' (he is troubled — literally, heart troubles him); 'a dat (or a dar) esit' (he rejoices.)

*   *   *   *   *

" Yours truly,

" WM. ANDERSON."

I may observe that the word Tibare is pronounced long (Tibaare) by the Efik people at Old Kalabar; and therefore it seems to me not at all improbable that this name, passed about amongst men who are entirely ignorant and unconscious of lexicography, may have been metamorphosed into Baari or Baati when dictated by word of mouth. As recorded by Dr. Baikie, there are some of the Bati tribe in Clarence, Fernando Po, and their characteristics are entirely different from those of the Batis described by Dr. Barth, or of the Baris mentioned to me by the Kameroons people.

Determined to pursue the matter further—to try to ascertain the identity of these hitherto mythical tribes—I wrote to the Rev. Mr. Crowther at Lagos, enclosing Dr. Barth's inquiries. The following is his answer:—

"I am afraid I cannot enlighten you much about Dr. Barth's queries. The name Ding-ding is familiar to me; we have a tribe of Yoruba living somewhere in the neighbourhood of Bargu—sometimes spelt Borgoo—on the right bank of the Kowara, opposite Bousa so called; but the mode of living, in huts erected in the branches of trees, leads me to think the Ding-ding must be another people, of whom I have no knowledge. Dr. Barth's Mbafu is in all probability the same as Mbofou of Mr. Koelle (see his map to 'Polyglotta Africana,' somewhere about the Ibo country. The name may not be known as such to the people of Old Kalabar and

Kameroons; if it be not this, I cannot otherwise guess it. From Dr. Barth's information, the Filatahs marched southward in that direction; and from the long intercourse the Kalabarese and Ibos have had with European merchants in the Bight of Biafra, they might, with all propriety, be said to have intercourse with Christians near the sea-shore. Considering the distance of Hamarrua and Adamawa from the Ibo country, the people of the latter might be said to live near the sea-coast."

I received further information respecting these unknown tribes and localities from the Rev. Mr. Anderson in December. From a letter communicated to me by Dr. Barth, he considers Koelles Ndob to be the Mburikum of which Mr. Anderson wrote in his first communication; and the latter gentleman, extending his inquiries still further, thus informs me :—

"1st. The Mburikum (or Mbudikum) call a tribe of the warlike Tibare Ding-ding; but they do not live in trees. The Tibare wear cloth, and ride on horses.

"2nd. Teka is the name of a tribe and country near the Tibare.

"3rd. Mbafum, or Mbafong, or Ekoi, furnishes many slaves for Old Kalabar.

"4th. Mburikum is the name of a large territory, including several other countries or towns, of which the following are the chief:—1st, Bamum, a fine, strong people, who frequently wage war with the Tibare ; 2nd, Ndob—big water at Ndob, and those who come here (to Old Kalabar) from that district can live in water, same as Kameroons; 3rd, Babuk; 4th, Bariki; 5th, Bangora ; 6th, Isa ; 7th, Bansok ; 8th, Bambo ; 9th, Balri; 10th, Banam ; 11th, Mfonsin ; 12th, Bandyn.

"All these places are to the east of Efik (Old Kalabar). They all lie 'on side where sun rises.'

"Yours truly,

"WM. ANDERSON."

On the occasion of a visit which I made to the Kameroons, in February of this year, on board H.M.S.S. "Merlin," I inquired of Mr. Johnson, a very intelligent *attaché* to the Baptist mission community there, if he knew anything of the Ding-ding, Tekar, Mbafu, Jetem, Mbudikum, Bari, or Bati, races. He informed me that the Bayon people who are of the Mbudikum territory, designated all the Filatahs as Baris. A man, from the Bayon district, was at that time near Kameroons—unfortunately, at the period of my inquiry, not accessible — who states that he met a white man and a black man in his country a few years before coming down.

I left Mr. Johnson a number of questions to ask of this Bayon man, but he has not been able to get any answers from him.

In a letter (Feb. 11th) which I had from Dr. Barth, he writes: "I cannot think that Mr. Anderson is right in stating the Ding-ding to be a section of the Tibare. They may be subjected."

Subsequent information received from Mr. Anderson proves that Dr. Barth is right, and seems to me to settle at once the identity of the Ding-ding.

When I paid a short visit to Old Kalabar, in the month of April, on board H.M.S.S. "Fire-fly," the subject came on in conversation, and Mr. Anderson communicated to me the following recent intelligence which he had obtained. A man was then in Duketown, who informed him that the word Ding-ding with the Tibare is synonymous with slave—that the story of their living in trees would seem to arise from the fact of some of the Mbudikums being constantly posted in the tops of trees to watch for the coming of the predatory Tibares, which they announce to their people by blowing horns, to give warning of the enemy's approach.

It may be asked by those who have followed me so far, what is the practical utility to be derived from investigations concerning these tribes, whilst these inquiries have tended to no ascertained conclusion? I answer, they may at least be considered as an impetus to future explorers, leading them to attempt the discovery of facts concerning people about whom we have hitherto been entirely ignorant; and that such inquiries may, in the end, prove as useful as the discoveries of Dr. Livingstone concerning unknown tribes on the eastern side of the continent. For I believe the rivers which traverse the hitherto great unknown tract of African land are destined to be the great highways by which legitimate commerce, and its consequent civilizing influence, are to be carried on. Even such slight information as this—be it only regarded by many in the light of crude conjecture

—may tend to increase our knowledge of the native tribes, as well as lead future explorers to gain clearer and more defined ideas respecting the Ethiopian people—a race the lowest in civilization of all created species; inhabiting a soil the richest in the production of such industrial resources as tend to the comfort of the great human family.

THE END.

R. BORN, PRINTER, GLOUCESTER STREET, REGENT'S PARK.

www.ingramcontent.com/pod-product-compliance
Lightning Source LLC
Chambersburg PA
CBHW021757110726
47902CB00006B/1549